William Wallace:

A Hero Through Time

Bobby Blackmore

ISBN: 9798572206005

Part I

When Am I?

Chapter 1

When am I?

William came to with an uneasy feeling that something was not quite right, even amongst all the obvious wrongs. Disregarding his own injuries, he immediately raised himself up to check on his brother.

"Malcolm, are you okay?" He hoped for, but was not expecting, a response. The last thing he remembered was his Ford Escort being hit from behind as he drove his brother home from the party. It flipped over as it left the road, and crashed down on the passenger side. Although he was praying that Malcolm was not dead, he knew that he could not possibly be okay.

Now that he was on his feet and looking around, that uneasy feeling began to solidify. It was not just that it was now daylight rather than full dark; he had no idea how long he had been unconscious. There was no apparent damage to the trees or undergrowth, no scrapes in the ground. Stranger than that, though, he could see no car, no twisted metal, no mangled plastic, no broken glass. Nothing.

Scanning the terrain, he spotted his brother and rushed to his side. "Malcolm, Malcolm, speak to me, Malcolm!" he beseeched the corpse-like body lying face down about fifty yards from where he had woken up. Aware that there could well be neck or back injuries, William carefully rolled Malcolm over onto his back. This would be no easy feat for the average man, Malcolm at six foot three inches and a front row rugby veteran represented a veritable man mountain. His little brother bested him by a couple of inches though, and while a little lighter on the scales, was all muscle.

William put his ear to his brother's chest, held his own breath, and listened. There was no sound of air being drawn in or expelled from Malcolm's lungs, but did his chest move just a little? He couldn't be sure, but it gave him a glimmer of hope. Moving his head up to Malcolm's face, William tried to detect any slight movement of air around the nose and mouth. Still nothing. He put two fingers on his neck, searching for a pulse. Was that one? Maybe. William waited, still barely daring to breathe himself, willing a response. There it was again; yes, he was sure of it. And another one, so faint and so long between pulses that it hardly seemed possible, but Malcolm clearly had the Wallace fighting spirit in spades.

William tried to put his hand in his pocket for his mobile phone, intending to dial 999. What! His pockets were gone. Torn off in the collision, he supposed. He scanned the ground, searching about, hoping against all available evidence to see his phone lying there, waiting to come to his aid. Again nothing.

"Got to get you to a hospital, old boy. I'll be right back. Don't go anywhere."

William climbed up the side of the gully, focussed on his brother's welfare, pushing to the back of his mind the missing car, the lack of blood, the plain unnaturalness of the whole scene.

When he got to the road that they had been so unceremoniously swatted off, who knows how long ago, unreality threatened to take him over. There was no proper road. Not a patch of tarmac in sight. No fencing or hedging either. When his car had left the road he had gone through both fence and hedge. Okay, at that point they would have been swept away, but it was the same for as far as he could see. No road, no fencing, no hedge.

What the actual fuck!

Not so long ago, William had been a highly trained member of the Special Forces. He had been trained to deal with all manner of scenarios, but nothing he had trained for, nothing he had experienced, had prepared him in any way for what his senses were screaming at him now. Concern for his brother had enabled him to focus and push back the evidence that was all around him. It wasn't just that the sights, sounds and smells that were engulfing him were so overwhelming now that he was accepting them. What made them so vivid, he realised, were the things that were not there. He could hear no engines, no cars or lorries on any nearby roads, no tractors toiling in fields on such a fine summer's morning. The air was pure and fresh; he could easily pick out fragrances like hawthorn and clover, and was that peat? Yes, he was sure of it. Someone had been cutting peat somewhere in the vicinity, which he knew was unusual this far south.

Where was he, he wondered, and how did he get here? It certainly looked familiar; he knew his home turf like the back of his hand and the general geography was right. Finer details, though, were off, as if he had just discovered a rash or extra hair on the back of his hand. It was still the back of his hand, but it just wasn't right.

Still, his overriding concern was for his brother. All other thoughts would have to wait until he had Malcolm under proper medical supervision. With no clues to go on, William set off in the direction of Craigie village. Assuming he was where the car incident had occurred, that would be the nearest place to get some help.

~~~

A few minutes later William spotted workers toiling in a field and set off towards them. But before he was close enough to shout for their attention, he heard the thundering sound of horses' hooves to his left. Turning towards that sound he saw a horseman galloping towards him, seemingly in as big a hurry as William himself. William raised his hand to his brow to shield against the glaring sun as he watched the horse approach. Fuck! The man bearing down on him had a sword, and he had it raised ready for action. Instinct took over. For all his training, he had never had to consider how to defend against an attack by a sword wielding horseman. Why would he? He had no weapon, and there was nothing close at hand that he could improvise with.

As the horse closed in William readied himself. The rider had his sword in his right hand, William got ready to move quickly to his own right. Out of range of the weapon, assuming his opponent was not agile and quick enough to be able to manoeuvre in the saddle enough to strike him on that side, he hoped to be able to grab the rider by the leg and unseat him. Only hoped; he was feeling very stiff and sore and had not tested his own abilities. Just as he prepared for his defensive move, the horse pulled up just short of him. Perhaps the rider had anticipated William's move and was himself improvising.

"Stop right there, stranger. Who are you and what is your business here?" the rider demanded, eyes wide and nostrils flaring.

As the workers drew nearer him, William noticed the coarseness of their clothing and the roughness of their tools. How long had he been unconscious? Was it possible that he had been out of it for so long that he had entirely missed some cataclysmic event, and the world had regressed into some kind of dystopian existence? No, surely such a change could not happen in days, weeks or even months. That being the case he could not have lived long enough to see it; he and Malcolm would have been dried out husks at best. More likely eaten by wild animals and maggots.

It occurred to William that the question he needed to ask was not where was he, but rather, when was he?

The guy on the horse did look strangely familiar, though. Long face below jet-black hair, with dark, slightly protruding eyes, a long, straight nose and thin lips.

"Walter? Walter Hose? Is that you? What—?"

"I do not know you, sir, how do you know my name? What is your business here?" and as William took a step towards him, "Stand still, stand still I say! State your business. You better have a damned good reason for trespassing on my land!"

William stopped walking towards the horseman. Walter Hose was one of a group of friends that he and Malcolm had hung about with back in the seventies, twenty or so years ago. This guy looked extremely like him and seemingly had the same name, but how could it be him? Riding a fucking horse? In any case, he certainly did not seem to recognise William and did not appear to be well disposed towards him. Possibly he was a relative of Walter; that would fit.

"Apologies, sir, you remind me of an old friend who appears to have the same name. I have no weapons and I mean you no harm. I do need some help though, if you would be so kind."

"You do appear to be unarmed, but your uncommon size makes you a threat in any case. Stay where you are and state your business, sir. Quickly now, or I will have them set the dogs on you, I have better things to do this day."

"My brother lies unconscious a couple of miles back, I need to get him to a .. to a .." William was trying to say hospital, but the word would not come out. Then an eerie realisation hit him. As a natural polyglot, he spoke many languages and could detect and reply to a stranger in his own tongue, if he knew it, instinctively. Didn't have to think about it. New languages he could pick up very quickly, from as little as a few days to a few weeks until he was fluent. This language, however, although it sounded very familiar, was still new to him, but he was speaking it immediately. There appeared to be no word for hospital! Only societies without one would not have a word for hospital.

"What are you havering about, stranger? My patience wears thin." By this point the field workers had surrounded William, brandishing their tools as weapons, although all were careful to stay out of his

6

personal space. The big stranger looked dangerous, unarmed or not.

"Who is he? Is it an Englishman?" the nearest worker asked, jabbing a hoe towards the intruder.

This was not going well and time was wasting. William had to get treatment for Malcolm or he would surely die.

"Look, I apologise for the intrusion, but please, my brother needs help urgently. I beg you, help me get him to the nearest place where he can get some attention."

"Sounds local, but he could be a collaborator. Says his brother is unwell and needs help nearby. Could be a trap," Walter told his people. "In any case he refuses to give me his name."

"I am William Wallace, and my brother is Malcolm. He needs urgent.."

Walter was slightly taken aback. He knew the names Malcolm and William Wallace, but surely they were dead? Unsure, he remained cautious.

"Sir William Wallace is that? From where?"

"Just plain William. Look—"

Once again Walter cut him off "Nothing plain-looking about you, nor your dress. How did you come about those clothes if you are indeed a plain man? Did you steal them?"

One of the workers said with a laugh, "Who could he steal clothes from that would fit that great lump?"

William looked down at his clothing. He was wearing the costume from the party, only now that he considered it, the cloth was somewhat coarser, and the finish was certainly not factory machined. All at once it struck him. Funny clothes, men on horseback, no vehicles or machinery. The party, his surprise birthday party, had been fancy dress and he had been given this outfit to resemble a historical figure with the same name, Sir William Wallace. He had never heard of him before. Although history was one of his interests, he was more interested in the history of warfare. Names like Alexander the Great and Genghis Khan were more familiar to him. Like most of his contemporaries, he knew very little of Scottish history.

The only logical conclusion William could reach was that he had been badly injured in the roll down the gully, and his mind was now building a fantasy world as an escape from the pain. It felt terribly real, though, and real or not he supposed he had to play along for now.

Sensing that the men facing him were becoming more agitated, William decided to have one more try to get their help. Failing that, he was quite prepared to take them on. He felt reasonably fit despite the circumstances and was confident he could easily unseat Walter from his horse, taking his sword from him in the process. The others had simple farm implements and did not represent a real threat. Probably with the boss subdued the others would scarper. He did not want to kill anybody, but he was prepared to do so if that was what it took to get back to Malcolm. He remembered the words of his mentor, Donald: "With death, it is always better to give than to receive."

"Please," William entreated, "do what you want with me, but please help my brother." Improvising on what had been said so far, he added, "We were taken by surprise by some English soldiers. I was knocked unconscious and when I came round Malcolm was lying close to me. I thought he was dead. He surely will die if he does not get some help soon."

Walter seemed to have a change of heart, and turning to the youngest of his men told him "Go bring a cart, we'll go and have a look for his brother." Turning back to William, he threatened, "You will lead us at the point of my sword. Any hint of trouble and I will not hesitate to part your head from your body, do you understand?"

William smiled back at him, relieved that at last he could get Malcolm some help, and answered, "Thank you, sir, I promise I will repay your kindness."

Chapter 2: August 1296

Fail monastery

"We will pray for your brother, William. He is in God's hands now, and by the Grace of God may he recover," the elderly abbot said reassuringly.

Malcolm had been taken to Fail monastery, that being the nearest location which offered any kind of medical experience, albeit not anything like what William had been hoping for. The monks were not hopeful of being able to do much more than pray for the poor soul, but at least Malcolm and William were made comfortable, in as far as they were able to be comfortable. Strange-smelling liquids and poultices were the order of the day.

"Thank you, anything I can do to repay you for your kindness I will gladly do." Malcolm was still unconscious, but his breathing now appeared more normal. At least it was noticeable as his chest rose and fell regularly.

"Oh, I'm sure we will be able to find plenty for you to do, William, and your brother should he recover, God willing," Walter said. "But it is not for us to decide. I have sent one of my men to give the news to our lord, Sir James the High Steward. He will decide what to do with you."

"Once again I thank you for your kindness and I look forward to meeting your lord. In the meantime, if you please, I would like to retire. I am not completely uninjured and would like to take some rest and let my poultices do their work."

William was not, in fact, at all tired. Adrenaline was still pumping through his body as his senses battled to come to terms with his current predicament. What he needed was not rest, but time to think and rationalise now that his brother was being attended to. He needed to get his shit together.

~~~

Next morning was a typical Scottish summer morning, in as far as the rain was somewhat warmer than at other times of the year. As William ate bread and porridge in the refectory, he heard a commotion in the corridor outside. It sounded like a lot of people, so he instinctively grabbed the knife from beside the bread, the only weapon in the room, and moved towards the kitchen door as the best means of escape. The door burst open and a wiry man with a shock of wavy red hair strode into the room at the head of a posse of heavily armed men. He had the kind of stature, William knew from experience, that masked a deceptively strong frame.

"Good morning, I am Sir James, High Steward. You won't be needing that," said the newcomer, nodding at the knife in William's hand, "unless you are going to cut me some bread."

"Walter there likes to point his sword at me, and the rest of your entourage look like they expect trouble. It seems to me that I need to defend myself."

Sir James looked round at his men and said, "I see what you mean, they do look rather intimidating. Understandable though. *Sir* Walter warned us we were meeting a giant. Of course, I assumed he was exaggerating, but you are a big man indeed."

William was used to standing out from the crowd because of his size, but looking around he realised that instead of being a few inches taller than most people around him, he now seemed to have almost a foot on most of the men he faced.

"I assure you I am no threat to anybody here. Quite the opposite in fact. I am dependent upon the goodwill of you all, my brother even more so. Be assured his welfare is my main concern."

"William, do you remember me? Alan Boyd. We used to meet up on market days when we were boys, do you mind?" The speaker moved forward through the group as he said this, and William was surprised to see that he did indeed know the face. Wide mouth with full lips, straight nose and sleepy blue eyes below straw-coloured hair. Another one of his childhood friends, but why did Alan remember him from a market? They had gone to the same school, lived in neighbouring streets. He looked more closely at the faces in the crowd and realised that a few more were somewhat familiar.

'I sure as fuck am not in Kansas now,' William thought. 'Best just play along until I meet the wizard.' Out loud he said simply, "The name and the face are very familiar. Sorry, but I am struggling with my memory, everything is foggy in my head right now."

"You are sure you know this man?" Sir James asked Alan.

"I haven't seen him since we were boys, but yes I am sure this is him. Look at the size of him, there can't be two. Malcolm was almost as tall. Sir Walter, you told me he looked familiar to you too, didn't you."

"Aye, although I really didn't recognise him even when he told me his name. Then when I saw Malcolm I remembered. I didn't say anything at the time, because I wasn't completely sure."

"That's good enough for me," Sir James decided. "You may all go," he said, waving his hand dismissively at the throng behind him.

"But, my lord, we still do not really know anything of this stranger. Should he turn on you, I will be responsible."

"It is okay, Sir Walter. I know what I am doing. This man is one of our own returned. He is a friend and I insist that he is treated as such. Wait outside, I will call you when I need you."

With that Walter and the others left the room, but not quietly.

"You know who I am, William, but I know next to nothing about you. Sit back down, please, and tell me about yourself, and your unfortunate brother. Where have you been, and more importantly, why are you back at this time?"

William had no idea how to answer these, or any of the other questions that were sure to be asked of him. Where had he been? He still had no idea quite where he was, or when he was, but he was entirely sure he had never been here before. Therefore he could not be back. Could he? Further, he did not know who Sir James was. Walter had referred to him as the High Steward, as he himself had done, but what was that? What did it mean? Wait a minute. Wait a fucking minute! The heir to the throne, usually referred to as the Prince of Wales, has many titles, one of which is High Steward of Scotland. This guy was not Prince Charles, so who was he, and why did he claim that title?

When you have excluded the impossible, whatever remains, however improbable, must be the truth. According to Sherlock Holmes anyway, but what would he say to this conundrum? Having excluded all other available explanations, what he was left with was still impossible! Could he really be living back in the distant past? So far, that was the only explanation that made sense, except that it made no sense at all. How could the impossible be possible!

Meantime Sir James had sat down opposite where William had been eating breakfast, and was watching him patiently. He spoke only to repeat, "Please sit back down, William." William did so, looked across to Sir James and wondered what he could possibly say that would not have him marked as a madman.

Finally, deciding it was better to keep quiet and be thought a fool that to speak and remove all doubt, he looked Sir James squarely in the eye and said, "I am sorry, but I can only repeat what I said to Sir Walter yesterday. That is, since the incident I remember almost nothing except my name, and my brother's name. To be honest, I am not even sure of that."

Sir James' gaze penetrated through William's eyes, as if he was looking directly into his mind in search of the truth. This was another new experience for William, but he instinctively remained still and did not drop his own gaze. At length Sir James sighed and called out, "Sir Walter, the sword."

William looked towards the sound of the opening door, and was more than a little surprised to see Walter re-enter carrying a familiar object.

"We found this close to where your brother lay. Given its length, our assumption is that it belonged to you or your brother."

During his birthday celebration William had been given an extremely long sword, made by the technical department at school where he worked as a teacher. Carrying on the theme, the sword was based on the description of the weapon allegedly wielded by the mediaeval warrior.

"That is indeed mine. May I have it back?"

Walter looked to Sir James, who simply smiled and nodded, and he reluctantly held out the sword. William had got up and walked round the table to stand in front of Walter. Taking the weapon in his hands, turning it over, examining it in the light from the window, he marvelled that what had seemed an impressive weapon on first sight, now seemed incredibly more so. It felt almost alive in his hands, shinier, sharper, now not just well balanced, but perfectly balanced. This was a weapon of the gods.

"With such a weapon, you must truly be a knight of the realm, Sir William." Sir James had approached and now laid his hand on William's shoulder. "I have use for such a fine weapon, wielded by such a fine man. When you are fully recovered, I will return, there are people you must meet, work to be done."

"I am sorry, my lord, but I cannot leave my brother."

"Do not worry, your brother is in good hands. Hopefully he will be awake and in better health himself soon. I'm sure he would not want you to remain here, where you can do very little of benefit except chop wood. The abbot will send word as soon as there is news. Sir Walter tells me you promised to do whatever you could in exchange for getting help for Malcolm. Well, I am here to hold you to your word"

He was right, there was nothing he could do here. Whatever the game that was afoot, he may as well get on with it. "Of course, Sir James, I am at your service."

Chapter 3: September 1296

Craigie Castle

There are still traces of Craigie castle to this day, although these ruins are from a much later building. In the thirteenth century it was little more than a rectangular hall, but still impressive for its time. Sir James was overlord of all of Kyle, that part of Ayrshire between the rivers Irvine and Doon, but Walter was the current holder of Craigie. He held it from Sir James, though, and when Sir James was in attendance he was the law.

As they approached the castle, for the first time William felt himself become involved in his new world. He knew this area intimately, and had often mused on what buildings such as this would have been like in their heyday. The monastery had not triggered this feeling because nothing of it remains in the present day, but now he could make a direct connection between the life he knew and his present predicament. Notwithstanding that he was not just caught in a distant corner of his own mind – that was still more likely – but for now he thought he may as well enjoy what he could. Having always been a country boy at heart, he was now really beginning to relish the sights, sounds and smells, unadulterated as they were by modern advancements.

"Welcome to my home, William," Walter said as they dismounted, still sounding not entirely sincere. Even before they had arrived, word had gone out and there were stable boys waiting to take the horses from them. Being the size that he was, William had been loaned a working horse, a giant in its own right, standing just short of nineteen hands. Walter had not been confident that any of his regular mounts would support the newcomer, or indeed keep his feet from trailing on the ground. Scottish noblemen tended to use coursours, really large ponies; they were smaller, but more nimble than the destriers preferred by their English neighbours.

As they walked towards the castle, Sir James, rather more enthusiastically, told William, "We have arranged a feast in your honour this evening, return of the prodigal son as it were. You will find much better sustenance than the basic fare they give you at Fail. With any luck you will also find much more interesting conversation. Word has been sent out to such dignitaries as are close at hand. Hopefully most will attend and we can plan ahead,"

"I do not understand, Sir James. You do not know me, nobody knows me. Why would you have a banquet for me? It just doesn't make sense."

"Ah, we don't know you, but we think we know *of* you. One of the most prominent guests will be Robert Wishart, the Bishop of Glasgow. The good bishop has been telling everyone about a dream he had, which he insists was a revelation from God. This revelation concerned a warrior who would come to lead all of Scotland to freedom. A giant of a man with a giant of a sword. Sound familiar?"

"You are doing all of this based on a dream?"

"Aye, and naw. This is not a first. Several years ago the bishop had dreams about the collapse of Scotland. He warned the rest of us of the threat from the King of England following the death of the old King, Alexander. Nobody took him too seriously, although most of the safeguards that were added to the treaties were at his insistence. A lot of good they did us in the long run. Events have proven him right. We would be foolish to ignore his messages from above a second time."

"You talk of *us* and *we*; who would that be?"

"The guardians, such as remain."

"Guardians, I'm sorry, but I don't understand. What is a guardian?"

Sir James stopped and turned to look directly at William. "You really have been out of it, haven't you?" Realising that William was sincere in his lack of knowledge, Sir James explained, "When King Alexander died, six of us were appointed as guardians of the kingdom, to govern until the new queen was old enough."

"Queen?" William had heard of Mary Queen of Scots – who hadn't? – but was not aware of Scotland being ruled by a woman before that.

"Princess Margaret was a child in Norway, the daughter of Alexander's daughter Margaret and the Norwegian King Eric, when her grandfather died. Not yet three years old. Sadly she died in Orkney on her way to Scotland."

Sir James paused and took another long look at William, clearly wondering what kind of man could be alive in Scotland and not know any of this. At length he gave a shrug. "Okay, there are many things you need to be reminded of, you clearly have lost much of your knowledge. I pray that you can remember how to fight. For now, just know that of the six original guardians, two are dead and a third is quite ill and may not live much longer. That leaves three, so Robert and I between us make up most of the government. I will fill you in on more later, but now let's go inside and meet our guests."

Not knowing what plans Sir James had, William followed him inside. He could not help but feel a little excited about what might lie ahead. Although he was still bemused, he was a pragmatic man, and had no trouble going with the flow of his current situation. There did not appear to be any immediate threat, but there was a sense of adventure. Teaching for the last few months had been such a drag. Many times he had wondered if he had made a mistake quitting the forces. He had been effectively press-ganged into service, and had come to resent that, among other things. With hindsight he could see that being a soldier had been a good move for him.

Chapter 4: September 1296

Banquet

The hall was buzzing, but went eerily quiet when Walter led William in. One and all turned to take in the big man that they had all come to see. It was Sir James who made the formal announcement.

"Ladies and gentlemen, here is our guest of honour, the recently returned Sir William Wallace. You will all get your chance to meet him after we eat, but for now please do not be too rude and let the man have some food."

William leaned over and reproached Sir James in a whisper. "I did say, Sir James, that I am not a knight, just William."

"This fine gentleman claims to be just a mere man, despite the clothes and the fine weapon he carried. Very well, we shall just call him William, for now. Soon, we will give him the opportunity to earn his title. Now eat, everyone, and drink. There is plenty of food and wine for all. Let no man hold back; this is a celebration."

Turning back to William, he pointed out a few of the faces that he deemed most important for his guest to know. As they reached their seats Sir James motioned to the dark man seated on the other side of Sir Walter. "This is Sir William, Lord of Douglas."

Douglas stood up and extended an arm to William. "Welcome, stranger. Bishop Wishart tells us that you have come to free us from those thieving English invaders. What are you going to do, tear down walls with your bare hands?" Commonly referred to as the Black Douglas, he had jet-black hair, dark, almost black eyes and a complexion so dark he did not look particularly Scottish at all.

"That will depend on the wall, I suppose, what sort of wall are we talking about?" William joked.

"Now, now, Lord Douglas," Sir James interrupted. "Let's eat and we can get down to business later. William, this is the man I told you about earlier, Robert Wishart, the Bishop of Glasgow. If he likes you, he will let you call him Robert." He gestured towards an older, barrel-chested, sombre-looking man, dressed in black robes." The bishop was already rising to greet him. Old as he was, he threw his arms around William and his bear hug actually squeezed air out of his lungs. A powerful man indeed.

Releasing William, the bishop stepped back and announced to the room, "This is indeed a great moment, my friends. Soon you will all look back to this night and realise that this is the day our world changed."

As every man rose, and shouted, and cheered, and drank his health, William, for perhaps the first time in his life, knew real fear. Not of these people, nor of defeat, nor of death. Fear of failure. Fear of letting others down. Sure, he had been in situations where his actions could mean life or death to his comrades, but that had been as part of a team. Part of a well-drilled team. Never before had anyone reacted to him in this way. Never before had he felt so small.

Sir James pulled him back to the moment when he said, "I had hoped that the Earl of Carrick would join us, but sadly he has not been able to attend. You will meet him soon, I am sure. He is a great man, and with so many of the country's leaders kept prisoner in England, it is good to have someone so dedicated to our cause to rally behind. I am assuming you are dedicated to our cause, William. Are you?"

"My lord." William was adapting to the speech patterns of those around him. "I am at your command, body and soul." He was still not entirely sure just quite what the cause was, but he was beginning to catch on.

"Give him your body, by all means," the Bishop of Glasgow interjected, "but I will have your soul, by God." The bishop was still looking sombre, and William was not yet sure how to read him. As William watched, he exploded in an uproarious belly laugh for several seconds before gulping down a huge swallow of wine and turning back to his food. He had plenty of belly to fill and seemed intent on doing just that.

The food was fairly plain, but plentiful. Lots of meats – venison, boar, beef and rabbit; birds such as pheasant, partridge and even swan. A multitude of fish, both freshwater and some saltwater varieties brought up specially from the coast. Various fruits and nuts and vegetables. No potatoes, though. Not a problem for William. He preferred rice and pasta to potatoes, only there were none of those either. Lots of wine, even though, he was told, trade with the rest of Europe was severely hampered by the English.

His thoughts turned to his family. He wondered what Malcolm would make of the food. His big brother was fond of spicier dishes;

he loved a good curry washed down with a few beers. Hopefully soon, very soon, Malcolm would wake up and he would find out. And his father, where was he now? Who was he with? Anyone? Was he on his own grieving for his wee boys? He always called them his wee boys, even though they were both inches taller than him. William was already concerned for his father's health. Alan Wallace had taken to drinking heavily after his wife died, although while his boys were still young they came first. As the boys grew, though, so did their father's drinking. By the time William left for university, he was aware that his dad was a functioning alcoholic. That is to say, he managed to do pretty much everything he needed to do while drunk, but could not do the simplest of things without a drink.

~~~

Later in the evening Bishop Wishart approached William. "Sir James tells me that you have forgotten much. Head injury, he suspects."

Not wanting to lie, but not knowing how to explain the truth, William replied, "I know almost nothing about anything it seems. I don't know who anyone is. I don't even know who I am."

"You feel like a lost soul, William. Don't worry, you are where you are meant to be. God has brought you to us. I know that because he told me he would. Trust in God. Trust me as his agent. Tomorrow you will accompany me and I will explain everything you need to know. We will go and see the people and places that are important, and you can show me why God has put you here."

Chapter 5: October 1296

Malcolm

"You should get over to Fail, there is news of your brother."

William had just returned from his travels with Bishop Wishart and had gone, as instructed, to see the Steward at his main residence, Dundonald Castle.

"Malcolm, is he awake? Is he okay? What is the news?"

"Best you see how he is for yourself. He is awake, but not very coherent."

William hesitated. Not because he did not want to see his brother; he did. For the second time he was slowed down by fear. As he had learned about the situation in Scotland he had begun to worry for his brother. William was a trained soldier. He had faced death before. He had killed before. Malcolm was a great guy, but he was not a fighter. To the best of William's knowledge he had never been in a fight in his life. Off the rugby pitch that is. Now that William realised what lay ahead for himself, he knew he had to protect Malcolm from it. For goodness sake, Malcolm was afraid of horses. How could he possibly face a cavalry charge?

"Are you okay? It sounds like good news. Your brother is alive."

"Aye, I will go to him right away." And thought, 'While I figure out how to keep him alive.'

~~~

"Wull, thank God you are here. What the fuck is happening? Where am I? Who are these weird-arsed dudes?" Poor Malcolm looked totally bewildered, and with good reason.

"Malc, it's okay, calm down. Please. It's okay." And he grabbed his brother in a hug and let him sob into his shoulder. Looking past his brother's tousled hair he asked the monks looking on, "Give us some time, please, I'll let you know if we need anything." The religious brothers, men of few words at the best of times, simply nodded, turned and left the room.

William just held his big brother and let him sob himself out. After a while Malcolm raised his head and asked again, this time more calmly, "What is going on, Wull, really? Last thing I remember we were at your birthday party, then I wake up in this weird place surrounded by creatures out of a horror film. Nobody knows anything, they treat me like some kind of a lunatic, but at least they mentioned you. Where were you? What happened? What is going on? Wull, am I mental? Am I in the loony bin? Where are the real doctors?"

"Ssh, calm down Malc, I'll explain what I can, but you need to calm down. There is a lot to take on board, you need to be ready to listen."

Malcolm sat down, took some deep breaths and tried to get himself under control. "I'm listening. Shoot."

"Okay, you remember we were at the party."

"Aye, was I really wasted ? Were there drugs?."

William chuckled. "You never know when to stop drinking, Malc. No drugs as far as I know."

"That's a shame, I was hoping I was still hallucinating."

"If only. You've been unconscious for weeks. In that time I have had to accept that whatever is going on, it's not a dream."

"So do you know what's going on? Where the fuck we are?"

"As far as I can tell, we are near where we were at the party in distance, but not in time."

"How do you mean, not in time?"

"Let me try to explain from the beginning. I think someone, no, I know someone tried to kill me."

"Tried to kill you? Who? Was it Andy McNab? Or are you shagging somebody else's wife, Wull? "

"Malcolm, please, be quiet while I tell you what I know. Don't interrupt. Just listen and try to take it in."

The older brother shrugged and made a zipping motion across his lips.

"Okay, my motor was forced off the road after the party. Something hit us, but it was travelling without lights, so I am sure it was deliberate. I was unconscious too. I don't know for how long, but when I came to I couldn't find any sign of the car, or an accident for that matter. Only you, lying lifeless nearby. Shit, Malc, I thought you were dead." Unusually for William he found his voice catching in his throat, and felt his eyes moisten. Malcolm still said nothing.

"Anyway, the thing is, Malc, you remember that film Back to the

Future?" Malcolm nodded, frowning, wondering why this detour. "Well, it seems that we have gone back in time."

"Fuck off." Malcolm laughed. "This is a joke, right? You were pissed off about the party, I wouldn't listen when you said you didn't want a fuss about being thirty. So you have slipped something into my drink and set up this crazy stunt. I suppose some TV presenter is behind one of these walls, waiting to jump out with a microphone and reveal that the weirdos in the hoodies are just actors."

"I wish that was true, Malc, I really do. You have been unconscious for weeks, look at yourself, you have faded away to a small hill." Malcolm had noticed that he was a bit – well, a lot – thinner. He had not dwelt on it. Now he looked down at himself and tried, unsuccessfully, to grab his beer belly.

"Bloody hell, what have you done to me?"

"Nothing, nothing at all. Your body has been eating itself to keep you alive, I suppose. Listen, Malcolm, we are now living about seven hundred years before we were born."

"Come on, this is not some crummy film, that kind of thing doesn't happen."

"It has happened, we are *where* we are. We are *when* we are."

"For real?"

"For real."

"So no schools, no roads, no hospitals. No friends and family. What about Dad?"

"Sorry, I don't know what has happened to Dad. I sincerely hope nothing has happened to him and he is still where and when we left him."

"So are we dead in Dad's time? Or missing? Poor old bugger! What is he going to do without us. He'll be all on his own."

"I know. Then again I don't know, that's the thing. We could be dead or missing in 1996, or maybe time has stopped somehow. Maybe we'll wake up one morning and everything will be back to normal. Shit, I can't even be sure you are really here. This could all be in my mind."

"No way, Wull. I'm not having it. I want to go home. Enough of this bullshit! Cut it out! Whatever is going on, make it stop!"

Malcolm was back on his feet, eyes wide and red rimmed, tears and snot all over his face. William had never seen his brother look so vulnerable and it shook him to his core. What worried him most was knowing that Malcolm was only vocalising what he himself had been suppressing.

William held his brother again and tried to reassure both of them "You'll be okay, Malc. Whatever this is we'll figure it out and we'll sort it."

Chapter 6: March 1297

Escape

Andrew took the berries out of the pouch he had hidden. They were poisonous, and as a child he had been warned never to eat them. Formulating a plan, he had collected a handful over the previous few weeks. Now he placed all of them in his mouth and chewed, grimacing at the foul taste of them. After taking a long drink of water he lay down on his bed and waited for the inevitable convulsions.

Although he was a prisoner, he was allowed out, accompanied, from time to time. He was not aware of it, but King Edward had plans for this esquire. His father had been a thorn in Edward's side for some time now. Taking a long-term view, Edward had asked that the son be given special treatment, intending to groom him as an ally. When the time came he would be taken back home to take up his rightful place – after pledging his allegiance to the King of England, of course – Andrew Moray senior having died, probably with some help, due to his own recalcitrance.

None of the young man's captors were aware that Andrew had been doing some grooming for himself. Aware that he was receiving preferential treatment, he played along and gathered favour with his captors. Especially the women of Chester Castle. He was a fine-looking man and he knew it. Tall, luxurious dark curly hair, noble features and the softest of brown eyes, he had known from a young age that most women found him attractive. He was a single man, heir not only of his father, but also of his father's childless older brother. Uncle William was known to be one of the richest men in Scotland. All of this made Andrew a very good prospect for a young lady looking for a husband, or indeed a gentleman looking for a son-in-law.

When the first screams of pain rang out, the door flew open and a guard approached the profusely sweating figure tentatively. Such were the force of the screams that they brought people from all over the castle, particularly, as Andrew had hoped, indeed had counted on, several young ladies.

"Is he dying?" Lady Eleanor asked tearfully.

"He is not good. Stay back, give him room. Let him breathe, for God's sake," snapped Elizabeth. "Don't just stand there like an idiot," she barked at the guard hovering behind her. "Bring water. Fresh water, and plenty of it." The guard rushed off to fetch some water.

"He is burning up. Help me get his shirt off, Eleanor." The younger woman hurried to help. She had dreamed of doing such a thing, but not under these circumstances. Over the course of the next two days neither woman strayed far from Andrew's bed, taking turns to wash the sweat from his head and body and trying to help the delirious patient drink some water. Finally the fever broke and the worst appeared to be over. Still the young women would not let anyone else near Andrew, and began to put aside their own truce as they battled to be the first face he would see when we came fully awake.

"Am I dead? Are you an angel?" Andrew asked.

Elizabeth tutted, but was inwardly delighted to be the one in attendance at this moment. Mopping his brow with a damp cloth, her face delightfully close to his, she replied, "It is only I, Elizabeth. You have been ill, Andrew, but you are not yet dead."

In truth, Andrew had been compos mentis for several hours, but had been concealing the fact, waiting for just such an opportunity. Over the weeks he had been building up a plan of the castle and surrounding area in his head. Most importantly, he felt pretty confident that he knew how to get out given an opportunity such as this. There was only one person standing in his way.

Andrew put his hand on the back of Elizabeth's neck and, pulling her towards him with absolutely no resistance, he kissed her passionately. Every nerve in her body tingling, Elizabeth prepared to surrender completely to her love. As her tongue probed his mouth, and her fingers caressed his head through his dark curls, Andrew eased her back from him and said softly, "Elizabeth, my love, we must be careful. We cannot be discovered like this. Especially not by Eleanor."

Aware of both women's feelings towards him, Andrew knew his best hope was to use that to his advantage. "Elizabeth, I must escape from here. Come with me."

Elizabeth recoiled from him. "You are playing me for a fool, Andrew. This is so cruel, using my love for you like that."

He reached out and took both of her hands in his and gazed deep into her baby blue eyes. "My darling, it is true I am using your love for me, but only because I feel the same way. They will never let us be together, you must know that. Your king has plans for me, and they include marrying me to someone closer to him. I don't want that, I want to be with you. Please come away with me."

Elizabeth hesitated. Deep down she knew he was right. She had heard some of the talk herself. What could she do? She could not leave, but could she let her love go? "Do you truly, truly love me?"

"With all of my heart. Come with me, we will be together always."

"But I cannot go with you, my love. Even though I know you cannot stay. Will you come back for me when you can?"

This was exactly what he wanted to hear. In truth he was fond of the pretty little blonde, but hey, all is fair in love and war. She might be in love, but he was at war. "Help me get out of the castle. I will go home and when I return I will be a great Lord and will claim you as my wife."

"They will kill me if I let you go."

"Go to your room and be surprised when they tell you I have gone. Tell them that you were overcome with fatigue and left me still soundly asleep. They cannot blame you alone. The guards will have to answer for their reasons for not still being here."

Elizabeth kissed him once more, took his hand and told him, "Come." Although he had already planned his escape route, he was delighted to find that there was an easier way. There is always another way. Once clear of the castle, it was a relatively simple case of finding a spot to get up and over the city wall. Since there was no sense of any imminent danger this was simpler than anticipated. After stealthily liberating a horse from a nearby farm he was galloping northwards and well clear before daybreak.

~~~

On his way home after his escape from Chester, Andrew took the westerly route, knowing that he was more likely to meet occupying forces if he took the easier route up the eastern side of Scotland. As he went he sought shelter and sustenance where he could safely do so and a few weeks later passed through Kyle. He stopped off at Dundonald where, as fate would have it, plans were being drawn up to begin an offensive to liberate Scotland.

When Andrew was brought into the hall where the meeting was in progress, Sir James greeted him enthusiastically. "This is a cause for celebration. Surely a sign from God that the English cannot keep a good Scotsman down for long. Andrew, I believe you know most of my guests, except this big fellow. Let me introduce you to William Wallace. William has also recently returned to us. You two have much in common."

William and Andrew embraced one another. Both men felt something pass between them. Although neither man said anything at the time, both had a strong feeling of deja vu. Impossible as it was, both were trying to remember where they had met before. William knew that, unlike Walter and Alan, Andrew was not a boyhood friend in the twentieth century. But there was something, for sure. Perhaps there was more than he realised to his cover story that he had lost a lot of memories. Could it be that he actually had? These days, anything seemed possible.

"Let us delay our plans for a day; this calls for a celebration," Sir James suggested. No one disagreed. "I am sure we are all keen to hear of this young man's adventures."

Part II

The Making of the Man

Chapter 7: April 1987–June 1988

Entrapment

At twenty one, William had not had a long-term girlfriend. Not that he didn't like girls, he did. He also liked a lot of other things and was not as willing as the other boys to give up the things he already enjoyed, just because a cute girl did not share the same interests. Had he met a girl who was into martial arts, hiking, fishing and camping, things might have been different. He certainly wasn't going to give up his personal freedom just for the hope of a regular shag. He recalled what a drunken neighbour told him and Malcolm one Saturday night.

"Don't get married, it's not what you think. Yous boys think that you get married and you get sex any time you want. You don't! You get sex when *she* wants."

In any case, tall, muscular, good-looking with a good sense of humour, there was never any shortage of girls willing, eager even, to give William whatever comforts he wanted. No need to be tied down for that.

That is, until he met Alice.

They were both students at St Andrews university. William was studying modern languages. He was a natural polyglot and had stunned his teachers at school when he mastered first French, then German in a matter of weeks. In no time at all they had run out of things to teach him; he had gone through all the language tapes and read all the foreign language books in the school library. For him it seemed all too easy and he began to get bored, but it was an easy choice to go on to university doing something that came naturally to him. It left him so much more time to do the things he really loved.

On a pleasantly dry and surprisingly sunny Thursday afternoon in April, William was walking purposefully back to his lodgings after handing in his assignments early. Since he had nothing scheduled for the next day, his intention, as it was every weekend regardless of the weather, was to gather his camping equipment and head off into the wild. Having already explored so many beautiful places in Fife and Tayside, and since the weather was so fine, he was intending to go a bit further afield and make a start on investigating The Mounth. Just as he reached the house he shared with five other students, a young lady appeared, seemingly from nowhere, and careered straight into him, spilling text books and papers all over the street.

"I'm sorry, are you okay?" William said, immediately hunkering down to pick up the girl's papers. As he handed them to her and looked into her emerald green eyes below a mass of soft blonde curls, his heart began drumming like Sandy Nelson in his chest.

"I'm fine, no thanks to you, you big galoot," she teased and gave William a playful punch to the arm.

Even although he knew it was not his fault, William heard himself say, "I do beg your pardon, my lady," and a part of him was astonished, even slightly embarrassed, as he felt himself make an exaggerated bow and add, "Please forgive your foolish servant, William Wallace."

The young lady giggled. "Hi, I'm Alice. You will be forgiven, but only if you buy your lady a coffee and a nice piece of cake."

William's head was swimming and his legs had gone all weak and wobbly, neither of which were due to the physical collision. The spiritual collision, however, was a different affair. Just like that, as if by magic, he was drowning in love. He could barely breathe for it, and seemed helpless to swim against it merciless tide. For the first weekend in a long, long time, William stayed home. For the first weekend ever, he barely got out of bed.

~~~~

Just over a year later William, recently graduated, decided it was time to do the honourable thing and ask Alice's father for permission to marry his daughter. For the first time he had been invited to the family home.

"Turn right just there, between the stone pillars," Alice directed.

"Here? Are you sure?" William was slightly overawed. He had just turned his aged Triumph TR6 into a long, sweeping driveway which had what he could only describe as a château at the end of it. "Alice Shirley, I always knew you were a posh bird, but really, this is ridiculous. I can't go in there, I won't know how to behave, how to speak even. You should have warned me."

Alice squeezed out that delightful little giggle that still gave him butterflies and explained, "I had to be sure you were not a gold digger or social climber, my dear. I wanted, no needed, to know that you love me for myself, not Daddy's money or influence."

Influence? Just who was he getting involved with? William wondered. A brief moment of clarity, something that had been sorely missing over the previous months. For the first time since they had literally bumped into each other, William was thinking critically of the girl smiling up at him.

"Come on, Billy boy, Daddy is just dying to meet you." Grabbing William's hand she propelled him up the flight of wide stone stairs towards the huge, ornately carved oak doors towering over them.

After dinner Alice's father invited William into his study for a chat. 'Here goes, it's now or never,' William thought, as he followed Sir Peter Shirley into the massive book-lined room. Once again William was overawed. Study? This room was larger, and appeared to have more books than his local library back home.

"Now then, young man, my daughter seems to be somewhat smitten by you. She thinks you may have marriage on your mind. Ah, I see you do," he added, picking up on William's slack-jawed response to his last statement.

This was not how William had planned it. He realised he was not going to be in control of this conversation. All those carefully practised words had just flown away in the wind. He was on the back foot and did not know how to turn this around.

"First thing first, William. As Alice's father, I am entitled to ask how you would intend to support my daughter, to keep her in the manner to which she is accustomed."

The manner to which she is accustomed! He was from a council estate in Ayrshire; he knew nothing of the manner to which she was so obviously accustomed. William was being railroaded. All at once he wanted out of there; he was completely out of his depth. But he wasn't a quitter. He would stand his ground and take what was coming to him and then leave with as much dignity as he still had. Rather meekly he replied, "As you are probably aware, sir, I have just graduated in Arabic language and Middle East Studies with first class honours. I have applied for several positions. My hope is to become an interpreter at the EU or even the UN."

"You sound a little defensive, young man. Relax, I am not your enemy. I know you are highly skilled and have the potential to do very well in that line of work. However, I may be able to help you to do better, if you will allow me."

Once more William was left reeling. A minute ago he was convinced that he was about to get the bum's rush; now suddenly Sir Peter seemed to want to be friends. His head was spinning. "Of course, Sir Peter, I am open to advice. What are you proposing?"

"You have been focussing on your academic skills, and no doubt the advisors at your university have been encouraging that. So they should, they want to see the university's work admired in the outside world. But you have other skills, William, and rare as your indisputable talent for languages is, your other skills can be just as useful."

"Other skills? Do you mean martial arts? I never really thought about it, it has just been my hobby since I was a boy. My brother Malcolm started taking lessons after seeing Bruce Lee in *Enter The Dragon*, and I just tagged along."

"It's not just a hobby, though, William, is it? You have black belts in several different martial arts, a couple of them weapons-based, do you not." William simply nodded; he did not like to brag.

Sir Peter continued, "In addition to that, you have survival skills. I know that you go off on your own all over the place, hiking, camping, climbing, even sleeping rough sometimes."

"Again, just a hobby. I love nature, love being in nature, being at one with nature. It's just something I enjoy doing."

"You are too modest. Hobby or not, you are probably as well equipped and experienced as any amateur survivalist in the entire country. Let's cut to the chase, shall we?"

"Er – please do." This was all very confusing, and William had no idea at that point in time what 'the chase' night be.

"A man in my position can't have just anybody getting involved in his family. You have been carefully monitored for some time now."

Sir Peter did not expand to say that 'some time' was considerably longer than the time since William and Alice had 'accidentally' bumped into one another. Or to be more precise, since Alice had 'accidentally' bumped into him!

"The long and the short of it is this, William. My daughter will not be marrying an interpreter. However, an officer in Her Majesty's armed forces is a different kettle of fish. A man with your talents and abilities can go a long way, William. Allow me to put you on a fast track to a long and successful military career."

Chapter 8: August 1988

SAS

"Here he comes, teacher's pet," mocked Gerry Clark, as William entered the barracks. Gerry walked over to William and shot his hand out towards him, as if to strike him. William did not flinch. He could tell this was for show; the older soldier would know better than to assault the new boy without provocation. Gerry ran his index finger behind William's ear, and turning to the rest of the room grinned and said, "Just like I thought, still wet behind the ears."

There were a few sniggers, it was always fun to have a laugh at a new recruit's expense. "So what's so special about you, Jock, that you can waltz in here with no experience and expect to play with the big boys?"

William knew the type, the wee hard man. Always seemed to have a chip on their shoulder, probably mostly down to envy. At five foot eight, Gerry was easily the shortest man in the room. Mousy brown hair, and average to ugly features, he was one of the kind who tried to make himself feel better by bringing others down. He was out of luck this time though.

William, surprisingly quickly and nimbly for such a big man, grabbed Gerry's right hand in his left, put his arm around his waist and started waltzing him around the room, la-la-ing a tune as he went. Now instead of a few sniggers, the whole place erupted in laughter as William bent Gerry backwards, lowered his face to almost kissing distance of his bemused partner and said softly, "Because I am a better dancer than you, darling," then kissed him briefly on the lips and then let him drop to the floor. William gave a twirl and bowed to the others. He knew first impressions were important, and wanted to ensure that everyone was aware that he was not there to be anybody's whipping boy, or even just to make up the numbers.

With a slow handclap, one man, with an air of authority, walked towards William and spoke to him, but for the benefit of all, "Welcome, William. I am Sergeant Donald McInnes. Some people," he said with a scathing glance at Gerry, "may resent the fact that you have been fast-tracked into the SAS when most of us have had to wait several years proving ourselves to get in. But the rest of us," he added, with a long, slow look around all of the faces around them, his stern look telling them that this was how it was going to be, "the rest of us, accept that you are here on merit, and will hold fire while you demonstrate that you are indeed fit to lace our boots. I have been tasked to ensure you are as capable as they say you are."

"If all I am going to do is lace boots, I will probably get bored quite quickly," the young man quipped.

Donald's expression changed abruptly as he snapped at his new charge. "I am not your friend, sonny boy, and you will not attempt to treat me like one. Henceforth, only speak to me when spoken to. And no jokes, this is not a playground. Do what I say, when I say, or sooner, and you will get where the brass want you to go. But one step out of place and I will come down on you like a ton of bricks. Your feet won't touch the ground on the way back home. Do you understand me?"

William snapped his heels together, made a salute and, looking straight ahead barked "Yes, sir. Loud and clear, sir."

"Don't make me dislike you, Wallace. You have had it easy up until now. Better get yourself a good night's sleep tonight, laddie, tomorrow the real work begins. Dismissed!" And with that the sergeant wheeled around and left the room.

The previous few weeks had been rigorous as William was put through his paces. The basic army training that he had received when he initially signed up were like a walk in the park though, compared to the onslaught he was put through in Wales. He knew those five weeks were designed to break men, but he also knew that he was equal to anything they could throw at him. Hell, this was just the kind of adventure holiday he would have paid for, if he could have found it, and if he could afford it. At the end of the stint he had the fastest time for the four-mile run and was third fastest on the two-mile swim.

Chapter 9: January 1989

Secondment

Sir Peter!

William and Donald were standing easy in a plush office with an outstanding view north over the River Thames. Turning to see who had just entered, who they were meeting with, William was astonished to see the father of his former girlfriend. The man responsible for him being in the forces. Not for the first time William felt a surge of anger at the realisation that he had been played. Should have known that Alice was out of his league. Should have known there was a reason for her interest in him. And here was the reason, this arrogant little cunt strutting around the huge oak desk, had had his daughter prostitute herself. Didn't make any sense, but he was sure that was what had happened. No sooner had he signed up than his ever-loving girlfriend started to make excuses to avoid him, before dumping him.

"Donald, how nice to see you again. And, may I say, you have done an excellent job knocking this young man into shape. Not that I doubted either of your abilities for a moment, you understand."

"Quite," was Donald's simple reply. William got the distinct impression that Donald was not a big fan of Sir Peter.

"And you, William. I knew you would suit that uniform. You do look splendid. Sit down, gentlemen, please. Let's not be overly formal. We are all friends here."

As the soldiers sat down Sir Peter continued, "I'm afraid I don't have a lot of time, got to get across to Downing Street shortly, so I'll get straight to the point. You will both be aware of the atrocity that occurred over your fine country just recently."

Both men nodded agreement. The Lockerbie bombing had been an outrage. A bomb had torn apart a jumbo jet over Scotland, killing all 259 people on board and another 11 on the ground.

"Right. Well, this is where you get the chance to put into practice all of that fine training you have been getting. You will know of the Popular Front for the Liberation of Palestine – General Command?"

William shook his head and said, "No."

Donald, though was nodding and asked, "Do you think that the PFLP-GC are behind the plane bombing?"

"Yes, we do, Donald. Yes we do. There have been rumblings about a revenge attack since the Americans shot down that Iranian plane last July. Much of our intelligence identified the PFLP-GC as the chosen vehicle."

Turning his attention to the younger man, Sir Peter continued, "Okay, it doesn't matter, William, that you don't know the organisation. Donald and I go back a long way and have come across so many of these lunatics. What is more important is that you do know some people connected to them. Indeed, it is your association with a relative of the group's ring leader, Ali Omar, that first brought us to your attention."

"Really? Not my relationship with your daughter?"

The older man allowed himself a chuckle. "Come, come, my dear boy. You do look put out. Are you miffed? Understandably so, I suppose." The amiable expression disappeared. "I'm afraid that I really do not have the time to do this delicately, so I will be blunt. Please forgive me for that. The truth is that Alice is not my daughter, but an undercover operative who was doing her job. Rather too well, I may add. As you grow and mature you will come to realise that we all have to do whatever is necessary in order to protect this great country of ours. She was doing her bit so that now you can do yours."

"Are you saying that you knew this was going to happen? My first meeting with Alice was, what, almost two years ago. That can't be."

"Of course not, but we were aware of Omar and his cohorts and were delighted to have an opportunity to get some inside information on them. They and several other monsters that they come into contact with. You look unconvinced. All you need to know is we like to play the long game here. We have agents all over the world infiltrating organisations, governments even, sometimes for many, many years. Our aim is not to react to events as they happen, but to anticipate and stop them before anyone gets hurt. Anyone innocent, that is. Of course the baddies do tend to get their comeuppance."

"But you are reacting to this," William said, stating the obvious.

"Yes, well, what a pity we didn't get to know each other a little sooner, William. Many, many lives could have been saved. With your help now, we can bring these men to justice and save who knows how many lives in the future. That is why you are here, to save lives. Can you work with that?"

"Yes, of course."

"Good. Now then, William, what I need you to do is re-establish contact with your university friend Musa. Tell him that you have been thinking about what you learned in your Integrated Year Abroad in Syria, and have been becoming more and more disillusioned with the Western way of life. You will say that you want to go back to Syria to learn more. Don't make it too complicated; you can improvise when you get there. How does that sound?"

"Sounds risky. Are you sure I am the right man for this job?"

"You are the only man for the job. Your friend Musa is a second cousin to Omar. Not only that, he is now part of his organisation, as we expected he would be. That is why we were keeping an eye on him, and why, because of your friendship, we began keeping an eye on you."

Sir Peter handed William a manilla folder with about an inch of papers inside. "This file here is an extract from our file on you. Oh, don't look surprised, we have files on anyone who is anyone. If we don't have a file on you, you don't matter. You should be flattered; there are senior politicians with thinner files than that. Take this with you, but not to Syria. Refresh your memory before you go. There are names, dates and times of meetings, prints of conversations where we could record them. All to do with your time in Syria, and a little background on some of the people we are most interested in. Not too much, though, it would look bad if you appeared to know of, or know about people you have not yet come into contact with. In any case, some of the stuff we have would prejudice your investigation. Best that you make your own mind up about things, we will amend our records as you find better information. Donald has all the good stuff in this file," he continued, as he handed an even thicker bundle to the sergeant, "and he is experienced enough to know better than to share any of it with you. It's all need to know stuff."

Looking at his Rolex, Sir Peter ended with, "As I said, I have to dash. You know the way out, Donald. God save the queen!"

Both soldiers automatically stood to attention, saluted, and echoed "God save the Queen."

When Sir Peter had left the office, Donald turned to William, put his hand on his shoulder and told him, "They are throwing you in at the deep end, son. If you are scared, and you should be, that is nothing to be ashamed of. Fear can keep you alive. Let's hope that when you get there, Musa's colleagues like you, and more importantly, trust you. God willing we will both come home soon."

The message, and the tone of the message particularly, did not comfort William. Nevertheless, he was old enough and wise enough to realise that he was in a job where people did get killed. This was the life he had signed up for. There was only one way to go, and that was forward.

Chapter 10: August 23rd 1996

Coma

"I'm sorry, Mr Wallace, but there has been no sign of any cerebral brain function whatsoever, and it is time to switch off the life support." Doctor Abernethy was suitably sombre as he informed William's father of the clinical decision taken by his care team.

Alan had been expecting this, but he was still momentarily distraught. Since he had lost his wife twenty years before, only his sons had given him any reason to carry on. Watching them grow into men, both good men he was very proud of, his happiness was always tempered by the knowledge that one day they would both leave to start their own families. Still, there was always the grandchildren to look forward to.

Only now, it seemed, there wasn't. Following the car accident Alan had buried his older son, Malcolm, while his younger son lay in a coma. Every day he had come to the hospital to sit with William and talk to him, as they said he should, but in all these weeks there had never been a flicker. Not on his face, not even a flutter of the eyelids. Not on his body, no twitches or spasms. Not on the array of machines around his bed; they picked up nothing more than what they put in.

Still, Alan knew that his son was still in there, somewhere, and he would be back. His despondency lasted only a few brief seconds. The Wallaces were fighters, never more so than when their backs were against the wall. He looked down at his son. He was only sleeping, he would wake up when he was ready. In all his life, William had never had to be woken. Ever. He was always up and at them when he needed to be.

"So what happens now?"

"Well, Alan, we will follow standard procedure. There has been no cerebral activity, but we have to check the brain stem. That controls a few things such as breathing and heartbeat. Two different doctors will supervise the tests, including switching off the machines on different days, and watching for any sign of life. In the absence of breathing or heartbeat, I'm afraid there is no possibility of William regaining consciousness. As I said, this will be done twice, by different doctors, to ensure that nothing is missed. However, Alan, you must prepare yourself for the worst."

"Can I be with him?"

"Of course. Do you want to go and get a coffee or something to eat while I make the preparations?"

"No. If these are my boy's last minutes, I don't want to miss a second." Alan spoke solemnly, but in reality, he wanted to be there to ensure nothing untoward happened. It was just a feeling, but come what may, he would be there when the wee man needed him.

~~~

Some time later Dr Abernethy returned with a few other serious-looking people in white coats.

'It's the death squad,' Alan thought as he stood up to face them.

"Mr Wallace, this is Dr Brown, he will be leading this test on William," Dr Abernethy said as the other doctor extended his hand.

"So sorry to meet you under these circumstances," the grey-haired gentleman said sombrely.

"No need to apologise, doctor. He's not dead, you'll see."

The two doctors exchanged a glance that Alan understood to mean that the task in hand could get messy since they both thought he was in denial. The doctors, though were in no doubt.

"Okay, lets proceed. We have had our briefing, you all know your roles. If we are all ready we should get started." Dr Brown looked around to check that everyone was in position, confirming their readiness.

"First test, eyes reaction to light."

Doctor Brown leaned over and pulled up each eyelid in turn, shining a bright torch into each eye.

"No reaction to light. Miss Toner, some cotton wool, please."

The nurse handed the doctor a piece of cotton wool. Once again the doctor lifted each eyelid, this time drawing the cotton wool over the eyeball.

"Second test, negative." The doctor then applied pressure to different parts of the patient's forehead and then pinched his nose tightly. Throughout this everyone's attention was on William, searching for the slightest sign of movement.

"Third test negative, are we all agreed?"

"Yes," they all responded in unison.

"Okay, syringe please." Taking the syringe, the doctor proceeded to insert ice cold water into both cars in turn.

"Fourth test negative, are we all agreed?"

"Yes."

"Plastic tube please, and can you assist me with this, please, nurse." The tube was inserted and pushed down William's windpipe.

Still no reaction whatsoever from the body on the bed.

"Fifth test negative. Final test, Miss Toner, if you please."

After the ventilator was turned off there was a pause of a few seconds when nothing happened. The room was eerily quiet, apart from the low hum of the monitoring equipment which continued to record ... nothing. It was as if everyone in the room held their own breath. Then a nurse gasped, "Did he move? Alan, did you feel something?"

With tears welling in his eyes, Alan looked up from his son's face towards the young nurse and said simply, "Aye." As if a spell had been broken the monitoring equipment came alive. To the incredulity of the senior doctors in attendance, within a minute the staff began giving verbal communication of what they could all see.

"Breathing normal."

"Heartbeat regular."

"Blood pressure normal."

And on the monitor showing cerebral activity, one tiny spike moving from left to right, showing the moment when William had given his father's hand a very soft squeeze.

Doctor Abernethy was first to recover his composure and tried to refocus with his favourite quip: "Well, that takes the biscuit." They had all heard this many times before, but most would agree that in this instance it was appropriate.

Most of the regular staff were in tears. Over the weeks they had grown fond of the father who came every day to read and talk to his last remaining relative. As they listened to the reminiscences, they started to empathise with the patient too. He changed, in their understanding, from being just another lump of lifeless flesh waiting to officially die, to a real person. A loving son who had lost his mother very young, but had grown up to form a close team in a male only household.

"What now, doctor?" Alan asked.

"Now, Alan? Now the ventilator will remain off. So long as William continues to breathe on his own, so long as his heart continues to beat, we will give him all the help towards recovery that we can. If he can. That single blip on the cerebral output was enough to be a game changer. I've never heard of anything like it in a case such as this."

"He squeezed my hand, doctor. He moved."

"Yes, but I still urge caution. Movements like that can be involuntary. Although in William's case such movements have been unusually absent to date. However, there is no doubt that it happened. The nurse saw it too, and it did seem to coincide with the cerebral activity. Quite remarkable."

Part III

The Making of the Warrior

Chapter 11: April 1297
Sanquhar Castle

"That is a useless waste of time and men!" William shook his head. "There has to be a better way. There is always a better way." The discussion at Dundonald Castle to plan the next steps had not got past the first target without disagreement over tactics.

"I like you, William, I really do, but I won't stand for that kind of insolence." Douglas rounded on the newcomer with eyes wide, nostrils flaring."

Wallace was a little taken aback by the ferocity of the reaction to his comment. "I mean no disrespect, Lord Douglas, but launching a full on attack against a heavily guarded castle is doomed to failure. Lives will be lost needlessly."

"So you are saying that we should just let the English keep all of the castles that they have stolen from us because we are afraid to die?"

"Not at all, I am saying that rather than rush in, we should take the time to assess the strengths and weaknesses of the building and its defences and come up with a plan that reduces our risks as much as possible."

"It is my castle, I don't need to assess its strengths and weaknesses. I know them already."

"True as that undoubtedly is, Lord Douglas, you nor I nor any of the others on this mission know how the current occupiers are using it. Chances are they are not using it as well as you would, and by having a look we can possibly identify a weakness, a way that we can get in with a minimum of fuss."

"Listen to him, Lord Douglas." Robert Wishart, Bishop of Glasgow, butted into the conversation. "This man is sent from God, as I told you already. Saint Andrew himself appeared to me in a dream and told me God was going to send us a warrior to free us. This is the man. We must listen to him. If God thought we were doing a good job as it was, he would have left us to get on with it. Just give him a chance."

The bishop was one of the few men Douglas truly respected. Not always one to toe the line, on this occasion he acquiesced.

Turning back to Wallace he asked, "So just what do you propose, man from God?"

William ignored the caustic remark. "You and I will go and appraise the current defences, try to gauge the numbers and probable locations of men inside, and identify its weakest spot. The rest of the men will hang back and wait for our order to proceed. Let's not give them any warning we are coming until they can feel our steel."

"Now you are talking my language, I can wait a bit, but not too long, so long as these usurpers pay for their impudence."

~~~

The young woman slipped out of the castle's postern gate and walked purposefully in the direction of the town. As she headed for home she went over her well-rehearsed excuse for being out, should her husband be awake when she got back. About half way to the small wood she began to fear that she was being followed and quickened her pace, almost running. Afraid to turn around when she became sure that there was indeed someone behind her, she broke into a run. The footsteps behind her hastened and she realised that whoever was behind her was rapidly gaining on her. If she screamed and alerted anyone close enough to hear, she would have to explain why she was out alone in the early hours of the morning. If she didn't scream she could be dead, or worse, in a few minutes. As she entered the trees she looked round to see whether her pursuer was her husband or someone from the castle or someone, something, else. Just as she saw the dark towering shape bearing down on her and opened her mouth to scream someone grabbed her around her waist and clamped a hand over her mouth.

Douglas had been waiting in the woods, and, as planned, the distraction of William following the woman allowed him to stop her easily. The terrified woman screamed into Douglas' palm, but no sound escaped it. Ever since she had been foolish enough to get involved with the handsome Englishman she knew that it must end badly. She closed her eyes and beseeched God to punish her quickly for her sins.

"Be still, woman, we do not plan to harm you, we just need to talk to you. I am going to release you. Do not run, and do not scream or yell, I do not want to have to hurt you."

Turning to face her captor, the woman's eyes widened in surprise.

"Lord Douglas, we thought you were still a prisoner at Berwick."

"Aye, the English like me so much they keep trying to hang on to me, but the feeling is not mutual."

William did not see the need for any small talk and got straight to the point. "So you are seeing one of the men keeping the castle. You are worried that one of the others might want some of whatever you are giving you 'friend', or that your husband, or another local will discover your secret."

Still speaking to Douglas, but responding to William's statement, the woman blurted out, "I am only doing this to protect—"

William cut her off; he wasn't interested in her excuses. What he wanted was a way to use this situation to get them into the castle quietly.

"Is this a regular liaison?" he asked.

"Every few days he will stop and drink from the well near the bakery. It is a signal that he will be by the back gate after dark."

"Not very subtle. He makes a show of stopping near your bakery and you disappear after dark. No wonder you are worried about getting caught." Before the woman could reply he added, "Continue as normal. Next time he wants a drink from the magic fountain go to the gate as normal. You will see us again, ignore us and make no signal to anyone inside. I take a very dim view of collaborating, in any form. This is your only chance to redeem yourself. Should anything go wrong the bakery will have a fire. Do you understand?"

Nodding her head, the woman began to cry, but William had become immune to womanly wiles. He ignored her cries and continued, "Good. Not a word or a sign to anyone, and all being well Lord Douglas will get his castle back and you can continue with your husband as if none of this ever happened. I imagine when you are having your liaison, there are not many soldiers about?"

"No, most of them are asleep. There is one soldier on the front wall. Two in the courtyard. The one I meet checks the back wall and the gate."

"So when he is supposed to be checking the postern gate, he lets you in and you have sex?"

"Yes."

"And nobody sees you?"

"I don't think so. I hope not, we are fairly quiet."

"The soldiers inside can't see the postern gate area?"

"No. There are walls nearby on both sides."

William looked to Douglas for confirmation. "There are stables on either side. The back gate is not normally used and should be heavily barred at all times."

"I suppose any muffled sounds the lady and her gentleman friend make could be construed as animal noise," William mused. "Okay, if you swear to be help us in the name of the King, go on your way."

Realising she was being offered a free pass, the woman brightened up noticeably and, bending to grab and kiss William's right hand, gushed, "I swear. Thank you, my lord. I will not let you down. This was not my choice—"

Once again William did not want to get sidetracked by excuses and said simply, "Go now, quietly, and do not mention us to anyone. Play your part well and all will be forgotten."

As the woman turned to go William added. "One more thing. I will leave a cloak close to the gate. Wear it, keep it tight around you."

"A cloak? I have a cloak. What is the meaning of this?"

"Trust me. If you are wearing a cloak, change it or just wear it over. But wear it. You will see."

~~~

William arranged for the men with them to take turns to approach the town and watch for any movement of English troops. After a few days Douglas became increasingly frustrated. He was a man of action and William's plan went against all his instincts. Still, he had given the bishop his word and he was determined to stick to it, however long it took. Better be worth it, though. Much as he agreed with the bishop that this man had something about him, he would feel much better if and when he saw tangible results.

About mid-afternoon on the sixth day, Alan Boyd returned to the camp. "A handful of English troops passed through the town. One of them did indeed have a drink from the well. I still don't understand why we don't just take the troops while they are out in the open."

William patiently explained. "No point taking a few and alerting the others to our presence. Let's get them all and make sure the castle is under our control."

To them all he said, "Our patience is to be rewarded. We go in tonight. Lord Douglas and I will enter through the postern gate. We will open the front gates to let the rest of you in."

"And if the gates don't open?" Walter asked.

William smiled, but replied flatly, "In that case we are probably dead. You can be in charge then, Walter. You decide what to do."

"That's not what I meant."

"Just be ready when the gate opens."

~~~

Later that night, as the baker's wife approached the postern gate she noted a pair of shadowy figures huddled a few yards away. She knocked lightly on the gate, as was usual, and as the gate began to open she was aware of the approach of one of the figures.

William moved as soon as he saw the gate begin to open. Keeping low, and trying to make as little noise as possible, none would be good, he sped to the gate. The soldier opening the gate was fixated on the woman standing just outside, only one thing on his mind. As he reached out to stroke her face he realised, too late, that something was not quite right. Turning towards the muffled sound to his right, and automatically reaching for his sword, he was stunned to see a shadowy figure rise from close to the ground to tower over him. Before he could react, before he could even cry out to raise the alarm, an arm shot out from the shadowy mass and grabbed him by the head, a huge hand covering his entire face and muffling any sounds that might try to escape. Without hesitation the attacker pulled the soldier to him, turning the soldier so that his back was against his assailants body and the soldier felt a brief moment of intense pain as a dagger slit his throat from end to end, and his life blood spurted from the gaping wound.

Turning briefly to nod to the traumatised woman, who had just witnessed her lover murdered in front of her very eyes, William turned back to the gate and disappeared inside, quickly followed by Douglas. The woman herself was covered almost head to toe in blood. Now she could see the reason for the cloak. It would be impossible to explain all that blood on her own clothes. Despite everything, she found herself silently thanking the big stranger for his thoughtfulness.

Inside the castle, everything seemed to be as advised. Peering round the walls leading to the gate they could see two guards sitting chatting to their left. The other guard was near the front right hand corner as they looked at it, unmoving. So still he could possibly be asleep on his feet, certainly not alert. 'Familiarity does breed contempt,' Wallace thought as he made a questioning expression at Douglas. The two or the one? Douglas would have preferred the two, but judging, wrongly, that his partners' size would make a quiet ascent unlikely, pointed to himself and then pointed to the upper guard. William nodded and immediately started towards the two guards talking together. Treading stealthily, he approached to within striking distance of the two men without being detected.

William had already drawn his sword and now, in one fluid movement, swung it above his head as he crouched slightly, and then brought it soaring down on his unsuspecting victims. The farthest away guard, sensing movement, turned just in time to see his comrades head fly past his face, splattering him with hot blood. It was no good as a warning though as William's weapon continued its arc and severed the second head before the soldier had a chance to react. Both men were dead, and William looked almost like a professional golfer after teeing off, only he had a bloodied sword rather than a driver over his left shoulder.

Meantime, Douglas had reached the last active guard. William turned at the sound of a shout as the guard heard Douglas approach. He was just in time to see the guard draw his sword half way out of its scabbard before Douglas plunged his own weapon into the guard's lower belly and drew it upwards, spilling intestines in its wake. Douglas looked over to William, grinned and winked. He appeared to take pleasure in the butchery, William less so.

This was almost too easy, but there was no room for complacency. Although there had been very little noise, William considered it unlikely that absolutely everyone was so soundly asleep that no-one had heard anything. He sprinted for the front gates, removed the bar, and threw them open. The other men had been inching slowly towards the gate all this time, helped by a low cloud cover that night. As soon as the gates began to swing open they were up and running.

Andrew Moray had delayed his journey home to join William and company, hoping to learn some skills to assist him when he did return northwards. Being swift of foot, he was the first to pass through the castle gate. Just as he entered the courtyard and saw the two decapitated bodies to his right, a door crashed open to his left. A bleary eyed Englishman, sword in hand, emerged demanding, "What is going on out here?" The sight of his two comrades lying in a pool of blood brought him completely awake instantly. He raised his sword towards the figure moving towards him, but before they could engage, Douglas, who had been walking across the roof of the building, dropped behind him, plunging his sword between his shoulder blades so deeply that he almost sheared him in two. Andrew looked at Douglas and told him, "I had him." To which Douglas smiled and replied, "But I saw him first."

More troops, by now aware of what was happening, were trying to come out of the lodging room.

Meantime, the remainder of the Scots whooped and yelled as they filled the courtyard, eager for a piece of the action. Few of them were able to get involved as the castle defenders were cut down mercilessly as soon as they exited the building. Soon it became all but impossible to even attempt to put up a fight and the English troops had no option but to surrender.

~~~

"What do you want to do with your prisoners?" William asked, nodding towards the dejected Englishmen standing in the middle of the courtyard surrounded by jubilant Scots singing and cheering.

"My prisoners?"

"Aye, it's your castle, and you are senior. What do you want to do with them?"

"I don't want them, there is no-one here who will command a ransom. We should just kill them."

"They have surrendered in good faith. We should not slaughter them in cold blood."

"I was in charge at Berwick last Easter when the English came and slaughtered for two days. Men, women and children. No quarter given. I gave up the castle, surrendering to stop the carnage, and still they continued. They must have killed more than ten thousand civilians. These men are soldiers. Who knows, some of them standing there might have been at Berwick then. Let their families know something of the grief they have inflicted on our countrymen."

William had already heard tales of the horrific events at Berwick and understood how Douglas must be feeling. Still, they had taken this castle back by doing things differently, with not a drop of Scottish blood spilt. Whatever he was here for, he was sure it was not to do the same things as everyone else.

Although his twentieth-century mind was not religious, William had taken note of the importance of religion amongst his comrades. He decided to try to use that to his advantage.

"God is on our side. Do we not ask him to forgive our sins as we forgive those who sin against us?"

Douglas scowled at William, not convinced.

"Longshanks is a barbarian. His actions cannot be pleasing to God. Let us not fall to his level."

Still Douglas declined to reply.

"Think about it for a minute. We are depleted and must make best use of our limited resources. If we kill these men, who will yield to us before death? On the other hand, if we show clemency, will not the next group we face be more likely to surrender and choose life, rather than stand firm and face certain death?"

"I think that if we kill them all it will deplete our enemy's resources. We don't need prisoners, we don't have the resources to keep them. As far as I am concerned we should all fight until death. I would not expect an Englishman to be less honourable."

"There is no honour in executing unarmed men. Let them go home and tell their friends and family tales of how they had to bow before the famous Lord Douglas."

"My name will not instil too much fear in their breasts. I have been at their mercy too many times."

Walking towards the prisoners, Douglas told William, "I do this for the bishop, not for you." To the prisoners he said, "Go home defeated. Go home and tell everyone in England that God has sent a mighty warrior to free Scotland. Behold, William Wallace, whose mighty sword kills men two at a time." Turning back to William he added under his breath, "You do realise that these men will head for the nearest stronghold and strengthen the garrison there?"

Before William could reply they were interrupted by the sound of a horse approaching at speed. William snapped, "Keep an eye in the prisoners!" as he strode for the open gates, drawing his sword as he went. Douglas, not one to take orders, was right behind him.

The rider pulled up and the pair saw that it was Alan Boyd. "Where were you? I thought you were still inside?" William asked.

"I was checking out buildings towards the back when I saw a man leading a horse out of the postern gate. I took a horse and followed him, but I lost him in the dark."

William frowned. "We must assume that he will go to the nearest place of safety, which will be Durisdeer."

"Our next target! Our chances of catching them unawares appear to have vanished with that horse. What do you propose now, William?"

"Let us work with what we have."

"And what might that be?"

"The prisoners. We will march them to Durisdeer. Let the garrison there see that we are generous and forgiving. Give them the chance to go home in peace with their countrymen."

"And when that doesn't work? We will either have to put them under siege, which could take weeks, or revert to my plan of all-out assault."

"We are more versatile than that, Lord Douglas. Importantly, we do not need to decide right now. We can discuss our options on the way tomorrow. Let us secure the prisoners and let our men have some rest. In the morning you and I will go meet the locals to ensure that they do not offer any assistance to any more foreign troops that come this way."

"How do we do that?"

"Carrot and stick. We reassure them of our complete forgiveness and amnesty for past actions that have aided the occupiers. At the same time, we make sure that they understand that any future actions will be dealt with harshly. Much as they may fear the English, we have to make them fear our retribution more. The English may come in large numbers and make a lot of noise, but we can return at any time, night or day, and be in and out without anyone else knowing we were here, until they find the lifeless bodies of the collaborators."

"Did you not tell me to be merciful?"

"Aye, I did. Understand the difference, though. English soldiers are here, on the most part, because they are ordered to be. For most of them, the reward is only the wages they receive. But Scots men and women must understand that the occupiers can only remain with the cooperation of the locals. Wilful cooperation, collaboration, is treason, and the penalty for treason is death. Always."

"Unless you are pretty, eh William?" Douglas chuckled, with a nudge and a wink. "Will you be having a tete a tete with the wee blonde lass?"

"That is not why I let her go. We had a deal and we will honour it. She has paid her debt."

"She might want to pay some more." Douglas persisted.

"You're a bit of a dirty old man Lord Douglas. Black by name and black by nature."

"And you are white as the driven snow I suppose?"

"There are many shades of grey, my friend."

Chapter 12: April 1297

Durisdeer

As they approached Durisdeer, William received an unexpected request. The commander of the Sanquhar garrison asked to speak to him.

"We would not wish to put your good humour to the test a second time, sir. But if you allow, one of my men has a brother here. He would like to approach to entreat them not to resist."

"Of course, we are not without compassion. I will accompany the two of you to the gates, but please do not try any trickery. My men here will put yours to the sword at the first sign of danger."

"You have my word."

"Good. Alan, come with me. The rest of you, draw weapons and should any harm befall either of us, do not leave any of these men alive before coming to our aid."

As they neared the gate a voice called down to them. "Brother, have you joined forces with these verminous Scots?"

Edmund, the young English soldier, looked up and replied, "Greetings to you, my brother. I bring bad news from Sanquhar. We were overwhelmed by this horde of Scotsmen, who appeared in the castle from nowhere. They very generously allowed us to live. If you fight, you will all die. Let us go home to our families and leave this foul country to its foul inhabitants."

"I am sorry to hear that, little brother. Sorry that you are alive to tell the tale. How can you yield to these creatures? We are real soldiers here and will fight to the death. Their death, not ours. Be gone from my sight, or I will come out and kill you myself. I no longer have a brother. Only one thing I ask of you: do not go home and bring shame on our father."

William had heard enough, and had not expected any better. To Alan he said, "Take these two back to the others. Place them as we discussed." And to the guards he shouted, "Brave words, my men over there hope that you have the courage to back up those words. Meantime, your countrymen have had all of the kindness they will get from us. They will be left in a field yonder, tied together until you come and get them, if you dare. All you have to do to release them is to get past me."

While the prisoners were being secured and the Scots were getting their camp organised William, Douglas and their lieutenants discussed tactics.

"Morton Castle is not too far from here, is it not? I assume that it also holds an English garrison?" William asked.

"Aye to both. It's about five miles from here," Douglas informed him.

"We must assume that our escapee has also alerted them, or someone has. That being the case, I would expect the commander here to wait for help, but to be ready to attack when the Morton troop arrives."

"We can't just wait and see and be caught in the middle." Walter, as always, anticipated the worst.

"Of course not. The attack from the castle will be straightforward enough. We will set some traps just this side of that small rise there. They should not realise until they are on top of them. We will need to assume that the attack from Morton could come at any moment so we have to work quickly. I would think that they will probably come through that small wood to the south; we will focus our efforts in cutting them off there. If we have time we should also make provision for them looping right around and attacking from the rear."

"That would not make much sense. We would see them well before they reached us," Douglas observed.

"Aye, but they may well expect to approach and have talks." William considered that the only useful purpose modern politicians served was to remove these useless conversations far away from the battlefield. He continued, "If they do, we need to send someone to them before they can have a look at our defences."

~~~

"They're coming!" the castle look-out shouted down from his vantage point as the troop from Morton Castle rode into view.

The castle commander strode to his horse and ordered his men "Right, mount up! As soon as the Scots are engaged we charge and attack from this side. We are all properly trained English soldiers, they do not stand a chance. Expect them to run like foxes as soon as they realise they are done for. Do not let them escape. Hunt them down and kill them like the wild animals that they are."

Half a mile away the Morton troops reached the end of a small wood and began their charge towards the Scots they could see camped up ahead, apparently totally off guard. When they had almost cleared the trees they heard a roar off to the left, and to a man they turned to see where the noise was coming from. Up ahead, on either side of the track teams of men heaved on either end of a long rope. As the rope tightened, looped over tree branches about five feet off the ground, the horsemen hit it at full gallop. Distracted as they were, and with the Scots winding the ends of the rope around tree trunks to hold it taught, the foremost attackers were scattered like bowling pins. Before any of the troop still mounted were able to recover any composure, the Scots were dropping from trees and springing from bushes with weapons at the ready.

Near the back of the charge, the horsemen began to slow as they realised the fighting had already started. Before any of them had a chance to react further, the blacksmith from Sanquhar, who along with many of his neighbours had joined Douglas and Wallace for this sortie, emerged from behind a giant old oak and swung his big hammer in an arc, cracking the skull of the rearmost horse, which collapsed to the ground, trapping its rider by the leg. The big hammer swung again as the horseman tried to pull his trapped and broken leg out from under his mount, crushing the helpless man's helmet almost flat while blood and bone and teeth and eyeballs exploded out of the crushed metal.

As riders attempted to manoeuvre around their comrades and closely packed trees and shrubbery all up and down the forest path, yelling Scotsmen materialised out of the gloom. First attacking the animals to bring the riders down and turning the armour of their enemies against the wearers as they struggled to move freely in the confined space. The Scots used their numerical advantage to overwhelm the enemy, beating and battering with a range of crude and improvised weapons.

While the Morton troop were being decimated in the wood, the Durisdeer troop emerged from the castle, expecting to attack the about-facing Scots from the rear. Once again, distraction got the better of the southerners. As they approached the Scots, their puzzlement as to why they were not moving to meet them was matched by the confusion caused by the screams and wails a few hundred yards away. The comrades who should have been ravaging the other side of the Scots camp had met some resistance in the wood. With the castle guard occupied getting ready to wage war, and the look-out concentrating on watching for the relief force, they were totally unaware of what the Scots had been doing.

Like the riders coming from the south, the castle troop realised too late that they had been hoodwinked. Expecting a straight fight they slashed and stabbed at the unmoving Scots and were thrown in all directions as horses stumbled into small pits. Riders were thrown clear to find that the figures they were attacking were the bound, gagged and terrified former garrison of Sanquhar. Wallace strode round the hillock, swinging his oversized blade in arcs around him, cleaving armour and cloth and flesh and bone. Dozens of Scots swarmed round either side of their leader and fell upon the bemused enemy in a killing frenzy. From the other side of the hillock Douglas led his men to fall upon the rear of the outmanoeuvred Durisdeer garrison.

~~~

"Surprise and speed have won the day, William. Good plan. Do we have any prisoners still?"

"Preparation is everything, Lord Douglas. A few men have escaped. I expect if we take a trip down to Morton we will find them ready to negotiate. It wasn't all one-way traffic though. We have a few brave men of our own to bury before we go anywhere."

"Did any of the prisoners from Sanquhar survive?"

"Walter is checking on them. I have told him to let any who can walk go on their way."

"Very generous, they could still be dangerous."

"Not today, though. They have suffered enough. Any wounded we will load onto carts and take with us to Morton."

"It would probably be kinder to kill them."

Chapter 13: April 1297
Malcolm and Mary

As soon as the fighting was over, William took his leave and rushed back to check on Malcolm. He found him chopping wood in the yard, whistling. Malcolm raised his head when he heard a horse approach, then smiled broadly and waved to his brother.

"There you are, I've been dying to see you, you'll never believe what's happened."

William was totally gobsmacked. He had left behind a quivering wreck, completely in denial of his situation, and returned to find a man who looked for all the world as if he was loving life. "I already don't believe it. Don't get me wrong, whatever it is I am delighted. But fuck's sake, Malcolm, I'm more worried than ever that you have finally cracked."

"Aye, it took me a wee while to get a grip, but what can you do? Life goes on."

"Seriously, big man, what is going on?"

"It's Mary."

"Mary?"

"Aye, you must remember Mary Barbour."

"Mary from the dairy? Here? Now? You're kidding me!"

"I shit you not. It's like she came back in time with us. Except, she has always been here. The wavy hair, the big blue eyes, those ruby red lips, I swear it's the same girl. Still a farmer's daughter."

"Did you speak to her?"

"Well, no. I bottled it. She came here to deliver milk. When I saw her, I nearly had a stroke. I started to walk towards her and then froze, I couldn't do it."

"What were you going to say? Not the same as last time I hope, 'The face of an angel with the voice of a demon.' What made you think that would flatter her?"

"I know, I know, I'm a twat. Then there was the carry-on with the horses."

William laughed out loud as he remembered Malcolm's attempt to ingratiate himself. Mary led pony treks from her father's farm and Malcolm had persuaded William to go on a trek with him. Malcolm got carried away and insisted they were experienced riders even though neither of them had ever been on a horse before. The horses all seemed quite docile until they got to a clearing where they knew they could have a gallop. The ponies took off and William had to be rescued by primary school kids while he clung to his mount's neck for dear life. Malcolm was not so lucky. He fell off and broke his arm.

"That's right. You have never been able to go near a horse since."

"Until now." Malcolm said stroking the nose of William's horse. He was trying to put his fears behind him, but he was touching the horse gingerly as if he expected it to bite him.

"Aye, full marks for effort, but anyone can tell you still don't like them. You'll need to get over that."

"I will. I am. I'm getting there. Anyway, now I've got added motivation."

"Mary."

"Mary, what a girl." Malcolm sighed dreamily.

"You've got an opportunity that probably nobody ever had before."

"What's that?"

"A second chance to make a first impression. Don't fuck it up this time, Malc. When you do speak to her, by all means tell her she has the face of an angel, but leave the demon bit out. Have you heard this Mary speak?"

"Aye, exactly the same, a deeper voice than me. That's what stopped me in my tracks when I was going over to see her. I remembered the face, but had somehow forgotten the voice." Malcolm shrugged. "But I'll be okay next time. I've been practising my lines for days."

"Good luck with that, Malc. I'm just so pleased to see you like your old self again."

~~~

After spending some time with is brother, William rode over to Dundonald to give the High Steward news of his actions with Lord Douglas.

"A good few days, William, but we should keep the pressure on." James the Steward was not one to become complacent.

"Of course, but can I make a suggestion?"

"So far all of your suggestions have been good ones. What are you thinking now?" This was the Bishop of Glasgow, obviously pleased that the man of his vision was doing so well..

"So far we've been looking at liberating places from the English occupiers, but the truth is that they can only stay in place with the support of locals. We need to hit the collaborators. Anyone who in any way helps, supports or encourages the foreign administration should be targetted."

"Excellent, that fits in nicely with our plans." The Steward beamed and turned towards the men warming up at the fire. "William, let me introduce you to Sir Richard Lundie and Sir John de Graham. They have a job for you."

Richard walked over towards William and saluted him. "It is a pleasure to meet the man in person. Your fame and tales of your deeds are spreading across the whole country. That is why I have come here to ask for your assistance with a problem we have over in Lanark."

"I am all ears, Sir Richard. What is the problem in Lanark?"

"It's the sheriff. One Andrew de Livingston. He sees his chances of advancement all coming from London. Not only has he embraced the occupying regime, his actions go even beyond those of the Englishmen in similar positions. No Scot has a position of any importance in his whole sheriffdom, all the good jobs having been given to Englishmen. Furthermore, when he sits at court his punishments become more and more severe the more they have any connection to any sign of resistance whatsoever."

"That's exactly the kind of target we should be hitting. No disrespect, Sir Richard, but I will want to have a good look at the Sheriff and his surroundings before making any firm plans."

"No offence taken, William. I will take you over there and we will see what you can come up with."

"Just one thing for now, Sir Richard: why come to me? Why not take this man out yourself?"

"Everyone hates him, and he knows it. That makes it very hard to get near him. Anyone he considers a threat, and that is a lot of people, is watched carefully. It doesn't take a lot to end up in his courtroom. From what I hear, despite your great size, you have a way of getting about with being noticed."

"It's not really that hard, I'll show you some of my techniques as we go. Mostly it's just distraction, you'll get the hang of it."

Sir James had not finished his own business yet, and before William rushed off he called him back "William, do not be in too much of a hurry."

"Apologies, Sir James, did you need me for something else?"

"Indeed I do. Andrew Moray and you have both scuppered my plans. I had planned a banquet and a ceremony for you both, but Andrew turned up by himself determined to get himself home."

"I don't understand. Andrew only delayed his trip home to take part in Lord Douglas' missions. I did not realise you needed to see us together."

"It was supposed to be a surprise. Andrew is now Sir Andrew Moray."

William interrupted to express his delight. "That is well deserved! He is a singular individual and should make a great impact in the north."

"Agreed." Sir James continued, "But he is not the only one deserving recognition. If you allow, William, take the knee and swear your allegiance to me and to the King." James drew his sword as William kneeled and dubbed him, saying simply, "Arise, Sir William Wallace, knight of Scotland."

Sir William stood and accepted the back slapping and congratulations from his peers. He felt a little bemused; he had not considered the title. Truth be told, in his previous military career, he considered that those men who had were peers of the realm were less capable of decisive action that the proper soldiers. He would not have swapped any of them for Donald. Hopefully the knighthood would indeed be an honour and not a curse.

Chapter 14: May 1297

Lanark

Market night was chosen as the best time to strike. Livingston always surrounded himself with English soldiers, day and night. The large crowds on market day made it easier to get men into place without attracting undue attention. The same large crowds made it difficult to launch an attack in daylight. Too many things to get in the way, too many bystanders would undoubtedly become casualties. Success was not guaranteed. Back in the modern world, a single bullet from a sniper's rifle would have been enough: William supposed that was progress of a sort.

~~~

Was it late spring or early summer? William wondered as he lay amongst farm produce in the back of a cart heading towards Lanark market place. Whichever, it was a glorious day. Almost cloudless sky, sun pleasantly warm, and just the gentlest of breezes whispering through the trees. A soft "Easy boy" and a rap on the seat was his cue to slip off of the cart and into the safe house where the men would gather throughout the day. One by one, steady, casual as you like. No rushing, nothing to attract any attention. The plan would fail if they were discovered before nightfall. No doubt they would fight their way out, but there would be increased casualties on the patriot side and the chances were Livingston would escape. Following that there would no doubt be a crack-down on anyone thought to be involved and the chances of a second attempt would be slim to non-existent.

"William, glad to see you. No problems getting here?" John Graham was among the handful of men who had already arrived.

"None at all, although I probably have more bruises from being bounced about in that cart than after a good fight."

"Aye, not the best way to travel. That's what you get for being such a big beast."

"I'm not complaining, I've had worse. Alan and Walter are taking a few men to scout the place before we make our final arrangements."

"You didn't see enough when Richard and I brought you up?"

"Can't be too careful. I may have missed something in the dark, or something may have changed."

John smiled and clapped William on the back. "It's the attention to detail that makes the difference, I suppose."

~~~

Throughout the day men arrived in ones and twos until everyone was accounted for. Alan arrived back before Walter and reported that everything was as expected.

Walter, when he arrived, reported the same but added, "I still don't see why we are skulking about like thieves in the night. We have about the same numbers and should be able to overcome them in a straight fight."

All eyes were on William to see how he would handle this dissent. "Maybe you should join with Lord Douglas? You will see more direct action with him."

"I have no wish to do that. That man is a barbarian."

"Careful, Walter, do not say anything you would not say to the man's face. Douglas is a good example of why we are doing this my way. He would charge in with weapons drawn and try to hack the garrison to pieces. On a good day he would succeed and get his man. But how many innocent men, women and children would be caught in the fight? On a bad day there would be more townsfolk and market traders dead than English soldiers, and Livingston would escape. Is that what you would prefer?"

"No, of course not. I just wonder if there is not another way."

"You always were a bit of a misery, Walter," Alan scolded him

"It's all right. We are all entitled to our own opinions. I would rather hear if anyone is unhappy." Looking around all the men, making sure he caught every eye, William continued, "If any man here is not happy with the plan, he is free to leave and should do so now."

Nobody moved and Walter shifted uncomfortably, aware that they were all waiting for his reaction."

William did not want to see his friend squirm, however much of a pain he could be. Patting him gently on the back he told them all, "We are all of one mind then. Anyone who is able should get as much rest as they can. There is nothing to be done now until nightfall."

At last the glare of the sun softened and darkened into night. Just a couple of days off a full moon, the light from a mainly cloudless sky gave all the light they needed to make their way the few hundred yards to the Sheriff's residence.

"Alan, you go first. Take your men to collect the posts; we will meet you there."

When they reached the Sheriff's residence, William watched as Richard and John directed their men into position where they could wedge the posts that they had collected against the window shutters of both buildings. Meantime Alan supervised the placing of straw around the outside of both buildings. It was all going to plan until one man took it upon himself to wedge his post against a shutter on the building housing most of the garrison.

"You are supposed to wait for the signal!" his neighbour hissed.

"Aye, but it was heavy. It was going to fall anyway."

"Oh well, I'm putting my down too." And as he did so others, fearing they had missed the signal, followed suit.

"Fuck!" William cursed, and as he did so his fears materialised. Shouts rose from the troops inside who had begun to awaken and realise they were under attack. With time now against him, he rushed at the door to the Sheriff's home and lifting his leg, roared "Saor Alba!" at the top of his lungs and took the door clean off its hinges with one almighty kick.

That was the signal for action, but most of the men had started without him. At the barrack building the door opened and some troops, now alert and armed, attempted to fight their way out. Duty told them that they must go to the Sheriff and protect him. Their exit was hampered by the cart which had been rolled in front of the door once emptied of hay. John Graham cut down the first of them to emerge as he clambered over the top of the cart. Others followed and a few made it up and over only to find that they were vastly outnumbered with most of the guard still inside.

Alan Boyd, although instructed not to start the fire until the women and children had been cleared from the Sheriff's building, took the initiative to set alight the straw stacked against the barracks. As the flame raced around the building the edifice itself was quickly alight, as was the cart blocking the doorway. Few of those still inside the building made it out and the screams and smell of burning flesh would live long in the memories of the watching townspeople.

In the main house William mounted the stairs three at a time and made directly for what he understood to be the main bedroom. Just before he reached the door a figure emerged from a doorway to his right and lunged at him with a dagger. William clasped the arm holding the blade and was about to smash his fist onto the face of his attacker when he realised it was just a boy on the cusp of manhood. The boy was screaming and kicking and punching, and while he did not have the strength to hurt William, the big Scotsman was nevertheless impressed by his spunk.

"Walter!" he called, turning to his old friend who was right behind him. "Take this boy outside and make sure he doesn't hurt himself or anyone else. Stay with him, he's a wild one."

"Behind him the door to the master bedroom had opened and a hysterical woman was screaming, "Leave him alone! He's just a boy! Do not hurt my son!"

William grabbed the woman and gave her a shake, he stopped short of slapping her because she was petite. "Your boy is okay, he will not be harmed. Go with him and get him clear of this place."

The woman then, slightly more calmly, turned back and said, "My husband! I cannot go without my husband."

Lifting the woman clear of the floor, William swung around and pushed her towards the stairs. "Your husband will not be joining you. Look after your son."

There was no time to debate further; sparks from the other building had set the straw alight and the sheriff's dwelling was already burning. William continued on though, he wanted to make sure the sheriff was accounted for. Entering the bedroom William was confronted by the backside of his target as he bent at the low window trying desperately to force the shutters open.

"There is no escape there into the fire. If you want out you must get past me."

Turning and straightening up to his full five foot six the Sheriff pleaded, "Do not kill me. King Edward will pay a handsome ransom for me."

"You are Sir Andrew de Livingston then?"

Livingston's mouth worked but no sound emerged. William assumed that he was trying to find the words to deny himself.

"No quick death for you, you worm." William took the Sheriff's own sword – he had not even taken the time to arm himself – lifted the man by the throat and pinned him, screaming, to the door.

Once back outside the now blazing building Richard informed him, "No one left alive in there, all the women and children are out."

"Good, Livingston is still in there, you can just about hear his screams over the crackle of the fire."

Some of the townspeople had arrived carrying buckets of water. William intercepted them. "Let these buildings burn. Save your water in case the fire spreads. Your houses are worth saving, these are not."

At the corner of the main building he found the Sheriff's wife crying over the lifeless body of her brave young son. To Walter he asked, "How did this happen?"

Richard Lundie answered. "Walter was bringing the woman out when the boy grabbed his sgian dubh and lunged at him. Instinctively I plunged my sword into his chest. Boy or not, he was dangerous."

"That is a pity. He was twice the man his father was. Get the women and children out of here. Walter, carry the boy to the churchyard. so that his mother can give him a proper burial."

Chapter 15: June 1297

Scone

"As I live and breathe, if it's not the bold Wallace!"

"Lord Douglas, always a pleasure to see you. You and your men look ready for action. I assume you are keeping the pressure on our unwelcome guests?"

Both men dismounted and embraced, the pleasure they declared was evident for all too see.

"Talking of action, I hear tell that you have had some of your own. You have rid Lanark of vermin, they say. I'm sorry I missed that."

"That is true, my Lord. We are now escorting the women and children to Edinburgh, from where they can be taken home."

"That is a long way, do you have to?"

"It gives me an excuse to have a good look at one of the few remaining English strongholds."

"That makes sense, but if you knew Edinburgh Castle you would know that you are on a wasted journey. There is no storming that place, and no way to steal up on it like at Sanquhar."

William did know the castle well, in its twentieth century incarnation. He had hoped that this early it might not be so impregnable. Douglas' comments removed some of that optimism.

"Still, I am on my way, may as well make sure these poor souls get there safely. There are a lot of mean men about who would take advantage."

Douglas looked across at the wretched bunch, many of them still sobbing. William knew of the horror that had taken place in Berwick and for a moment feared that Douglas would have no compassion for them. Looking back to William, Douglas shrugged and said, "Looking after children is no work for a warrior such as you, William. Let your men continue without you. I have something much more suitable to a man of your stature."

"You do? What could be more fun than a trip to Edinburgh?"

"We are going to Scone to visit Longshanks' chief justiciar in Scotland. I hear that he is sitting on rather a large sum of money, ready to be sent to London for his king."

"That certainly is tempting. How accurate is your information, do you think?"

Douglas laughed. "Never mind how much money there is, William. The English administration in Scotland is dwindling fast. Remove Ormsby and they do not have much left at all. Possibly no way to channel Scottish taxes south."

"That will do for me. I'm in."

"Excellent! You can tell me about Lanark on the way."

~~~

Before they reached Scone the pair once more had a disagreement over tactics.

"Your ways have worked well, I admit that William. But this is my mission and this time we are doing it my way. I promise you the outcome will be the same in the end."

"Without proper planning so many things can you wrong. I implore you, let's take the time to size the situation up properly before we go in."

"It is reported that Sir William Ormsby has a great fortune, taxes and fines collected from Scotsmen to pay for their subjugation. We have a duty to relieve him of that, and if we delay we may miss it. Should we wait a day, two days, longer, and then find the place empty we will have lost a great opportunity to use Longshanks' ill-gotten gains against him. We are going in now. If you do not like it, wait here. You will be a great help to us, but we can manage without you as we originally intended."

"Lead on, my Lord. I feel duty bound to ensure that you don't get yourself killed." William grinned.

Douglas simply smiled back, wheeled his horse around and spurred it onwards the last few miles towards Scone.

~~~

Douglas and his pack arrived at Scone at a gallop. Meeting no resistance outside, they drew swords and headed on in. Their blood was up and there was a genuine need to use up their adrenalin with some action, but they were to be disappointed. Ormsby was nowhere to be found. Nor was there a single English soldier to be found anywhere in the vicinity. All that remained were a few locals who had been forced into service – reluctantly, they assured the two Williams.

"Where are Ormsby and his men?" Douglas demanded.

"My Lord, news of your approach reached here and Sir William flew into a panic. He demanded that the captain of the guard select his best men to protect him on his way home. They were gone within the hour. Such was the fear that spread throughout the whole city of Scone that even those not selected as part of that guard soon followed after them."

"They all ran away?"

"They were left with no orders to stay and defend. I heard them discuss the stories they had heard of Douglas and Wallace. The great size and incredible strength of Wallace and the savage aggression of Douglas filled them with dread."

"Savage?" Douglas feigned hurt.

"They were like children telling each other ghost stories. The more they talked, the less they felt able to resist you. They are only men doing a job, and with no-one to direct them they did not see the point in waiting here to die."

Wallace looked directly at Douglas as he asked, "Did they take everything with them? All the money?" Douglas returned his stare as they both realised that the gung-ho approach had probably cost them dearly.

"Money? I don't know, Sir Willian. They left in such a rush that they did not appear to take any provisions even."

A brief flicker of relief flashed on Douglas's face before he smiled. "Sounds that they may have left us the prize. Let's get looking for it."

Wallace halted him as he turned to begin his search. "Even if we get the money, we have still lost the man. Such a high-ranking prisoner would have been worth even more to us."

"Unless he died in the fight."

"Sounds unlikely given his rush from battle."

"Even so, Longshanks may not have been prepared to pay for his return."

"Perhaps not, but if not, we may have been able to trade him for some of our own still held in England."

"Okay, I concede. Sometimes it may be better to do it your way."

"Sometimes?"

"Aye, sometimes. Come on man, don't rub it in. Let's go find the treasure."

~~~

As it turned out, Ormsby had indeed been in such a panic that he had not taken anything. William and Douglas were drinking some of his finest wines when one of the men interrupted their celebration.

"Lord Douglas, a rider approaches."

"Only one?"

"Yes, my Lord, but he is in a terrible rush."

"Let's go see what he wants, then."

As they reached the courtyard, the horseman pulled up and threw himself from his mount. It was Alan Boyd again. Douglas walked forward to greet him, but he rushed past and addressed Wallace. "Sir William, you've got to come. There is going to be a massacre."

"Calm down, Alan. A massacre? What can be that bad? Things are starting to go well for us."

"Well, when we got back from Lanark there was news of an English army crossing the border."

"That is not good, we were not expecting that big a response so soon. Longshanks is still in Flanders, so who is raising an army without him?"

"I do not know that, Sir William, but I do know that an army is indeed on its way. Not only that, but the High Steward, the Earl of Carrick and the Bishop of Glasgow have mustered an army to fight them, but they are heavily outnumbered."

William turned to Lord Douglas, the joy of an easy win blown away by news of impending stupidity. "I need to go right away. By the Grace of God this news has reached me in time to stop this foolishness."

"I'm coming with you. Can't miss this."

"I go not to fight, but to stop the fight, Lord Douglas."

"Whichever way it goes, I'm with you Sir William." Douglas quickly barked orders to his men, detailing who went to Irvine and who stayed at Scone to secure against an English return.

Chapter 16: June 1297
Near disaster at Irvine

"This is the last thing we need! Has no one listened to a single word I have said?" William had arrived at Bourtreehill to find the Scottish forces ready to give battle. On the other side of the loch Sir Henry Percy led an army that outnumbered the Scots by about four to one.

"Who died and made you king?" William noted that the questioner was a very dignified man, with a definite air of authority. Standing as tall as any of his peers, he had the luxurious wavy black hair, dark complexion and piercing, almost black eyes that declared his Gaelic heritage.

"You must be the Earl of Carrick. My Lord, I mean no disrespect, and certainly I cannot rebuke you for not listening to things I have not spoken to you of directly."

"Nevertheless, as a newcomer and only recently knighted, I demand to know what gives you the right to speak to your superiors in such a manner. Men have died for less."

William brushed off the clear threat in this statement. There was no time for bickering. He motioned across the loch and said instead. "My Lords, there must be over twenty thousand men on the far shore." Then sweeping his hand in the direction of their own troops added, "And we have less than five thousand souls on this shore. The numbers are against us."

Bruce remained argumentative. "Since the Romans came, we Scots have been overcoming greater numbers of well trained and greatly experienced armies. I see no one of great renown facing us. We fear no one."

"You speak true, and truly we Scots are a nation of great warriors. However, even should we take on and defeat the army opposite, at what cost that victory."

"What do you mean at what cost? The cost will be to the losing side."

"Even in victory, many of our men will die. How many will be left for the next battle? For there will always be a next battle, until and unless you defeat King Edward himself. You rightly point out that there is no one of great note facing you. That only means that if they lose half their men and half their leaders, it will have no great bearing one way or the other on the situation in England. On the other hand, if we Scots lose half the men and half the leaders, who is left for the next battle? Who will lead the nation to its freedom if there is no Earl of Carrick, no High Steward, no Bishop of Glasgow, no Lord Douglas?"

"Listen to him, my Lord, he speaks sense," the Bishop of Glasgow entreated.

"Yes, your man from God, Robert. Forgive me if I do not completely share your enthusiasm."

"Still, what he says is true. This is a battle we cannot afford to lose."

"And you should never start a fight that you cannot win," Wallace insisted.

"We are not starting it. They came up here looking for a fight. We should not disappoint them."

"So far, nobody has started anything. Do not let pride force you into making a bad decision."

Sir James spoke up. "It is not unknown for armies to come to terms without coming to blows. Perhaps we should speak to them and see just what they want. In truth, they may have been sent up here against their wishes, with no wish to die here."

"If we do negotiate with them. If. What are we looking for?" Carrick wanted to know.

"Time," William said simply.

"Time? Time for what?"

"Time to get ready. We are not ready to win today, but given time we can put ourselves in a position to win."

"How so?"

"We must choose the location carefully to give us the maximum advantage."

"In what way?"

"Our numbers are depleted after heavy losses. Wherever and whenever we fight we will almost certainly be heavily outnumbered. Outnumbered in men, outnumbered in horses, outnumbered in weapons. Therefore we must do all we can to swing the balance of power in our favour."

"And you have a plan to do just that? This is all just talk if you do not have a plan, Sir William."

"I have a plan, but I need time."

"And how do you plan to get time? No man, not even the famous Sir William Wallace, can manage time."

"That is where you are wrong, my Lord Carrick. No man can make time, or stop time, but we can all manage the time that is available to us, and make efforts to lengthen that time."

"I'm listening. What is your plan?"

"Many men have been coming to me as news has gone abroad, offering their services. Men who may not have not been involved in warfare before for various reasons. Many of them have been displaced by the incomers. These men have a real desire to fight for our country, but have had no one to follow. I propose to base these men in Ettrick and mould them into a coherent force."

"That is all good and well, but how can this untrained rabble overcome a highly trained English army? How can you sustain them through training and through a battle?"

"Good question, and I am glad to see that you are not dismissing it out of hand."

Lord Douglas interrupted. "As for sustaining them, Sir William and I have just returned from a successful outing to Scone. The city is now in our hands, as is a great deal of money that will not now be going to London. Sir William has that to sustain his men. In addition I will give him horses from my own stables, and as many weapons as I can reasonably spare. I urge you all to do the same."

William was humbled, but before he could express his gratefulness others spoke up.

"I also can spare some horses and weapons," said the High Steward.

"Perhaps I can offload some of my excess, but make it look like a robbery. If we are going to sue for peace here, we cannot be seen to actively encourage the opposite. I'll speak to you about it later, Sir William," put in the Bishop.

"Are you all completely mad?" The Earl of Carrick was wide-eyed with dismay. "A stranger turns up and starts ordering everyone around and the best you can do is help him to create his own army. An army that can defeat the English can also defeat any noble in Scotland. This man you all admire so much might just turn round and declare himself King of Scots. And you will all have handed it to him on a silver platter."

"Sir Robert." The High Steward advanced on the Earl of Carrick. "Not everyone wishes to be King."

"Really? So what do most men dream of? Do you think that men only have hopes of adequacy?"

"Sir Robert, I assure you that I have no dreams for myself. Whatever regard the common people of the country may have for me, I could never be King. I have no royal blood, no connection whatsoever. In any case, as I understand it, your main opposition for the crown is safe and well in the north, a long way from here. Should you fall here today, who is left to oppose the Lord of Badenoch?"

The mention of his great rival served to focus the young Earl's mind. All at once he stopped just objecting and really started to listen to the advice the others were giving.

"Okay, let's say I agree with Sir William's ideas. Just what is the plan?"

"On the way back here from Scone it occurred to me that anyone wanting to relieve Stirling Castle has to approach it over a bridge. If we can lure an English army to cross the river Tay over that bridge we can limit the numbers we have to face and fight them on the marshy ground where their heavy horses will not be able to manoeuvre. Assuming it will take several weeks for this army to return home and several weeks more for another army to form and travel up to Stirling, I will have enough time to train my men in the tactics they will need for such a battle. Each man will be trained to do one thing and one thing only. But they will be able to do that one thing to a very high level."

"I'm sure we would all like to be at that battle," Sir Richard Lundie told William, to shouts of agreement from most of the others.

"Good. I have had exchanges with Sir Andrew Moray and he is also keen to join the fight. He has been having as much success up north as we have been having here in the south west. Indeed, my idea is to use his success to lure the English by way of Stirling."

"I will not fight at Stirling and leave my home undefended," Robert Bruce stated defiantly.

'You will not fight with me, you mean,' William thought, but kept it to himself. To the others he said, "I ask no one to fight away from home, and I understand completely the Earl's reluctance to do so. My plan is based only on my own men, and I will not change that for any reason, because I am sure it will work."

He stopped and had a good look at them all. Here he was, a boy from a council estate being treated as an equal by most of the great and the good of the country. What he was about to ask could risk all the good will and respect he had gained. "There is one part of my plan that is very risky and I will need a volunteer."

They all looked at him expectantly. What could possibly be more risky than all-out war?

"My plan relies on the English arriving at Stirling by the correct route. I need someone to pretend to switch sides in order to send us information and to feed the other side with information that will guide them to us. Anyone up for that?"

"Are you out of your mind? You can't really be asking one of us to ride with our enemies? Have you any idea how those people speak of us? It wouldn't last a day before someone said something that deserved a dagger. It's a suicide mission."

"Clearly you are not in, Lord Douglas. In any case, you would be an unlikely candidate. It is not uncommon for nobles to change sides, but that happens mainly at a crucial event, and usually under pressure from Edward himself. What I need is for someone to come up with a good reason for switching sides now. A credible reason that would give credence to that person becoming very forceful in their opposition to the rest of us. Maybe a couple of you could stage a fight and one of you leave following that."

"We don't want anyone to get hurt though, do we. And if no one gets hurt, it's not going to be enough of a fight to be convincing," Richard Lundie argued. "How about this: we delay to allow Sir William and a few others to leave and start making their preparations. Then we delay some more, then some more again. At length I will vent my frustration at the lack of progress and make a show of leaving the camp. I then go alone to the English camp and express my frustration, surely echoing their own, at the complete lack of progress in the Scottish camp."

"Done correctly, it could work. Knowing Sir Richard as I do, I am sure he will do it well. Does everyone else agree."

"Aye," they all echoed, although not all sounded completely

convinced.

Part IV

Disillusion

Chapter 17: January 1989

Syria

Musa was easy to spot. He parked his car and strode casually towards the airport terminal. As soon as he was well clear, and Donald was sure no one was watching the vehicle, he slipped out of hiding and made his way across the car park. Another quick check and he bent down to place a tracking device under the vehicle.

William too was easy to spot, being head and shoulders above most of the other passengers. Musa started waving long before he cleared the arrivals exit.

"William, over here," he called, waving his arms wildly.

The two old friends embraced warmly. "I saw some snow on the hills on the way down," William remarked. "Makes me feel at home."

"You are home now, brother. When you learn the whole truth you will never go back."

"That is why I am here, to discover the truth," William answered honestly.

From Damascus airport it was a short hop to the barren conditions that William remembered from his student days a couple of years earlier. As the friends drove and reminisced the Toyota suddenly slewed to the left, leaving the road and jolting across the rough terrain until Musa managed to bring it to a sliding halt.

"Whee! That was fun!" William laughed as Musa slowly exhaled. "You did good to stop us rolling."

"Not funny at all!" his friend retorted. "This is my uncle's car; he will go crazy if it is damaged." William noted that Musa was frightened, almost terrified. If Omar invoked that reaction from his relatives, how must others fear him?

The pair got out and walked around the vehicle, relieved to see no apparent damage to the bodywork. "Fucking puncture!" the Syrian exclaimed, kicking the flat tyre.

"No problem, easily fixed," the Scot reassured him. "Where's the jack?"

Placing a flat rock below the jack to stop it sinking into the dusty ground, William began to raise the car while Musa finished unscrewing the wheel nuts.

"What the fuck!" Musa spat, horror on his face. This time there was no mistaking the pure terror on the young man's face.

"What's the matter?" William asked, following his stare, expecting to see a snake or a scorpion or some such.

It was much, much worse than that. Attached to the underside of the vehicle was a small metal box that both men realised must be a tracking device. Just at that moment two vehicles appeared and sped towards them.

"I assume that is not the AA," William joked, trying to keep it light.

"My uncle has lookouts everywhere, especially this close to his place. He will have heard about our incident and sent help." Musa looked from William to the tracker and back again. "Please tell me that this has nothing to do with you? We will both be in trouble!"

William feigned hurt and surprise. "It has nothing to do with me, you have my word. For goodness sake, I am just out of university, what could I know about these things? Why would anyone put such a device on your car? Is there something I should know?"

There was no time to answer, Omar's men had arrived and immediately spotted the problem.

~~~

When Donald arrived some time later he found the car still jacked up with doors open.

"No sign of them, but with that wheel off there is sure to be a problem. Fuck! We were 95% sure they would come this way, we should have left things alone," he lamented.

"We couldn't be totally sure. If they had taken him anywhere else we would not have been able to follow closely enough. We could have lost them completely," one of the Israelis stated with a shrug.

"What makes you so sure we haven't? Let's spread out and search the area."

As the five agents spread out to search the area for any sign of a struggle, the jacked-up car shot into the air, spraying glass and metal in all directions.

The men were all close enough to the vehicle to be hurled through the air. Donald landed in a slight depression, shielding him from the second blast as a missile from a hand-held rocket launcher obliterated their jeep. Cautiously raising his head above the parapet, Donald noted that two of his fellow operatives had sustained serious injury and were not moving. The legs of a third were protruding out from below the wreck of the Toyota which had come down several feet from its original location. Collins, the only other man still mobile, spotted Donald and began to snake towards him. Immediately he moved there was a burst of machine gun fire and he slumped to the dirt, lifeless eyes still looking at Donald.

~~~

Omar grabbed William's jaw and lifted his bruised and bloodied face. By that time it could have been anyone's face; one of William's eyes was completely closed and the other partially closed but misted with blood from a cut on his eyebrow. But he didn't need to see to know who the voice belonged to. "It would be better to tell me now while you can still speak. When you are so battered that I cannot make out your words I will have to kill you."

William spat out blood, phlegm and a tooth that had lost the fight to stay attached to his gum. "You may as well just kill me then, because I have no idea what you want from me. I don't know anything about electronics. I don't know anyone who does, I did not mix with the geeky types. I have no idea who would want to track me or Musa, or why anyone would."

Omar straightened up, letting William's head drop back to his chest. He took out his handgun, released the safety and placed it against the prisoner's forehead. "Do you really want to die, Englishman?"

"I'm a fucking Scotsman!" William croaked, raising his head as far as he was able, trying, unsuccessfully, to look his assailant in the eye.

All the watching men laughed. Omar put the safety back on his pistol and holstered it. "For that you get to live another day. We love Scotland," he proclaimed, spreading his arms, nodding and looking around his colleagues for confirmation. They all agreed.

When the door unlocked and opened the next morning William braced himself for the next round of torture and interrogation. He wondered what it would be today. He had already been subjected to all of the methods he had been trained to expect. Maybe they would invent something new just for him. But instead of the armed guards, a grey-haired man in a white coat crossed to his bedside and introduced himself.

"Good morning, I am Doctor Samaan. How are you feeling?" The medic bent to examine his patient.

William briefly considered a sarcastic reply, but decided to play safe until he figured out what was going on.

"I am sore and very confused. Can you tell me what is going on?"

"I only know that I have been brought here to examine you and treat you as necessary."

As the doctor continued the examination, William grimaced, gasped and winced in pain almost every time the doctor touched him or asked him to move in any way. Although he had developed an extremely high pain threshold, he thought it prudent to act as much as possible as a civilian would.

"Well, the good news is that there appears to be nothing broken. I am going to give you a painkilling injection and I will leave some pills with your friends. Take it easy for a few days and you should be fine."

Just after the medic had left Musa came in and sat on the edge of the bed.

"You look like shit, man."

"Thanks, you look a million dollars." William laughed, hurting his ribs despite the painkilling injection.

"I am really sorry about all of this. My uncle is a bit paranoid. He thinks everyone is out to get him."

"Everyone? Who in particular?"

"The Americans, the Brits, the Jews."

"Sounds really popular. What has he done?"

"Nothing to worry about. He is just outspoken. People do not like to hear the truth."

'I wouldn't mind hearing some,' William thought, but said, "Does this mean he is not going to kill me?"

"It seems some friends of his have been looking into the tracking device. It is Israeli, and they have failed to find anything to link you, or any British agency, to it. Also, the trackers who arrived later were all Israeli."

"Were?"

"Unfortunately they all died so could not be interrogated. But the ones we could identify were known Mossad operatives."

"Have I arrived at the start of a war?"

"Just an unfortunate incident. I had been so looking forward to you being here again. Uncle Ali was going to kill you when he realised that you had nothing to tell him."

"Nice family you have. Why didn't he kill me?"

"I persuaded him that you are a good man, deserving of mercy."

"And he just accepted that?"

"Okay, I also had to remind him why he was keen to have you here in the first place."

"So, are you saying that I am free to go?"

"Do you want to go? I thought you were turning your back on Western ways?"

"I thought I would be welcome here. Not beat to within an inch of my life. Tortured in ways that you don't even see in stupid American films."

William had sensed, he still could not see very much, that someone was lurking outside the room. Confirmation came when the figure of Omar approached the bed and said, "If you are still that radical young man who is disillusioned with the greed and inequality that drives the West then you are very welcome here."

"Are you crazy? Do you really think that I would want to stay here after what you have put me though?"

"Of course not. You have been badly treated and I have not even apologised for the misunderstanding."

"Misunderstanding? Are you serious? I was viciously attacked, tortured and beaten for days *before* you found out whether whatever was on that car had anything to do with me. Now you want to dismiss it as a misunderstanding."

"Look, William, you came out here having stated that you were disillusioned and were considering joining us. You are an educated man, you know that there are many things going on in the world. Maybe you did not expect anything to occur so quickly, but you must have known that just by coming here you were putting yourself in danger."

William did not want to overplay it; he would be no good to anyone dead. "Just tell me one thing. If I want to go back to Scotland now, or at any time, am I free to do so?"

"Absolutely," Omar assured William, but the young Scotsman knew it was a lie. "Come," he said, extending an arm. "Let us feed you and nurse you back to full fitness. When you are well we can begin your training."

~~~

In the early hours of the next morning William was awakened by a hand closing over his mouth.

"You're in a bad way, laddie," Donald whispered. "Let's get you out of here." He lifted his hand away now that he was sure his protege would not make enough noise to alert his captors.

"Where the fuck have you been while I was getting the Spanish Inquisition?"

"We got ambushed. The others are all dead. I was lucky. Managed to find a dip and enough scrub to cover myself. Fucking amateurs walked right past me and didn't see."

"How did you get in here?"

"It's my job, remember? I've been in and out for days trying to locate you. This is the first night that there hasn't been a guard on your door. Let's get you out of here. Can you walk?"

"I can't go."

"What do you mean you can't go? You're three-quarters dead! We need to go now."

"No. If they were going to kill me, I'd be dead already. As it is, I'm in. Apart from the minor hiccup, it is now going to plan."

"You can't be serious!"

"You know that I knew some of the people from Lockerbie who died. That makes this personal. I won't give up until we get them justice."

"Even if it kills you?"

"That's *my* job."

Chapter 18: March/April 1989
Changed priorities

Omar had found William to be a good student and had named him Walid, meaning newborn. As confidence in Walid increased he was allowed greater freedom to wander off by himself to study and meditate. In time William and Donald settled into a routine of whispered exchanges almost every evening. Donald had managed to secure a hiding spot within the roof space of an outbuilding which allowed him to see without being seen, so that they could be confident of not being overheard as the younger man paced, reading his Quran seemingly in reverie, back and forth in front of Donald's refuge.

"You are not going to like this."

William stopped pacing and almost turned to look at the spot where Donald was concealed, the tone of his voice had alarmed him. Stealing a quick glance across the compound, he was relieved to see that none of the others were looking his way. Although he was by now generally accepted by most, there were still a couple of men who remained suspicious of his every move.

"What am I not going to like?"

"We are ordered back to London."

"Why?"

"No reason given. It is not a request, it is an order, it is not our place to ask questions."

"But we are on the verge of confirming the actual bomber, surely that is the reason we are here? There is no point in anything less. Even if they come after the group, surely they need to be sure they get everybody involved?"

"Just be ready to go tonight."

~~~

A few days later Donald and William were ushered into Sir Peter's office for a debrief.

"Ah, come in, sit down, gentlemen," Sir Peter enthused, walking around his desk, indicating the leather sofa to his right. "Drink?"

"No thank you, sir" the pair said in unison as they sat at either end of the sofa.

"Okay, well, straight to business then. First of all, well done both of you on an excellent mission."

"Thank you, sir. Just doing our jobs," Donald clipped back. William, noting the response, coupled with the sofa and offer of a drink, was only slightly behind the more experienced soldier in realising that something was off.

"Now then, you are both aware of the sensitivity of all this and the need to leave the rest to those with the right skills." Sir Peter paused for confirmation, but neither man reacted, waiting to see what was coming. "Before I continue I hope I do not need to remind you that you are both prohibited by the Official Secrets Act from discussing any of this with anyone. That at least is clear, I hope." This time both men nodded.

"Good. Now, as you know, things are not always as they seem. I have been advised that the information we had that led to your operation in Syria was flawed." Donald and William exchanged knowing looks. "Apparently the Syrians had nothing at all to do with the Lockerbie bombing."

"With respect, Sir Peter," William interrupted, "I had spent many weeks with the people who were directly responsible. I have passed on details that put that beyond any doubt."

"William, I will allow your impudence just this once. This is not an open discussion. There are those who would question your judgement on this. Those who suspect that your time in Syria has impaired your judgement. Be careful not to give those people an excuse they would welcome to damage all of us.

"Your orders, gentlemen, and I do mean orders, are to put this behind you and move on. New information implicates the Libyan dictator Gaddafi as the mastermind behind the Pan Am 103 outrage."

"Why?" William again. One word was enough. They knew why the Iranians and Syrians did it. There was no obvious motive for Libya.

Extremely vexed that his previous censure to William had not had the desired effect, Sir Peter's face hardened and he barked, "This meeting is now over. Go back to your unit and do as you are told. And keep your mouths shut."

"What about the Syrians?" William persisted in forcing the issue while trying to remain calm. Inside he was seething; it was personal.

Sir Peter did not answer William, but looked at the senior man with an expression that Donald understood to mean that it was now up to him to set his charge straight.

William had had enough. It took all of his self-control to walk out of the office without saying or doing something he would be made to really regret. As Donald rose to follow him, Sir Peter affirmed, "Get him under control before this gets out of hand! Better you bring him to heel than I have to."

The implied threat was not lost on Donald "No need for you to concern yourself, sir. Look upon this as part of his learning process. He will be better for it in the long run."

Chapter 19: 1995

School daze

Alan Wallace had not been this happy in years. There was a time when he could not have imagined being happy again. A widower at thirty-six, he had suppressed his own grief in order to put on a brave face for his boys. As the boys grew into adulthood they naturally spent less time at home, unaware in their typically teenage outlook that although they did not need their father, he certainly needed them. Long before his younger son followed his brother to university, Alan had turned to Johnny Walker for solace. Now though, they were both back, and here he was, for the first time in years, having a night out with both of his sons.

"There you go, Dad, a nippy sweetie for you," Malcolm said as he placed the amber liquid on the beer mat. "I got you a Black Label, since it's a special occasion. And a pint of heavy for you, Wull, there you go."

William lifted the pint glass. "Cheers, here's to family."

"Slainte," Malcolm said as he lifted his lager.

"A bheil Gaidhlig agad?" William asked cheekily, knowing the answer.

"Whit?"

"Do you have the Gaelic?" William repeated in English.

"Naw, just 'slainte'. Stop showing aff, Mr-I-speak-every-language-in-the-world."

"You pair bantering is just like old times." Alan beamed as he clinked glasses with his wee boys. "Slainte."

"Don't you start," William laughed.

"So, it's definite, you're going to work at the school with Malcolm. Will that not be boring after all your globe-trotting?"

"I wasn't on holiday, you know. Globe-trotting makes it sound exotic. Getting shot at in Basra, Bosnia and Belfast is not fun, I'll have you know."

"Come on, I've seen the adverts, skiing in Norway, sunbathing in Belize, all that kind of stuff, it's a breeze."

"That's only to con you into signing up. If they showed you boys getting shot and blown up, nobody would enlist. Anyway, I'm sure there are tougher folk at the school than some of the fannies that sign up for the army"

"You're not kidding," Malcolm laughed "They're talking about putting bars on the staff room windows."

"Is that to stop the teachers escaping?"

"You can laugh, Wull, but some of the teachers are a bit rough too. Talking of dodgy teachers, see that wee redhead over there that keeps giving you the eye?"

"I could hardly miss her, she's a bit obvious. She's filed under 'later'." William laughed and winked.

"That is Janey McNab. A right wee firecracker. Flirts with everyone."

"You mean I'm not special?" Pretending hurt feelings.

"Causes more fights than anyone I know. Her husband is a Physics teacher. Good enough guy most of the time, but with a tendency to jealous rages."

"That's a bad combination."

"Aye. It's said that the headmaster is afraid to get rid of him. Rumour has it that he has something on the boss."

"I haven't started yet and, here I am being pulled into school politics."

"You can't avoid them. Just, whatever you do, be discreet."

Chapter 20: July 1996

Glencoe

Donald retired not long after William left, having served for twenty-four years. The pair kept in touch, and William took every opportunity to visit his old sergeant at his home just past Glencoe. On a balmy July evening with just enough breeze to keep the midges at bay, after devouring some tasty trout which they had caught earlier, Donald enquired, "Do you ever miss the Service?"

"Of course I do. The camaraderie, the travel, the challenges. Probably much the same as you. Why do you ask?"

"It just seems such a pity that things went so bad for you so early. You were a great soldier. There will always be a need for a man like you. You must have regrets."

"I've had a few, but then again, too few to mention," William sang, badly.

"You are no Frank Sinatra, that's for sure. But seriously, you never got over the Lockerbie carry-on. You just couldn't let it go, could you?"

"We had them and somebody let them go, what was the point? Everything we went through only to find that justice for those hundreds of lives didn't really matter."

"You can't take things personally. Those people died, and nothing we did, or could have done, will ever change that. Whatever happened or did not happen at any time after the event, they are still just as dead."

"For fuck's sake, Donald. That is such a crock of shit."

"But true, nevertheless. You have got to accept that there is a bigger picture. We are, or were I suppose, just very small cogs in a very large machine."

"Do the cogs and wheels drive the machine, or does the machine grind on regardless, forcing all the parts to comply?"

"Don't get all philosophical on me," Donald mocked, taking a long swig from his bottle of single malt. He still drank his local Ben Nevis, despite his misgivings about it now being owned by a Japanese company.

"It never fails to amaze me how much whisky you can put away without showing any outward signs of being drunk."

Donald smiled, taking the comment as a compliment. "It's like anything else, sonny boy, you have to keep practising to stay good at it."

"Have you never had any doubts? Or were you always the model soldier?"

"We all have our moments. I too had reason to question the motives of the machine. Not all that long before you joined us, actually."

"Even you, Donald? What could possibly have driven a man like you to question the system?"

"As soldiers, we all follow orders, do as we are told. That is the job. But everyone, or most of us at least, are asked to do things that go against the grain."

"There can't be many with a grain straighter or truer than you Donald. So what was it that worried you?"

Donald took another drink and stared out across the loch. William left him to his thoughts, not sure if he would decide to tell or not. At length the older man sighed and carried on.

"I was home on leave in 1985 when I got a call. Something urgent had come up and I was the only man close enough to deal with it before it got out of hand."

"Nothing unusual about getting pulled off of leave."

"No, it was not the first time and not the last. Anyway, as you would expect, everything was need to know and all I was told was that an elderly gentleman had been given some documents that were potentially embarrassing to the government. He was travelling to the Dornie area from Glasgow in a maroon coloured Volvo saloon car. My mission was to make the car and driver disappear and return the papers to London.

"I knew the road well so I had no trouble formulating a plan. I took an old Triumph that I kept covered up at the back of my garage, for use when I did not want to be spotted by anyone who may know me, drove to a lay-by on the A87 and popped the bonnet. It was a bit risky because anyone could stop, but it was the best I could do at such short notice. In those days the traffic was fairly light at that time of the year, early April it was. If anyone else had happened along I would just have started to close the bonnet and told them I was okay, problem fixed. I fully expected the Volvo to stop when I flagged it down, it would just be common decency.

"I got into position, smoked a couple of cigarettes and waited. There were no other vehicles until the Volvo came trundling along, which it did sooner than I expected. They had told me that it was already en route, but it must have been well on its way by the time that they called me.

"Anyway, as the car approached I stepped out from behind the bonnet of my car, wiping my hands with a rag as if I had been tinkering with the engine, and waved both my arms to indicate I needed help. The Volvo slowed down and started to pull in, but seemed to take fright and swerved back out onto the road with a screech of its tyres. Getting in my car and chasing him was very risky, too many things could go wrong, so I took out my hand gun and shot at him before he could get too far away. A car is a fairly easy target at that distance, but hitting the driver was asking a bit much. Nevertheless the car swerved and plunged off of the road. I sprinted after it knowing I had to reach it before the driver could escape, if he was able to. If he got out and got any distance at all I was totally exposed if another car had come along.

"Although it had sounded like such an easy task to take a briefcase off an old man, my target had other ideas. Before I got close to the car I heard a crack and the unmistakable sound of a bullet whistling just past my right ear. You can imagine how annoyed I was at that! I later found out that it was well known that the guy owned a hand gun, but no one had bothered to tell me. Just one of those details I did not need to know, I suppose. There I was running across open ground towards what I thought was an old duffer in a Volvo, when in fact not only was he armed, he was either a very good shot or very lucky to come so close to a moving target at that range. Either way I was not waiting to find out which it was. I threw myself into a roll and got myself out of his line of sight behind the car. I knew the shooter was squatting behind the open driver's door. I made my way carefully around the car. The old boy had no idea where I was until he felt my arm go around his throat. I kept the pressure on until I felt him go limp."

"There is no satisfaction in overcoming a civilian at the best of times. You must have felt like shit beating up an old man. What were you then, about thirty-five and in your prime?"

Donald accepted that the younger man was sympathising and was not taking the piss. He had another swallow of his whisky and continued without answering the interruption.

"Now that the car was stuck in a bog, there was no way I was going to make it disappear. I had to improvise. Shoving the driver back behind the steering wheel, I fixed the gun in his hand as best I could, placed the muzzle against his head and put a bullet into his brain. The positioning was a bit awkward and in the process the gun dropped and I could not locate it. It was a shambles, the whole mission had descended into chaos. I grabbed the bags off of the back seat, did a quick check of the boot and headed back to my own car as quickly as I could.

"Now, had everything gone according to plan I would have driven the Volvo and put it in Loch Cluanie, then walked back to my car and headed off to hand over the documents. I had taken the fan belt off of the Triumph so that if anyone happened upon it, or me walking towards it, I could say that I had gone to get a replacement. As it was, I had to make the best of a bad job. I went home, telephoned London and explained what had happened. They told me to sit tight and they would send someone to collect the briefcase."

"I've been listening and trying to figure out what your dilemma was. Nothing about the job seems too off the wall. I have heard much worse, some of the stuff that went on in Ireland for instance. The timing though. I would have been in first year as St Andrews. Are you telling me you killed Willie McRae?"

"You know about it?"

"Well the media did not make too big a deal about it and if I had been elsewhere it might not even have registered. But the university was buzzing about it. All those political activists, not just the SNP, but Labour too I remember, talking about conspiracy theories and claiming murder."

"Aye, that was the guy. And they were right of course. It was a political assassination. The car was not found until the next morning. Poor bastard lay all night, and it turned out he did not die until the early hours of Sunday morning. I was sure he was dead, but like a complete amateur I did not check his vitals before leaving the scene. In due course I was brought in and given an almighty bollocking."

"Sorry, Donald, but I still do not understand your quandary over a messed-up murder. Is it because he was a civilian? It is unusual to hit a civilian, but not unknown."

"He was acting against the government, so he was not a civilian in the true sense of the word. It wasn't the killing. What came afterwards put a different perspective on it. You see we are all a little bit curious, and there I was sitting alone at home, enjoying a wee dram and that damn briefcase seemed to be mocking me. In my head I could hear it say 'Aye, look at you. Big hard man eh? No bother to you, you were just following orders. Well so were the fucking Nazis! At least they knew what they were killing for all the same. What did you kill that poor old man for?' Eventually it got too much so to shut the damned thing up I opened it and read the papers."

"So what were they? What made this man such a threat?"

"Take your pick, it was a mixed bag, excuse the pun. It was well known, not to me at that time, I found out later, but it was well known that McRae was very active against the nuclear industry. And there were all sorts of documents concerning that. Radioactive waste at nuclear power stations. Accidents and leaks. Information about nuclear submarines accidents. I found out later that he had been under surveillance for ages and he was a bit paranoid, if that is a good word when his fears were well founded, that the police and MI5 spent more time in his house than he did. That is why his briefcase was crammed full of papers, he was afraid to let anything important out of his sight."

"So there could have been something in there that was worth killing him for?"

"Possibly, but there were a couple of other things. Firstly, he had a copy of the McCrone report."

"You say that as if it should mean something. I've never heard of it. What is it?"

"It is a report commissioned in the mid-seventies about potential North Sea oil revenues. Apparently the claims made by the nationalists were not accurate in that their estimates of the wealth were way too low."

"So why is that a problem? It must have been about ten years old."

"You are too young to remember, I suppose. In the seventies the UK government had to run cap in hand to the IMF for a bail-out. A few years later Margaret Thatcher was claiming Brits could live the dream. What do you think paid for those dreams?"

"Ach, but surely they could have spun that away. It was still an old document, presumably people had been saying much the same anyway." William was beginning to think that maybe Donald did not handle his whisky just as well it usually seemed.

"You're right. Actually, I only put that in to make you feel a bit better. You were upset about the Lockerbie cover-up because they shit on Scotland's needs for the greater UK good. I am just showing you that I understand. That's why I defended you so vigorously to Sir Peter and others."

"Okay, thank you. I always just assumed that you had a soft spot for me as a younger version of yourself."

"Don't flatter yourself, laddie." Donald laughed. "You still couldn't lace my boots. I may have taught you everything you know, but I didn't teach you everything I know."

"So, come on then, you said there were a couple of things. You're clearly saving the best for last. What else was there?"

"Best? No, not best. Worst. There was a large manilla envelope full of notes, documents and photographs relating to a paedophile ring."

"Fuck! Really? Kiddy fiddlers. Bastards!"

"Aye. That was my dilemma. Oil and nuclear waste I could ignore as none of my business, like terrorists and foreign wars. Those are things for people way above my pay grade. But children, and some of the poorest souls at that. Children in care homes that should have been getting looked after were being supplied to a bunch of perverted cunts for their amusement."

"Who? Who would do such a thing? Surely that was something that should be eradicated."

"If only. Politicians, judges, policemen. Royalty even. You name it. I couldn't believe it. I cried."

"You cried! I would have put money on you never having cried in your entire life."

"And until then you would have been right. But that night. Those photographs. The realisation of how widespread it was and therefore impossible to stop. Oh, I cried all right. I cried all fucking night." Donald had taken on a haunted expression. All these years later the anguish was still acute.

"That was what, three years before I met you? Conscience or not, however many tears, you must still have passed the envelope on."

William, for the first time, was unsure of how he felt about his mentor. Everything he thought he knew about him was riding on what he said next.

"It was a long night. In fact it was several long nights before I slept again. I wanted to go to the newspapers, the television companies, the police. Anyone and everyone. But they were all there, in that envelope. There was nowhere I could go, almost certainly still isn't, that would have made any difference."

"They would have killed you just as surely as they killed Willie McRae," William stated matter-of-factly.

"To be honest, right then, that would have been a kindness. I've lived with that knowledge for over ten years now and I know that it will probably be the last thing that I think of when I do die. No, I didn't keep quiet for my own safety. More importantly, there were things that identified witnesses. I said nothing to protect them."

"Saying nothing would not save them though."

"No, it wouldn't. That's why I spent all night doctoring the papers. I removed whole documents or pages of notes where I could without making a material difference to the overall package. Despite everything, there was still a tiny part of me that hoped that someone would see it that would act on it, so I didn't want to lose any evidence against any individual."

"And where you couldn't?"

"I took the briefcase outside and found some ground that was roughly comparable to where the killing had taken place. I emptied the contents out and let them blow about a bit, there was just a gentle breeze. That way I was able to smudge and deface names without, hopefully, making it too obvious. When I handed the briefcase over I told them that McRae had been running off with the briefcase and during the struggle it had burst open and the contents emptied. I said I had to run after some and jump on them to catch them. Also that I could not be sure that I had got everything, but I thought I had."

"You must have done a good enough job, here you are now."

"I was under a cloud for a while. I know for a fact that I was very closely monitored for over a year and I was kept close to base during that time. That did not worry me too much and that is probably why I got through it. To be honest, if someone had decided to terminate me I would have been glad to be free of the burden that knowledge still places on me."

Chapter 21: 30th July 1996

Party

"Surprise!"

William was actually speechless. Not the 'OMG, I'm speechless, I don't know what to say...' kind of speechless that prattles on for several minutes. For almost a full minute he stood trying to lift his jaw off of his chest and form proper words. None came. Even when Malcolm asked, "Well, what do you think?" he could only look back at him and do an impression of a fish, mouth opening and closing as if gasping for air.

Today was William's thirtieth birthday and his brother had insisted on taking him out to celebrate. It was supposed to be dinner with their father, but William had been suspicious of Malcolm's behaviour, deducing that his brother was lining up another blind date. But this! How could anyone have kept all of this secret? The function room had been totally decked out to look like a medieval hall with long tables, wall hangings and everybody dressed up to look the part. He had been suspicious of Malcolm for a while, knowing something was being planned. Now he was looking at what seemed to be the entire staff of the school, and even a few of the older pupils.

Eventually, as colleagues queued up to wish him well, he found his voice.

"Malcolm, what is this? I've hardly been at the school for five minutes, why are they doing this for me?"

The headmaster was first to reach the pair and offer his congratulations. He answered for Malcolm. "Actually, as you are aware, we had a school wide project covering this period of Scottish history. Just by chance, one of the history teachers, Miss Pringle... you know Emma, don't you?"

"Yes, we've met," William answered, looking round and spotting the petite brunette who was smiling sweetly at his brother. He wondered if the headmaster was aware that the pair had been an item for while now.

"Well, Emma came across a little-known figure with the same name as you. Apparently this man was a giant for his time, coincidentally probably about the same height as you, although most regular men were much shorter than they are today. Anyway, long story short, we decided it would be fun to culminate everybody's hard work with a night out, and your birthday gave it a focus."

"I feel a bit underdressed," William said, as he shook hands with more of his friends, all of whom had made the effort to dress up for the period.

"Don't worry about that," Emma told him. "There is a room for you and Malcolm to change in. Malcolm's costume is a good fit, and yours, we hope, will not be too far out. Certainly none of the outfits are tailored."

~~~

Throughout the meal, an array of meat and vegetable dishes that suited William nicely, the headmaster bored William with an almost unbroken monologue that must have covered every detail of the preparations. Everything was described in great detail, right down to which pupils had sewn together William's costume. At length there was a drum roll and a voice announced over the speakers:

"And now, ladies and gentlemen, the main event of the evening, the presentation of Sir William's birthday present."

There was a further fanfare and the doors at the far side of the hall opened to reveal a line of three teachers with arms outstretched carrying what was clearly an offering. As they neared the top table William saw to his astonishment that they were carrying a sword that looked to be about six feet long, longer than most of the people on the room.

"Sir William!" the headmaster shouted out for the whole room to hear. "It had been our intention to knight you with this fine weapon, but to be honest we were all afraid of injuring someone. Therefore, please accept this replica of your namesake's weapon of choice as a gift from everyone at the school."

"Are you kidding me?" William asked incredulously. "What am I supposed to do with that?"

"Well, actually we can't let you keep it. It remains the property of the school and will become the focal point of our display. Your present is to have it for the evening."

"So generous, I'm sure. Am I allowed to even touch it?"

"If you are very careful. We are not insured for any resultant injuries; I wouldn't want anyone to end up in court."

"You know that I do martial arts, headmaster, don't you?"

"Yes, why do you ask?"

"Well, if you had looked into the disciplines I have studied you would know that a couple of them are weapons based."

"That is nothing like a Japanese sword, William," Malcolm pointed out.

"No, but nevertheless I would like to take it outside and try some moves. Think of it as a thank you to all of you."

"What do you think, Mr Johnstone?" the headmaster asked the head of the technical department and main manufacturer of the sword.

Harry Johnstone, head of metalwork, was a short, squat man with a round head totally immersed in tightly curled dark hair. Incredibly skilful at his art, school legend made him a direct descendant of the Tolkien dwarves.

"It's heavy, but he is big enough to handle it I reckon. Won't do any harm if everyone keeps well back. It's obviously not nearly as sharp as an actual weapon would be."

William did not wait for further confirmation, but hurried around the big table and took the sword in his hands.

"Now, be careful!" the headmaster cautioned, already regretting even contemplating such a high-risk activity.

"To the car park!" William enthused. "Let's see what this can do." He had been out of the forces for what seemed like forever now, and had almost forgotten what a kick he got from weaponry.

There was not enough room in the car park so William climbed the fence into a neighbouring field. This was a comfort for the headmaster, who now had his charges safely behind a barrier. William began by slowly moving the sword from side to side until he had the feel of it and then swirled it around his head few times. When he felt happy with the length, weight and balance of the weapon he improvised a kenjitsu routine which ended with him appearing to cartwheel over the sword as it remained stationary three feet off of the ground. His peers cheered and whistled in appreciation.

Walking back towards the party, William was bringing up the rear.

Most of the other teachers were already inside. Thrilled as they were by his display, the bar had the edge in entertainment value. In any case, nobody likes a show off. Just as he reached out to grasp the door handle a much more delicate hand fell on his.

"Impressive display, William. Why don't you take me round there and show me what else you can do with that big weapon of yours?" It was Janey McNab, the glasses of Prosecco making her even bolder than normal.

"What about your husband?" The grumpy physics teacher was already inside, probably first back to the bar, but William was reluctant to risk causing a rammy on what had been a good night so far.

"What about him?" she said and, grabbing her prey by the crotch, pulled him towards her.

'Fuck it, it is my birthday,' he thought simply as he allowed her to pull him by the cock around the back.

~~~

William waited a few minutes after Janey had gone back in before returning in a futile attempt to be discrete. He was only two steps into the hall when pain exploded in a lightning flash as Andy McNab, who had been waiting for William's return, sucker punched him on the back of the head. Despite the pain of the blow from the sixteen stone cuckolded husband, William took a quick step forward and spun quickly ready to defend the follow up punch. Andy had sunk too many pints to launch a coordinated offensive though, and the speed of William's move left Andy off balance as he punched fresh air. Instinctively William jabbed his assailants chin, sending him sprawling across a table, bottles and glasses flying in all directions. Before Andy had fully regained his feet, oblivious to. the blood seeping through his shirt, several teachers had taken hold of each man in an attempt to prevent further blows. William raised his hands in a gesture of compliance, while a groggy Andy allowed himself to be pushed, pulled and cajoled towards the door before jabbing a finger towards William and spitting "I'll get you for this, arsehole! You better watch your fucking back!"

The headmaster was apoplectic. "There will be serious repercussions over this outrage, Wallace!"

"I was just defending myself from a cowardly attack, headmaster."

"My head doesn't button up the back, you are not innocent in this. I cannot condone *any* of this behaviour on an official school event."

"Official it may be for you, headmaster, but I just came out for my birthday. Nothing official in my invite. In any case, it's school holidays."

"That is as may be. I had hoped that it being a week night it would have been a less boozy affair. Make sure this is all sorted out before term time. Report to me first day back."

~~~

Chucking out time came without further incident. William had had a couple, but Malcolm was sozzled. As William half-walked, half-carried his brother outside, Bill Yates, one of the PE teachers and a good friend of Malcolm's, grabbed hold of Malcolm just as his foot missed a step.

"You really should be taking a taxi. How much have you had?" Bill asked William.

"Relax, Bill, I've only had a couple. I'm fine. Wouldn't want Malcolm to throw up in a taxi. Just help me get him into my motor. That blue Escort over there." Nodding across the car park. "Who the fuck is that?" William was alarmed at the sight of a Middle Eastern man loitering next to his car.

"Your turn to relax," Bill reassured him. That's just a taxi driver. He'll be waiting for his fare."

"Aye. Right." Still, William did not like the way the man had been watching him.

Bill added, "I'll bet he's glad he's not picking up Malcolm. Probably wouldn't take him by the look on his face. Wasted trip out here to get a no run."

"Okay, can you just hold onto him while I get his belt?" William asked after they had manoeuvred Malcolm, bawling out 'I would walk 500 miles' into the passenger seat.

William rushed round to the other side and slid into the driver's seat, leaned over and pulled the seatbelt around his brother. When it clicked into place he smiled and said, "Thanks, Bill. Give him a ring at the weekend, he should be recovered by then."

"Take it easy. Look after him, we've got a game on Saturday," Bill told him and slammed the door, thumping a final goodbye on the roof as William eased out of the car park.

A few minutes later Malcolm abruptly stopped singing 'Gonna Be' and announced "I'm going to chuck, Wull."

William took his foot off the gas, turning to look at his brother to work out if he had time to stop and get him out of the car before he vomited. Before his foot had reached the brake the car lurched as it was struck from behind, knocking the rear end out towards the far side of the road. Before William could make a correction the Ford struck the flimsy fence and launched into the trees, taking branches off of those at the top of the slope and trimming the tops off of those lower down as it turned in the air and came crashing down on the passenger side of the roof, before rolling to the bottom, flattening everything in its path.

Part V

Battle To The Top

Chapter 22: September 1297
Dundee Castle

"Welcome, Andrew, how are things in the North?" William was delighted to see his friend bring a sizeable force to Dundee. The pair embraced warmly, for there was genuine affection between them.

"Very well, William. Better than here it would seem." Andrew nodded in the direction of the castle that William and some of his men were keeping under siege. "There is not a castle north of here still in English hands. Looks like an easy castle to defend. Steep slopes on three sides and sheer cliffs at the back. Do you need some help here?"

"Thank you, but no. As you surmise, there is little to be gained by assaulting it, waiting it out is our only real option. Cressingham is expected to reach Stirling in no more than five days, so we cannot tarry any longer."

"It will be a shame to give up now. Do you think they can hold out much longer?"

"We don't know how long their supplies might last. However, I have no intention of letting them restock. Alexander Scrymgeour over there –" William pointed out a tall, thin, hook-nosed man busying himself directing proceedings " – will take charge of the siege with a handful of my men. He has raised volunteers from the town to come and make the place look busy and keep the pressure on. He is making the final arrangements now. Come, I will introduce you."

As the pair walked up the hill, Andrew's thoughts went ahead to the forthcoming clash. "When do we head across to Stirling?"

"First light. Alexander will swap his people under cover of darkness. I'll tell you what we have prepared so far, then we can discuss the deployment of your troops. You have brought many horses as promised, that is good. Your men will not need to be lying waiting in bogs like most of mine."

"They will be glad of that, although no-one surpasses we northerners when it comes to such tactics. What of the others? Has anyone else promised support, or is it just you and me?"

"We still have some friends, Andrew, but I do not want the English to know that. All I want them to see is us stationed high above the bridge. Let them focus on us to draw them on. Most of our warriors will be unseen by them until it is too late."

"What news of Lundie? Are you sure he still has their trust?"

"It is my belief that Sir Richard has the English eating out of the palm of his hand. He has been impressing him with his knowledge of the route and the best places to rest and find sustenance. Of course, we have been helping with that; our opponents are well fed."

"Is that wise? To me it goes against common sense. Surely we want our enemy to be under strength if possible?"

"Normally, yes, of course. But this is not a normal fight. Part of our plan is to restrict our enemy's ability to fight. My argument is that the heavier the buggers are, the more they will sink into the soft ground."

"I'm not convinced. I would rather they lacked strength by being undernourished."

"Let's not get bogged down in minor details, Andrew. How well fed they are will not make a great deal of difference either way. A man fighting for his life will fight just as hard regardless of the contents of his stomach. What I think is more important is that Richard has their confidence and that they themselves are overconfident, thereby underestimating us. Part of the reason for keeping Lennox and the Steward out of sight is to make them think that they are up against nobody. Their arrogance will tell them that we do not have the experience to resist them."

"Okay, so we have the Steward, we have Lennox and we have Lundie. If Lundie is with the English and the others are holding back, what assistance will they be able to give us when the fighting starts?"

"Lundie's task is to draw some of their cavalry off into an ambush. The Steward and the Earl of Lennox are about three miles upstream with almost two thousand horse. If we can lure most of their horses across the bridge and the others take care of most of the rest, it becomes a straight fight between infantry. By that time we will certainly have the advantage."

"If that works, all good and well. If it doesn't?"

"Either way, we will draw enough of their horses across the bridge so that our reserve force can defeat what is left. Upstream or downstream, it does not matter. We will make them fight on our terms."

Andrew considered for a bit, then admitted, "I am glad we are on the north. Having been there when we were soundly beaten by Surrey at Dunbar, I would not relish facing mounted English knights again in open battle. I hope that Sir James and Lennox fare better."

"I do not believe in starting a fight I cannot win, I would ask anyone to die for nothing." Then, William stopped and turned to face Andrew, asking him earnestly, "Do you have doubts, my friend? You have a duty to take care of your men. I would not ask you to risk them unnecessarily, but it is your decision whether to take them into battle or not."

Andrew smiled back and replied, "It is not that I do not trust your judgement, for it has been sound this far, but let us survey the field together tomorrow and finalise our plans then."

Chapter 23: September 1297

Stirling Bridge

"They are not coming. Maybe they are not as over-confident as we expected." Andrew Moray was exasperated by the wait. The English had arrived, the Scots were ready, but after two days nothing had occurred. It was now approaching sundown on the tenth of September.

"Let us go down and goad them then; we can't wait indefinitely," William replied and, turning to Alan Boyd, who had become his most trusted lieutenant, he ordered, "Have the men withdraw as inconspicuously as yesterday, Alan. Let them get dried off and fed, ready for another attempt tomorrow. I will speak to them myself on my return. For now we will go to the enemy and try to shame them into attacking in the morning."

~~~

Half an hour later, on the other side of the Tay a shout went up. "My Lord Surrey, two horsemen approach under a white flag."

Smiling broadly, the Earl of Surrey, John de Warenne, answered the messenger. "Thank you, I will be out to meet them directly." He turned to Edward's treasurer and beamed. "Well, Sir Hugh, it seems we were right to delay. The Scots have wilted under our show of strength and are surrendering. Let us go and give them our terms."

"Our terms? We are giving these upstarts terms?"

"No. We are giving them nothing. Rather, we will be telling them what they are giving us, which is pretty much all they have short of their lives and the clothes they stand up in."

"Clothes? You call those rags clothes? Yes, well, they can keep them, save us the trouble of burning them. Let's go and get this over with, the sooner I can get out of this damned country to somewhere civilised, the better."

Warenne and Cressingham were smug as they approached the visitors. "Gentlemen, we accept your surrender, of course. Won't you join us in our tent where we can relay our terms to you?"

Wallace and Moray looked at each other, dumbfounded. Andrew quipped, "Now, now, Sir William, it would be rude to laugh at our guests. Be polite." Turning to the invaders he told them, "Surrender? Us? Forgive us, but that is the funniest thing we have heard in a long, long time, is it not, Sir William?"

"Aye, indeed it is. We did not come here to give you our surrender. Quite the opposite. We have been patiently waiting for you to attack for days now. The conclusion we have reached is that you are afraid and just too shy to come to us with your terms for us allowing you to return home safely."

"Look here, sir, this is ridiculous. You are seriously outnumbered by every conceivable measurement. You cannot possibly hope to overcome us. Just tell all your men to lay down their weapons and go home, and we will say no more about it. You two, of course, will have to come with us." Warenne was aghast at the impudence of the Scottish leaders. He had heard that one of them had been among those he took prisoner the previous year. How anyone could have come through that comprehensive defeat and become so arrogant he could not fathom.

Nevertheless the two Scots could not hold back their laughter and let fly uproariously, much to the disdain of their English counterparts.

"You may think you are superior to us," William glowered, his demeanour changing instantly, making Cressingham visibly flinch as he leaned towards him, "but it is beholden on you to prove it. After all, your countrymen, and their Scots allies, thought they were superior to us common folk when you defeated the nobles last year. Yet here we are, a commoner and an esquire a year ago, leading the army that has all but removed English administration from most of Scotland. As you will be well aware, north of here only the castle behind us and Dundee are yours. Some of our men are still at Dundee where they expect to accept its surrender any day now. Stirling castle there will only remain loyal to your King if you get past us to relieve it."

Surrey was more circumspect than Cressingham. "Look, we will attack, and we will defeat you. There is no doubt about the outcome. However, we are gentlemen and we are quite prepared to come to terms, as we did with your chaps at Irvine. Perhaps your men may retain their arms, and you your freedom. But we will need both of your guarantees, as gentlemen, as to your future good conduct."

Turning back to Andrew, William shrugged and asked, "What do we have to say to get it through to these people?"

"Beats me, I was told they were intelligent men, but if so, they are hiding it well. Do you want me to try? I have spent some time as a guest in their land, I know their language."

"By all means, please do."

Andrew advanced towards Surrey. "My dear sir, unlike you, we do not have the patience to stand about talking nonsense for hours and days on end. We are not like our countrymen at Irvine. You will see none of them here, you saw none of us there. Our meeting here is over, we return to tell our men that you are too scared to come to us, and therefore the victory is ours."

"Okay, gentlemen, if that is how you want it, so be it. We attack on the morrow, and our men will be told not to hold back in any way. The two of you will accompany us back to London, dead or alive."

William approached Surrey and leaned down so that their faces were almost touching. "If you do return to London, and I doubt it, it will be because we have not come face to face again. But if you do, tell your King that we, and I speak for the common folk of Scotland, for I am proudly one of them, will never surrender, but will fight to defend ourselves and free our country to the last man. Let him come himself and we will prove ourselves to his face."

~~~

The following morning Surrey roared as he stomped furiously through the smur towards Cressingham. "What is going on? Who gave the order to advance?"

"Well, you did," the treasurer replied. "You must remember, last night you told those Scots oafs that we would attack today. Time is wasting. I am not prepared to continue paying these soldiers to do nothing. The King will be outraged when he learns how much this is costing him."

"Get them back! Get them back!" Surrey barked at the lieutenants around them. Turning back to Cressingham he continued, "The King will be more concerned with losing a battle than losing a few shillings, I assure you. You are his treasurer and should be concerned for his money, but you have no right to commit these men to battle. That is my decision, and mine alone. Get everyone back." With that he headed back towards his tent. "I will give the order when I am ready. No one moves before I am."

High above the bridge, from his vantage point William sighed and informed those around him, although they could all see for themselves what was happening, "Looks like they are retreating. Will this battle ever happen? This is a huge test of our men now, if just one man breaks cover to chase them, the game is over. There is not nearly enough of them across the bridge to make it worthwhile, and since they are already starting to recross many of them would escape anyway."

"You have trained them well, William. Their discipline is unshakeable, like their belief in you. If anyone was going to crack, they would have done so by now," Andrew reassured him.

"Aye, they are the best of men. Perhaps they will not need to fight. I yearn for a big victory to boost our cause throughout the land. On the other hand, many of these brave souls will perish and each one will be a sad loss. Maybe it will be for the best if we do not fight. Let us wait and see what the enemy proposes to do next. Whatever it is, they must come to us."

~~~

The English horsemen were not long fully back on the south bank of the Tay when finally the Earl of Surrey emerged from his tent ready for action. Already there were murmurs of discontent among them. Like Cressingham, they were keen to get things over with. Unlike Cressingham, it was not for the money, they just wanted to go home. Scotland was such a wretched place.

As Surrey signalled the advance, Sir Richard Lundie approached him once more. "My Lord, will you not reconsider my advice? Look at the field, see how our men are strung out in a line. That causeway is almost a mile long and there is high ground on either side towards the end of it. Surely our men will be bombarded from above even before they reach the Scots. Let me take a few hundred men and cross a couple of miles upstream where there is a ford wide enough to cross dozens at a time. We can attack from the rear and divide their forces. That will give the main attack a better chance of breaking through. Most of the men we face are unused to warfare and are reliant on their leaders. We should go all out to get Moray and Wallace. With them dead or captured I am sure the rest will quickly surrender."

Surrey had had a bad feeling about the forthcoming battle since they arrived and was becoming less and less confident with each passing minute. He had been rash when promising to attack today. Simply put, he was just not sure, despite his advantage in men, horses, weaponry and experience, that this was going to be an easy victory. Lundie waited patiently on Surrey's reply, knowing that if he pressed him he was likely to dig in. At length he sighed and once again cried out, "Pull the men back across the bridge."

On the Abbey Craig the Scottish commanders watched the second withdrawal with exasperation.

"Are this lot never going to get bored going backwards and forwards over the bridge?" Andrew asked William. From their vantage point they could see the enemy spread out on the opposite bank of the Tay, before funnelling in to cross the bridge two abreast. They could also see what the enemy could not, thousands of Scotsmen hidden on either side of the narrow causeway that led up towards them from the bridge. It had never occurred to the southerners that there should not be so many bushes or shrubbery only on one side of the river.

"This is only the second time they have started to advance and turned back. We must let them do so as many times as they wish. Our plan will only work if there are enough of them across to make our attack worthwhile. If we start too soon, and especially if we let them lure us across the bridge, we will lose. We do not have enough horses for a straight fight. Even if Lennox and the Steward are pulled back from their position we are too heavily outnumbered."

Back on the south bank it was Cressingham's turn to be outraged. "What is it this time? Why do we still not attack? It's only a few thousand Scottish peasants we face, not the King of France with an array of well-organised and experienced knights."

Surrey was not in the mood to listen to the treasurer, especially on battle tactics. "I will not tell you again, you may be in charge of the purse strings, but I, and I alone, am in charge of the battle."

"Is that so, or is Sir Richard in control? You gave the order to advance and it seems to me that he has overruled that decision. Are you sure whose side he is on?"

Lundie said nothing. He was aware that delays would extend the hardship of the Scots lying in wait on the other side of the river, some of them almost totally immersed in water. However, he was also aware that indecision, infighting and confusion in the English camp were all to the good for the patriots. Let Surrey and Cressingham fight all day long if they so desired. Far be it from him to intervene and offer any solutions.

By now the Earl of Surrey was wishing he had stayed home. Whatever the outcome, it could not possibly be worth all this. After all, they were not facing anyone of note. "Sir Hugh, I believe we are being too hasty. We have let those peasants shame us into acting before we are completely ready. There may be some merit in Sir Richard's plan. Let us take the time to hear him out and give it proper consideration. Whatever your misgivings, Sir Richard has proven himself to me."

Cressingham was not to be placated. He raged, "More time! More time! Well, why not just open the King's chests and let everyone help themselves? At this rate the end result will be the same, there will be no money left and we still will not have brought theses rebellious Scots to heel."

"There are more important considerations than money..."

Cressingham cut him off curtly. "Not to me, there aren't. If we reach the same spend as it cost us for your grandson to do nothing at Irvine, we will both be lucky to keep our heads when the King returns. No, Sir John, no more delays. No diversions. No side fights. I refuse to pay for one more hour than is necessary. Either get yourself across that bridge and sort that lot out, or let us just pack up and go home."

"You cannot do that."

"I can, and I will. I mean it, sir. Get this battle done or I will be writing to the King forthwith and denouncing your actions in the strongest possible terms."

The term between a rock and a hard place would not be coined for several hundred years, but it explained precisely the Earl of Surrey's position.

~~~

"Looks like they are serious this time." William told those around him. "Soon I will signal the attack. You all know your roles; go to your positions and may God go with you."

The judgement on when to attack was not based on any count but rather by weighing up the speed of ascent with how far up the first English knight was. William wanted to have as many horses on his side of the river as possible, while still being confident he could stop any of them completing the ascent and reaching ground where they could manoeuvre properly. Because the charge was faster than he anticipated he moved slightly earlier than he had planned.

Raising his standard overhead, a saltire flag attached to a sharpened stake, William threw it high in the air, where it arced and fell, embedding itself in the ground. As it landed he roared, "Saor Alba!" and his soldiers began to emerge from their hiding places, shouting their own war cries.

"Alba gu brath!" Andrew added as both men kicked their mounts from standing to gallop and charged downhill to confront English with their own cavalry yelling and cheering behind them.

The advancing English knights responded by urging their own mounts on as they raised their weapons ready for the clash. As they did so missiles began to rain down on them from both sides as the common Scots folk appeared on the slopes and bombarded the enemy from above. Although this resulted in very few direct deaths, many riders were injured or unseated and the confusion meant that the formation, such as it was, was lost.

William and Andrew led the Scots' downhill charge. They went two abreast, not because of the space, but because the smaller, more agile Scottish horses allowed them to charge between the larger English beasts, forcing them to the edge of the level ground. Their first strike was not necessarily to kill outright, rather the emphasis was on speed to build the confusion amongst their enemy. William was swinging a heavy hammer, Andrew an oversized axe and they ploughed into the enemy, unseating as many riders as they could. The unseated knights found it hard to manoeuvre in the melee, weighed down by their own armour and surrounded by riderless horses trying to find their own safe passage out of the battle. As wave after wave of Scots riders descended on them they found themselves being hacked, hammered and hewed from all directions. For the few who survived this first vicious onslaught there was no respite. Bold knights were overwhelmed by weight of numbers as the wee folk swarmed down the slopes and battered them mercilessly with crude weapon, sticks and stones.

Further downhill hundreds of soaking wet Scotsmen emerged from the bogs, jabbing at the horses from below to bring them down and dismount the riders. They carried a variety of weapons; many were simple farming implements, others were improvised or as basic as a sharpened stick of varying lengths. Few of the Scots ventured up onto the causeway itself, allowing the knights to come to them and find that they could not move easily in the bog. Those knights bold enough to remove armour in order to move more freely only found that they died more quickly as the Scots swarmed over them, daggers stinging, hammers bludgeoning and axes hacking in a bloody frenzy. For the few overexcited Scotsmen who ignored the order to remain off of the solid ground the battle was over very quickly, having no real defence against the sharpened steel of the English knights.

One knight, Sir Marmaduke Thweng, realising all was lost, was able to avoid the jabs and stabs from the bog by weaving down the middle of the causeway and reaching the comparative safety of the bridge. When the dust settled he would discover that he was the only Englishman to have crossed the bridge and survive. Unbelievably, more riders were trying to cross the bridge, urged on by their commanders to certain death. Sir Marmaduke, struggling against this tide, sought to deter his countrymen, yelling, "Turn around, go back , there is only death on the other side of the bridge! Are you fools? Can you not see what is happening. Save yourselves!" When he finally cleared the bridge he entreated his superiors, "My Lords, we are overwhelmed, do not send any more men to their death."

Surrey, who was already regretting not paying more attention to the foreboding he had felt since even before he crossed the border, had no heart to argue with Thweng. Why had he allowed that idiot Cressingham to push him into attacking when he knew it was not a good move? Should he have listened to Lundie and sent a force to attack from the rear? There was no way of knowing, but he could see that most of the men on the other side of the bridge had perished before the Scots horses had even reached them. Still, if he had sent some of them around at least they would have had a fighting chance.

With the Scots cavalry now most of the way down towards the bridge, Surrey saw an opportunity to recover the situation. He could see that the Scots were not well armed and he still had his own infantry in reserve, along with the few hundred horse that had not yet crossed.

"Get our men off of the bridge. Have them get into formation to face the Scots when they cross. Line up the infantry behind them."

Marmaduke interrupted him. "Excuse me, my Lord, but you might want to reconsider that, they seem to have reinforcements."

"Reinforcements? What.. oh shit!" Surrey exclaimed as he followed Thweng's pointing finger to where he had spotted a large company of horse galloping towards them. "Attach ropes to the bridge. Let's pull the damned thing down before these heathens can cross. We have enough to deal with already on this side."

"Are you a fool or a coward, sir?" Cressingham demanded of him. "We cannot yield to these peasants! Furthermore, we will need to cross this bridge to relieve the castle."

"If you dare to call me either of those names after this day I will give you a slow and painful death, you arrogant little shit," Surrey spat at the treasurer. "In about ten minutes we will be fighting on another front. Look upstream."

Cressingham now saw what had worried Surrey. "Get that bridge down!" he screamed at those around him who were awaiting the outcome of the row between their leaders. "You men, protect the wagons. Get them out of here."

Arriving in the vicinity of the bridge a few minutes later, the Scottish noblemen were as surprised as their English counterparts at the carnage that assaulted their eyes. The bridge was now down on the south side and most of the fighting was done on the north bank. Thousands of Englishmen lay dead on the causeway; more littered the bogs on either side. On that far bank the Scots were mostly busying themselves doing one of two things. Many of them were jeering the retreating English.

"Aye run away, son, away hame to yer mammy."

"Any time ye want a good kicking, come back and see me."

"You better run fast, boys, because when we get across this river we are coming after ye."

But most were lining the river bank directing their taunts at those soldiers who had managed to escape to what they thought was the relative safety of the water. However, as most of them could not swim and the water was too deep to wade across, the river took their lives. Those that could swim were hampered by the weight of their own armour, the thrashing of other men and horses only thinking of their own escape, and the missiles being launched by the Scots. Helmets, weapons, arms, legs, anything and everything was thrown at them by a jubilant Scottish army revelling in what would become a historic victory. Never before had such a traditional army been bested essentially by lightly armed infantry.

Few of the fleeing soldiers would have made the far bank in any case and some of the Scots were wagering against each other on who would last the longest.

"I'll bet you two pints that that one there with the curly beard will beat the one next to him with the big scar down his face."

"Yer on, yours is half drowned already. Hey, that's cheating!" as the first man caught scar-face right on the side of the head with the detached head of one of his countrymen. "Great throw, though."

"Thanks, but you still owe me two beers."

Back on the south bank the remainder of the English army had ignored the command to get into formation and were making haste on the road south. Surrey realised very quickly, as the trickle of retreating soldiers became a stampede, that the battle was lost and was already well clear before the Scottish Lords reached the camp. Cressingham had delayed his departure only long enough to ensure that the wagons containing the King's gold were not left behind. It was a costly delay. He was less than half a mile from the bridge when the first Scots reached him.

"My Lord Cressingham," Lennox purred and made an exaggerated bow in his direction.

Cressingham's face collapsed as he turned to face his pursuers.

"Take the money, take it all. Please don't kill me," he beseeched the grinning Scotsmen.

"Oh, don't you worry, we are taking the money. All of it."

"I will be worth a sizeable ransom to King Edward…"

"For myself, I neither need nor want anything from your King, save him stopping meddling in our affairs. You should try to convince those men." Lennox gestured to the dripping wet Scottish folk who had not let a broken bridge stop them joining in the chase. "What do you say, boys, do you want to keep this fine gentleman and sell him to Longshanks?"

With cries of "Naw", "Kill the bastard", "Fuck Longshanks", "Fuck the English" and the like, the crowd advanced on Cressingham. As he collapsed, blubbering and pleading for his life, the wee folk of Scotland reduced him to an unrecognisable mass of blood, bone and flesh as they jostled with each other to get near enough to batter the quivering wreck that used to be a treasurer.

~~~

With the battle won and the English baggage train captured the Scots were jubilant. Lennox and the Steward returned to the scene after chasing their fleeing foe for several miles. Surrey was either too far ahead or had taken a different route to avoid being hunted down.

"What of Sir Richard?" William enquired of Lennox.

"I know not. He did not appear upstream as we had hoped and by the time we got down here there was no sign of him."

"Perhaps he is still chasing Surrey. He will return soon, no doubt," the Steward ventured.

However, Sir Richard Lundie, instigator of the attack on the Sheriff of Lanark would not be seen or heard from again.

Chapter 24: October 1297

Stirling Castle

"My Lords, we find ourselves here today in a much better position than many of us would have dared to hope for a year and a half ago. Then, in a short space of time, we lost many of our barons and our King. Some were killed, most were taken captive by our great enemy the King of England. The weeks that followed saw Longshanks exert almost total control over our country. Dark days indeed.

"Now, though, we find ourselves once again almost free of foreign influence and on the verge of a great new era for Scotland. Most of us here have played our part in that success, but there can be no doubt that we all owe a great deal to the two young men who have done more than most to earn Scotland her freedom. Let us all shout our appreciation for Sir Andrew Moray and Sir William Wallace." With that the High Steward stepped aside to join in the praise for the two heroes.

Not everyone attending the parliament was as enthusiastic as Sir James, but those men knew better than to dissent. John Comyn, Earl of Buchan, son of a previous Guardian, was the first to speak up as the revelry subsided. Stepping forward, he told the gathering, "While it is all good and well that we have enjoyed tremendous success, we must look to the future governance of the country. With no disrespect to Sir Andrew and Sir William, they are great young fighters, but what we need now is experienced heads to lead us forward. It is time to formally reinstate the Guardians."

Sir James countered, "That may seem like a reasonable step to you, but it is not at all that simple. While I and your cousin were elected Guardians all those years ago, it is not a hereditary position. You should not assume that because your father was a Guardian that you are in line to succeed him to that position." James held up his hand to stop Buchan's interruption and continued, "No doubt you are in a strong position to claim a place, but that would be on your own merit, you understand, and not as a right. Other Guardian places are still less clear cut. The young Earl of Fife obviously does not fit into the 'experienced heads' category, being still a boy, so cannot possibly 'inherit' his father's place. And how would you choose for the Bishop of St Andrews, who died recently in France, and the Bishop of Glasgow, who is imprisoned in England?"

"I was not proposing that," Buchan replied, although it was clear to most that he was lying "I was simply saying that we should take the time to elect suitable people and not rush into a hasty decision based on euphoria."

"You are exactly right, then. But first we must decide if we even want to have Guardians." There were murmurs throughout the meeting at this, but James ignored them. "Our King gave up his crown, maybe we should decide on a new King ourselves, as we should have done last time, without outside interference."

The Lord of Badenoch, John Comyn, commonly known as the Black Comyn, glowered at the Earl of Carrick as he rose to his feet. "Gentlemen, I cannot agree that King John gave up his crown freely, and we have no right to remove the Kingship from him." And once more pointedly looking at Bruce he added, "Even if I, myself, am the obvious choice to replace him."

Bruce was on his feet immediately. "Not so, my Lord. John Balliol was a bad choice, the wrong choice. No point continuing on that path. Had the parliament seen sense and agreed that my grandfather was the rightful heir after the death of Alexander's granddaughter, or indeed after the death of King Alexander himself..."

There were shouts of disapproval at this and the rest of Bruce's words were lost in the hubbub. It was Wallace who brought the meeting back to order. "My Lords!" his big voice boomed as he stood and walked to the midst of the gathered nobles, "Please show each other some respect. Let us treat each other as equals and allow everyone to be heard. If you do not agree with someone, say so during your own turn to speak. Do not drown a speaker out. Let us all be civilised here."

John Strathbogie was first to his feet to respond. Wallace raised his hands to quiet those who attempted to speak over him. "Let the Earl of Atholl speak. You will all have a chance to reply."

"Thank you, Sir William. Nevertheless, the point I want to make is this: notwithstanding your military prowess, what gives you the right to intervene here? You are not even a landholder."

Once again Wallace raised his hands to quieten the room. Calmly he replied, "I do not claim to be an equal in the sense that I am not an

Earl or a Lord. I am here at the invitation of the Steward, but I will not be voting with you as an equal."

Now Andrew Moray stepped forward, limping due to a wound on his left thigh that he had received during the fighting at Stirling. "I am here in lieu of my father and I intend to vote in his place. Do any of you dispute my right to do so?"

Nobody dared question Andrew's right to be there, so after pausing to ensure everyone was in agreement he went on, "Good, for I have proven myself by doing more to rid us of our enemies than any of you." Again he paused and looked at them all one by one. "Any of you, except this man, Sir William Wallace, and I challenge any of you to give one good reason why he should not be ranked as an equal amongst us." This time he looked direct at Atholl and asked him directly, "Well, Sir John, do you deny that the man most responsible for Scotland being free today is as worthy as being heard as any of the rest of us?"

Atholl knew he was going to lose any argument about this. Other than the Comyns and a handful of close allies, he could see that the whole room was in awe of the big man. "What the hell, he still has only one vote, let's get back to business." Then, turning, he asked Wallace what many were wondering. "If the vote goes against King John, would you be King?"

"I am a soldier, and a good one, but I am not a King. Nor would I wish to be. So the answer to your question is simply no. How about you, Sir Andrew?"

Andrew laughed. "There may be a dozen or more men in this room who would kill anyone chosen. I'm too young to die. Give it to an old man!"

Sir James took back control of the meeting, holding up both hands and calling for quiet. Admonishing his peers he scolded them, "It is all good and well putting yourselves forward as leaders now. But where were you all this last year and a half? How many of you led the revolt against the English administration Longshanks imposed on us?"

The shouts began to subside because of those present none had done as much as the Steward himself. They had been cowed, not wanting to be taken south like their comrades at Dunbar, or indeed the Bishop of Glasgow and William Douglas, who had both suffered for their continued resistance.

When the room eventually became calm enough he told them all, "We may feel we are in control of the country now, but Longshanks will eventually return from Flanders, and when he does he will not accept it quietly. We have won a lot of small battles recently, aye and a very great one, but do not be fooled into thinking that we have won the war. There is more fighting to be done, and I propose that the men best placed to continue the fight are the men who have brought us to this point, Sir William Wallace and Sir Andrew Moray."

There were limited murmurs of approval, but overall the mood was restrained. The question of the crown had been raised, and with it the spectre of a likely civil war. Reading the mood well, Sir James continued, "Let us all join together and give these two as much support as we can. Hopefully we can gather again soon and discuss the long-term future of our country. Until then, let us all work together to reach that point. I propose that Sir William Wallace and Sir Andrew Moray assume the positions of Guardians, with the power to proceed as they see fit until such time that the King of England is defeated or renounces all claim to any piece of Scotland. At that time, and not a day before, we will gather again and decide, peacefully, the question of the Kingship."

~~~

As the meeting broke up William was not feeling overly confident. "We will be doing well to get any of that lot fighting beside us, if you ask me," he told Andrew.

"That's as may be, but we need to try. If they are not fighting with us they are likely to end up fighting against us. They are too powerful to allow that to happen. Give them time to cool down a bit, then we must go to them and allay their fears. Assure them that we are not after the crown."

"Glad to hear that," a voice behind then informed them. They both turned to see the Earl of Carrick had been listening to their conversation.

"Now, now, let's not get ourselves worked up." The High Steward put an arm around the shoulders of Bruce and Moray. Wallace's shoulder was a bit too high. "Time to celebrate our victories and drink a toast to the young men who will lead our country to real freedom." Then to Willian he said, "That was a cruel remark about you not being a landowner."

"Didn't bother me at all"

"Probably not, but nevertheless we should right that wrong and avoid any further unpleasantness. Some land has become available back in Kyle. Now it is yours."

"I am very grateful, my Lord, but I do not have time for that. I am a soldier, not a farmer."

Sir James chuckled. "Is that what you think we are, William? Farmers?"

"Apologies, Sir James, I meant no disrespect."

"Of course you didn't. Do not worry about it. You really are a remarkable man. Nobody has any idea what makes you tick. Anyway, a knight of the realm should have some substance behind him to support him and provide the means for him to do whatever it is he does, whether fighting or not. None of us actually farm. That is what the peasants do."

"Peasants are people too. I was one myself a few weeks ago."

"You could never have been a peasant, William!" Andrew was genuinely shocked that his friend had such an idea in his head.

"Why not, what is wrong with peasants? There but for the Grace of God, after all. We are all just men, we come into the world with nothing and we take nothing with us when we go. Everyone has the same potential, why should anyone be limited by birth?"

The others looked at each other and then laughed out loud. Bruce clapped William on the back and noted, "No wonder the common folk love you, Sir William. You must have them all dreaming of becoming Lords and Earls."

William stopped and turned towards Bruce, relishing the chance of a proper debate, but the High Steward cut him off. Taking him by the arm he told him, "Let's leave this for another time. For now we should celebrate. Do not worry about farming. I will install your brother to look after things in your stead. You do not even ever need to go there. Just take the income."

"I will go when I can, I must at least see how Malcolm is doing. But there is a lot of work to be done now. We have won a battle, but we still have a war to win. As long as we have food in our bellies I have no need of any more."

Chapter 25: October 1297

Wallace seals it

"Here is my seal, William. Where is yours?" Andrew asked.

"My seal? I don't have one, do I need one?"

"Of course you do. We cannot send these letters without a seal. We cannot send out anything official without a seal."

"You've got a seal, what's wrong with that?"

Andrew laughed "You really have come from nowhere, haven't you? We are both signatories to these documents, we must both seal them. Every family has a seal, and every branch of a family has a variation on it. But you don't have a family do you? Not here, I mean."

"No, not here. I have never seen a Wallace seal. What do I do?" It had not occurred to William when they set out to send letters assuring continental traders that Scotland was ready, willing and able to trade as an independent nation, that he could not just scribble his signature on the bottom.

"Then you must make one, and quickly. There will be a tradesman somewhere close by in such an important port that can make one for you, but he must have a design."

A seal. A family seal. His family seal. William cast his mind back, or was it forward, to the last time he saw his mother.

~~~

Alan Wallace was holding back the tears. His heart had been ripped from his chest, and now he had to do the same to his poor boys. "Malky, Billy, come and sit down, there is something I need to tell you."

The boys looked at each other and fought back the tears. Much as their father was trying to put on a brave face for them, he could not disguise the sadness he was feeling. Their mother had been ill for a while. Malcolm was old enough to realise. William too, although he had only turned ten that day, was mature beyond his years. It was he who spoke first

"It's Mum, isn't it? She's dead." Not a question, a statement of fact. No tears yet, he was being brave for his dad and brother.

"Aye, your mammy has gone to heaven. She is not hurting any more."

Malcolm was the first of them to cry. He threw himself into his father's arms with a howl and buried his face into his shoulder and sobbed. William stepped in a daze into the other shoulder and let his own tears go. Alan's dam burst and all three stood in the middle of the living room holding each other for an eternity, all too choked to speak, and cried a loch.

When the tears had subsided, for now, Alan made them some breakfast, which none of them had the appetite to finish. "Can I see her?" William asked his dad. "Can I say goodbye?"

"Are you sure you want to? It might be best to remember her as she was."

"She was in pain, hurting all the time. I want to see her not hurting any more. I want to kiss her goodbye."

"Okay, I'll come with you."

"No, it's okay, Dad, I'll be fine."

When William went into the bedroom his mother was at peace. For months now she had been making a big effort to smile and be cheerful for her family, but that mask could not fully hide the pain she was feeling as the cancer ate her way. Now she was peaceful and William was glad he had come up. Now it would be easier to remember the beautiful smile on his mother's lovely face. Now it would be easier to remember how soft and soothing her voice had been, and remember the songs she used to sing to them at night.

Leaning against the bedside table was a parcel wrapped in brightly coloured paper. His birthday present. 'To our wee Billy Boy, Happy Birthday Mum & Dad xxxxxxxxxx' It would be a few weeks before he could bring himself to open the uncompromisingly cheerful package. A bow and arrow set. A proper one. He had been desperate to get one, but believed his parents when they said he was too young.

~~~

Bringing his mind back to the present (past?) William finally answered Andrew. "A bow, I'll have a bow as my seal."

"A bow? Not a bloody big sword? I didn't know you used a bow."

"It's been a long time, but it's not for me. It's for my mother."

"William, you appear to have come over all melancholy. Do you want to talk about your mother?"

He did, but could not. "No, there is no time to become maudlin. We have much work to do and not a lot of time to do it in."

"Okay, tell me about it later, if you want to. Meantime, what about the reverse?"

"The reverse?"

"Aye, these seals are double sided, you didn't know that?"

"I do now." William considered for a bit. The bow was for his mother. He should have something for his father. Outside of his family Alan's only real interest had been football. He had been so happy to see his team win the domestic treble just before his wife died. "A lion. A red lion. That will do it, will it not, a bow and a lion."

"The lion rampant is the symbol of the crown since the days of King William the Lion. I do not think that the others will be very happy about that. It might look as if you are indeed making a claim for the crown."

"Let them think what they like. As Guardians do we not speak for the King?"

"Of course."

"Then let us not waste time arguing about trivialities. Let us just say that the lion represents my commitment to the King in whose name we fight. I do not have time for petty squabbles. When the fighting is over will be time enough to argue about symbols."

"If that's what you want, let's go get it organised and get these letters despatched."

Chapter 26: October 1297

Haddington

"That man over there who has all the women a flutter," William enquired of the landlord, indicating the dashing young man with glossy black hair and a thin scar down his left cheek. "Is he the one they call the Red Reaver?"

"Indeed, Sir William, that is the renowned pirate in the flesh. Although when he has time to pirate I don't know. If you ask me, he is just a seducer of women."

William could see that the women gathered around the dashing young man were not all, or even mainly, the type you would normally expect to see unaccompanied in such an establishment.

"Thank you. I must introduce myself. Give me a bottle of whatever he is drinking."

"Most sailors like their rum, but that one is very fond of the brandy," the landlord told William as he handed him a bottle. "Why on earth would you want to speak to that sort?"

"The French are our friends. They have almost as much against the English as we do. An enemy of your enemy should be your friend."

"You can't trust a man like that. He would stab you in the back as soon as look you."

"Then I won't turn my back on him."

William crossed the inn and the ladies reluctantly parted to allow him access to the young man regaling them with tales of his derring-do. As he neared the table he noticed how remarkably vivid the pirate's eyes and teeth were. An unremarkably plain face was transformed by the glaring green of his eyes and the brilliant whiteness of his teeth. 'I must ask him how he manages that,' William thought to himself, becoming conscious of just how bad his own personal hygiene had become. What would he not give for a nice warm shower?

The pirate stood as William approached, gave an exaggerated bow and said, "Sir William Wallace. I am very pleased to make your acquaintance."

"You have me at a disadvantage sir, you know me, but I do not know you."

"You are famous throughout the whole world, Sir William. I am but a humble sailor. Sir Thomas de Longueville at your service, my lord. I see you have brought me a gift. Very kind. Thank you." Thomas reached out and took the brandy.

Turning back to his audience he disappointed them by saying, " Ladies, you are all very lovely and I would like to continue our chat, but I sense that my new friend would like my full attention. Please excuse us, I will catch up with you all later."

As the women reluctantly left them alone the Frenchman sat back down and indicated the seat opposite "Please sit. You look like you have something on your mind. What can a wretched sailor possibly do for you?"

"You are far too modest. And I misled you. I do not know you, that is true, but I have heard many tales of you. From what I hear you are an extraordinary man. They say you are the greatest sailor the world has ever seen."

"Nonsense! I am not even a sailor. I was forced into it a few years ago, but that is a story for another time."

"Nevertheless, your fame is such that it must be built upon truths."

"You are too kind. But let's assume that I am a capable mariner. What could you possibly want with me in any case? You are surely not thinking about leaving Scotland just when things are getting interesting?"

"I have need of a skilful seaman, if you are agreeable."

"I am certainly listening."

"Right now I have need of someone to ensure some letters we have written are properly delivered."

Thomas feigned indignant outrage. "You need a messenger? Sir, you mock me!"

"I do not need a messenger. I have messengers. I need someone to ensure their safe passage to various ports on the continent. You know better than most that the seas are not safe. We are keen that our letters to our European partners are not intercepted. There are other things I need to attend to, things that will be of more interest to you on your return. If you agree to go, of course."

"And if I do agree to chaperone your messengers, what is in it for me?"

"You will be well rewarded. More importantly, when you return we would like to retain your services for the ongoing war with the English."

"Now that is indeed more interesting. Explain to me what you mean by retain, and how a humble sailor can possibly help in a war."

"I know that you have been effectively homeless since your exile from France."

"I like to think that Scotland is my home now. When I am not aboard my ship, that is."

"Indeed it is, but we would like to make it official. There is some land available not too far from here. We would like to make you a Scottish landowner with the resources to support our cause."

"You honour me, Sir William, and I am intrigued enough to accept the job of helping deliver your letters. I assume you expect some trouble en route."

"I hope there is not, but I must allow for it."

"I hope there is; sailing in itself is not really that exciting. You keep saying 'we'. Where is Sir Andrew? Am I not important enough to meet both of you?"

"Sir Andrew sends his apologies. He would certainly have come, but he is unwell. He has a wound in his leg which refuses to heal. It does not look good."

Actually, William was pretty sure that Andrew had sepsis. He had been cut, not too badly, during their charge through the English cavalry. Not an unusual occurrence, a typical hazard of the job. Some time later he began to feel ill and deteriorated worryingly quickly so that he was now bedridden. What he really needed was a course of antibiotics. A week of those and he would probably be as right as rain. "He has a fever. Have you, in your travels, come across any exotic herbs or ointments that might give him some comfort?" William asked hopefully.

"I can ask my ship's doctor to have a look at him if you wish. He is up to date with the latest techniques brought back from the Crusades."

Chapter 27: October 1297

Sole Guardian

The ship's doctor could not save Andrew. In truth, no-one could have saved him at that time. It would be more than six centuries before a Scotsman would discover the penicillin that would save the lives of countless people around the world.

After the ruling class had laid the young hero to rest, William called a snap parliament. Parliaments were not regular events as we would understand them today, but rather were ad hoc meetings called by the King or Guardians mainly to get agreement on anything that required money or men from the nobles.

"Friends, it has been a very sad day, and a tragedy to have lost such a capable young man who should have led the fight to win and maintain our freedom for decades to come," William told the gathering.

No dissension to this. Andrew was a bona fide member of the ruling class and well liked by all. William was neither. Seen by some as a saviour, and admired, even revered as such, many were nevertheless suspicious of him. Many others resented the hold he appeared to have over the people. And not just the common people; many of the nobility and clergy seemed just as thrilled by him as anyone else.

"After such a short time I find myself having to make decisions on my own. Don't get me wrong, I am not averse to doing that, but I want to give you all the opportunity to hear the plans that Andrew and I had made, which I intend to carry out still."

"Do you intend to continue alone as sole Guardian?" Unsurprisingly, the question that was forefront in most minds was vocalised by a Comyn, John, Earl of Buchan.

"That is something we will discuss once I have laid out my plans."

"If you are not sole Guardian, your plans may be subject to revision," said John Comyn, Lord of Badenoch..

"No, my lord, they will not," William responded forcefully. "I know there are those amongst you who feel that since we have regained control of most of the country that the war is over. That is a naive and dangerous stance to take. There will be retaliation when the

English King returns from the continent, as he must, and we must be ready for it. The country cannot afford otherwise."

"But still, that is just your personal view, and any other Guardian chosen today may not agree with that view."

Now the Earl of Carrick joined the debate. "You do not seem to realise that this is not your choice, not our choice. We chose Sir William and Sir Andrew as Guardians. Now Sir William is alone it makes little difference. The Guardians, or Guardian, speak for the King. The Guardians' decision is final. We can propose anything we like, but Sir William has a veto."

"That is outrageous! One man cannot have all this power!" The irony of Buchan's statement was not lost on all those present. They all understood it to mean not that one man could not have such power, since they accepted that a king had, but that no common man should wield such power over his superiors.

A few nobles agreed with Buchan's statement, but Bruce said, "When we chose Sir William and Sir Andrew we did so because of the way that they had led the fight to free our country, and because we did not feel the previous Guardians could do a better job. Nothing has changed in that respect."

"How can you say nothing has changed when Moray is dead? Wallace cannot continue on his own," Buchan persisted.

"Nothing has changed in that the old Guardians do not have everyone's confidence and I do not see that we will be able to reach agreement on new Guardians any more than we could last time. You and your kin will not work with me nor any of my West Coast neighbours. That feeling is mutual. Let's not pretend that anything has changed in that respect since Alexander died. With John Balliol—"

"You mean King John, surely?" Buchan interrupted.

"If you wish, but we all know that *King* John was stripped of his kingship by Longshanks and is held prisoner by him. I don't see any of his kin making plans to recover him."

"You are being facetious, Carrick. How can we possibly march on London?"

"There are other ways. Has anyone contacted Longshanks and tried to negotiate a ransom?" Bruce paused and looked round the room, knowing that the answer was a definitive no. "Have any of his kin made any other moves to release him?"

"You know well that the Bishop of St Andrews is on the continent on a diplomatic mission to get the King freed."

Wallace interrupted. "That is the new Bishop that you and your kin argued against. The man you dislike because you think he is my Bishop is the man leading the efforts to free your kin while you all sit back and do nothing. It is all good and well to come to these meetings with a lot of talk, but what Scotland needs is action. While you sat safe in your castles, Andrew Moray was removing the English from your part of the world." Wallace held up his hands to stop the Comyns replying to this. It was not completely true, he knew, but the point had to be made that he did not feel that they were pulling their weight. "While the nobles in the west, to a man, partook in the efforts in that area and the MacDuffs did the same in Fife, you only bothered with your own possessions. Even accepting help from Moray for some of them. Bear in mind that I fight in the name of King John until and unless there is a new king. It makes no difference to me, for I fight only to free Scotland. We should all fight for the lion."

He paused for effect, looking each and every man in the eye, daring each one to contradict him. Despite the resentment felt towards him by many, the whole room , to a man, immediately remained quiet in order to hear him out. For most it was respect, for the others it was fear. "I say again, I am happy to share the responsibility, but whether we decide to elect additional Guardians or not, be assured that I will expect every man to pull his weight, and anyone who does not can explain it to me face to face."

Another pause, much shuffling of feet, but no dissent. No one was in any doubt now that the big man was in charge and was not only willing, but exceptionally able, to enforce his will on any individual. For those that were not already fans it only confirmed their fears about him.

"Okay then, let me tell you of my plans, which are not up for debate, and then we can discuss who will join me in carrying them out. I have many thousands of men who will follow me only, enough for the tasks I have planned for the winter. We will be raiding into the North of England with two intertwined goals. To increase our war chest and to leave nothing for Longshanks when he eventually comes to us."

There were a few whispered comments, but none of them dared argue this time. William had his business face on. For most of them, this was the moment they accepted him as their leader, even if they did so reluctantly.

"It is madness to campaign over the winter. You are letting your success go to your head," Badenoch declared as he strode up to William.

"I'll tell you what is madness," William replied, looking past Comyn and speaking to the rest of the gathered nobles. "Doing the same thing over and over again and expecting different results." Now directly to Comyn he asked, "How many times do you want to wait for an English invasion before readying and army? How many times do you want to ask your brave men to face a bigger, more experienced and better equipped enemy? How many battles must you lose before you realise that you are doing it wrong? A few months ago I had a similar conversation at Irvine. We could have lost a lot of men there, but we didn't. Instead we fought on our terms, at a site we chose and prepared and we won convincingly. Not so convincingly that our enemy will have given up. But surely convincingly enough that you all can see that it is the right thing to do. The only way we can win, not just the battle, but the war. Make no mistake, Longshanks himself will be coming to try to reclaim what he mistakenly believes is his. I intend to show him then, once and for all, that Scotland is not, and never will be, a possession of the King of England."

"Longshanks is in Flanders. Nobody is going to attack us over the winter. There is no need to take unnecessary risks when the weather will be against us."

"Do you know when Longshanks will return? No, nobody does. For all any of us know he could be on his way back now and we haven't yet heard. Or next week, or next month. Nobody knows, but I'll tell you what I do know, what we all should know. When he returns we must be ready. My plans will take many months. If we wait until he gets back he will be upon us long before we are ready."

"Months! Surely you exaggerate. Now can it possibly take months to get ready for a fight?"

"This is exactly why you have been losing. Do you think that Longshanks will get back from Flanders one day and be on his way north the next day? Of course not, nor the next week, or the week after. You can be sure he will take many weeks, months even to prepare his campaign before he starts the march. It is our job to anticipate him and defeat his plans even before we face him in battle."

Buchan turned to face the meeting and asked, "Am I the only one here confused by this?" There were a few mumbles of agreement, but not one individual dared speak up. Let Buchan take all Wallace's wrath.

By now William was losing his patience. There was a lot to teach them, but this was not the time.

"It is clear to me that nobody here wants to commit to an invasion of the North of England over the winter. Do not concern yourselves with that, my men will do that. Since no one wants to join in with that then I assume that no one wants to be put forward to join me as Guardian?"

As he looked around waiting to see if anyone would challenge this, he realised that, even if not consciously, he had already put them in a position where they could not do so.

"That is decided then. I can tell you that some of my men have already set off, some for Cumbria, some for Northumberland, to begin this operation. I will not call another parliament until I know of Longshanks' plans, but I will be visiting many of you to discuss the next stage of the campaign, which will be to clear the south of the country of supplies."

Now Buchan felt he had something he could speak up about and challenged William. "Do you intend to ravage your own countrymen?" He looked around the others trying to encourage their support, but most remained tight lipped. Instead it was the High Steward who chastised him.

"Maybe we should let Sir William finish what he is telling us before arguing with it. I'm sure he has a good reason for this."

"Thank you, Sir James. I do have this well planned, if you will allow me to explain," William said, with a pointed look at Buchan. He would be the first to receive a personal visit when time allowed. "We all know that when Longshanks comes he will bring a larger force than the one we will be able to face him with. Even if you all join the battle with your all your available men." Again he paused to let them realise that he was aware that many of them would not back him, but that he was prepared to take on Longshanks without them.

"That army will be well supplied. Anyone who has faced the English will know that they always have a baggage train with supplies and money. However big his supply train is they will still expect to pick up supplies on the way. In addition I would expect for a large army led by the king many supplies will be sent by ship. We will spend the winter removing potential supplies from the other side of the border. Anything that can keep for a long time will be brought north to bolster our own supplies. Monies recovered will be used for the next phase, and here I need the agreement of those of you with lands in the border country. The second phase will start as soon as we have news that the English are getting ready."

"How will you know that?" William could not see who asked the question, but it was a fair one. He replied, "We have spies in most of the counties we expect to be involved. As soon as any one of them informs us of preparations we start to remove everything we can. Anything that can possibly be useful to the enemy will be moved north. If it can't be moved it must be destroyed."

"No, we cannot steal from our own." Badenoch was taking over from his cousin as lead dissenter. William was not fazed at all. "Of course not, Sir John. We will pay a fair price for everything we take or waste. No one will lose out. There will be hardships, of course, but we must all make sacrifices for the greater good."

"Is it really necessary? You said yourself that he will only send supplies by sea, bypassing your wastelands."

"Indeed I did say that. My Lords, let me now introduce you to our newest ally, Sir Thomas de Longueville. You may have heard of him by another name, the Red Reaver." Thomas appeared out of the shadows where he had been trying, with reasonable success, to keep his presence unknown up to that point.

"But he's a pirate, an outlaw!" Badenoch exclaimed.

"He has had his disagreements with our friend the King of France, that is true. However, far from being a pirate, he has remained loyal to his king and attacks only English vessels. That is not piracy, that is war. Sir Thomas will lead our efforts to stop supply ships reaching any invading army."

Chapter 28: Winter 1298

Hexham Priory

"My God, what has happened to you, Prior?" William was grieved to see that his visitor looked to have been the victim of a serious assault. His face was bruised and swollen and he had his hand clasped to his right side where his robes were blood-soaked.

"Forgive me for bothering you, Sir William, but I am outraged and cannot keep quiet."

"Speak up, we are your friends. I promise you that whoever is responsible for this will pay for it."

"Sire, some of your soldiers came to the priory. When I heard the noise I rushed to the chapel to find a handful of men overturning benches and removing anything of value. I told them that you had assured us that we would not be touched, but they laughed in my face and pushed me aside."

"They will pay for this. How did you get your injuries?"

"When they would not stop I left to fetch the letter you gave me and brought it back to them. When I produced the letter most of the men dropped the goods they had and left. A couple of them remained and I admit that I got carried away with my success and got more forceful with them. told them that if they did not fear you then they should fear God himself as such acts of sacrilege would surely be punished."

"They were not put off by this?"

"No, Sire, they were not. Laughing and telling me that they had never seen anyone struck by lightning after stealing from a church, they started hurling me about, spinning me around and kicking and punching me. It was when one of the monks came to my aid that they drew their weapons. Sadly Brother Luke lies dead and I myself am wounded."

William was moved by many emotions. Sadness for the sacrilege. Pity for the dead monk. Shame that his men were responsible. Rage at the men who were involved. "Prior, you have my deepest apologies for these acts. I will arrange for some men to come and make good what they can. Your property will be located and returned. Be assured that the men responsible will be found and dealt with. Do you want me to bring them to you before I deal with them?"

"That won't be necessary. Indeed, as you talk about punishment I realise that I really should be finding a way to forgive them. I must go and pray for them."

"You are far too kind, Prior. I, on the other hand am not required to forgive, and I cannot and will not."

~~~

"What do you think he will do with them?" one of the gathered men asked Alan Boyd, who was known to be close to the Guardian.

"I would expect he will give them a flogging, shame them in public and send them home," Alan replied "but I really don't know. Sir William has a habit of doing the unexpected. Whatever it is, I am sure it will be the right thing at the right time. That is what makes him great."

William strode out, walking in front of the two men who were being heavily guarded just outside of Hexham Priory. "Fellow Scotsmen, I have called you all together here to share in our shame. You will all remember that before we came I told you of our aims for the campaign and gave you rules to follow. Not a lot of rules. I appreciate that we all have our emotions to deal with. However, it was made quite clear that there should be no unnecessary suffering. No killing or injuring for the sake of it. Definitely no harming of women or children. Lastly, no harm to be done to any religious person or building. It was all made very clear and I can accept no excuses for breaking any of these rules."

He pointed at the prisoners. "These men, against clear instruction, ransacked the priory there, wounding the Prior and killing – yes, killing – a monk. How can we claim God is on our side if we kill his disciples? How can we claim to be better than our enemy if we let ourselves fall to their level?"

Seeing the Prior standing at the priory door William pointed him out as he continued. "The prior, being a man of God, has asked for forgiveness for these men." At that the two perpetrators looked at each other with a look of hope on their faces. Maybe the punishment would not be as bad as they feared. Neither of them, despite their bravado in the priory, relished being on the receiving end of anything from their leader. "For myself, I cannot forgive these actions. Nor can I ignore such a direct challenge to my authority. Be in no doubt that I will not be denied."

Walking to a cart a few feet away, William lifted two lengths of rope. The intention was clear for all to see and a wave of excitement spread out as they all saw the nooses on the end of each rope. With no further comment William placed a noose over the head of each prisoner and threw the other ends of the ropes over a thick branch of an oak tree. As he took up the slack on the ropes, one in each hand, draped over his shoulder he walked steadily away and the crowd gasped as both men were hoisted into the air.

When the two men had stopped kicking, and William was reasonably sure they were dead, he lowered them to the ground. During the time the men were suspended from the tree there was barely a sound from anyone watching. Calling to the Prior, William asked "Prior, do you have forgiveness enough to bury these men?"

Caught off guard by this request the Prior could only reply, "Yes, of course."

To Alan, William ordered, "Have some men carry these two to the priory and place them at the Prior's direction. Tell him that we will dig the graves as he directs. Make sure that no one shows any more disrespect. Let us draw a line under this unfortunate episode."

"I notice that you did not just drop the bodies. Why were you so gentle with them?"

"Their sins have been punished. No need for anything further. It saddens my heart to lose two otherwise good men. Let's hope their examples stops any further problems."

Chapter 29: January 1298
Wedding

"Welcome to your manor, my Lord, how does it please you?"

"Fuck off with that 'my Lord' shit, Malc. If our dad thought either of us was swanning about playing lord of the fucking manor he'd take his belt to us."

"Thank fuck you haven't changed," the older man said as he hugged his brother. Then, stepping back, he continued, "Sole Guardian though, you are nearly the fucking King! You must feel at least a wee bit different."

"Things have just happened so fast, and they will probably continue to change just as quickly. From a Jack to a King is all good and well, but I could still end up the six of clubs."

"At least you won't fall all the way to a deuce then," Malcolm chuckled. "Come away in and see your new house. No inside plumbing or central heating, but it's pretty roomy."

"Aye, looks good. Are you comfortable?"

"After the monastery the only way was up. This is great."

"I think I'll have a look about outside first; you can show me the layout. If I am right, we must be pretty near to where we grew up."

"We are. I think I have figured out just about exactly where our house would have been, and it's in our land. Over there a bit." Malcolm pointed roughly east. "We own most of our council estate land, and this side," he continued, now indicating the lands to the west of where they stood, "will be Caprington Golf Course."

"We own the golf club?"

"You own the golf club, and way past it. It is fucking huge. What we knew as Caprington, Riccarton, Shortlees and a bit more. Welcome to Ellerslie."

"Come on, Malcolm, what's mine is yours. Anyway, it seems you are doing all the work running the place."

"Welcome to the landed class, Sir William." Malcolm made an elaborate bow.

William punched his brother on the left arm. "Dead arm, ya cheeky cunt."

"I'll get you back for that, you big bastard."

"Have you been back on a horse? You'll definitely need that skill."

"You've been away a while, meantime I'm turning into Clint Eastwood."

"You're a cowboy?" William was laughing.

"Always was a bit of a cowboy, aye, but I mean I'm getting quite comfortable on a horse. Need to be, we've got a lot of land."

"Good, that's one less thing to worry about. Get your horse then, you can show me around."

~~~

Later, after the tour of the grounds, the pair entered the big house to the aroma of baking. "That smells great, Malc, who does your cooking?"

Malcolm beamed and his wee brother realised that the excitement bubbling away inside of Malcolm was not just about the land at Ellerslie. "Mary," he answered, and his big face broke into a huge smile, showing all of his remaining teeth.

"Mary from the dairy? Well done, big man, no wonder you look so pleased with yourself."

"I plucked up the courage to talk to her just a few days after you left. We get on great, soul mates. I never dreamed I could be this happy."

"It's well serious then?"

"Aye, we're getting married. I'm glad you're back so you can be my best man."

William gave his brother a big hug, even bigger than when he first returned. "I am so pleased for you, Malc. Congratulations. You'll make a great dad."

"Whoa, steady on. We're not even married yet, there is plenty of time for all that later."

"Aye, of course. You just took me by surprise, I don't know what else to say. Can I kiss the bride? Where is she?"

Right on cue Mary emerged from the kitchen, bringing in beer and some freshly baked bread.

"Congratulations, hen," William said, scooping up his future sister-in-law who, giggling, slapped him about the head and insisted, "Put me down, you brute. Any man that lays a hand on me will have Malcolm to answer to."

William placed her, gently, on a stool. "You look after my big brother, he's one of a kind. I know he'll look after you, he adores you."

"Oh, we'll look after each other well enough. Nice to finally meet you, William. I'll away and feed the hens, let you talk in peace."

When the door closed behind Mary, William asked, "Things going well with the farm?"

"Never mind about me, the stories I have been hearing about you! It's like a film. I wish I had been with you."

"It's not at all like a film. People get killed. Or horribly injured with no real medical treatment. Andrew Moray died after a wee cut in the leg, not much more than a scratch. Poor cunt. It took him weeks, he fought it right to the end, but sepsis is a horrible thing. You don't want to see that. You don't need to see that."

"Come on, Wull. A man's a man for all that, remember? I'm back to full health, fitter than I've been for years. If I don't fight, what are people going to think about me? I won't be able to look folk in the eye. If you don't take me, I will go with somebody else."

William knew his brother was right, and it scared him. The best he could hope for was to put it off for as long as he could. With a bit of luck it might all be over before Malcolm had a chance to go into battle. "Okay, but not right now. Let's get you trained well enough to keep you alive. We'll start tomorrow. Do you remember your karate training?"

"I was never that good, Wull, you were the black belt."

"Aye, but you know the basics, and you would have made black belt if you'd kept going. I'll show you some moves to practice. It's all about poise, balance and awareness. We'll concentrate on defensive manoeuvres. Later I'll teach you about weapons."

"So, this being Guardian, it must be really heavy. I need to ask you, are you sure you need to do it all on your own?"

"You mean, should I share it with other Guardians? I'd love to, it's just that there is nobody who wants it that would be right for it. Don't think that I don't wish that Andrew was still alongside me. I'm not doing it for the glory, I'm doing it for Scotland. Anyone, and I mean anyone, who had the abilities and the commitment is welcome to join me. So far the only nobles I have met only have one or the other."

"Seriously? You think that men like Bruce, Sir James and the Comyns are lacking in either of those departments?"

"Naw, and that is the really sad and frustrating part. Any of them could do it, but you know that there is an almost complete lack of trust among most of the ruling class. If they don't trust each other, and they know each other better than I do, how can I trust them?"

"You will probably have to trust somebody at some point Wull. However good you are, you cannot do this all on your own. You are going to need some help."

"You are probably right, Malc, but it's not even that straightforward."

"How no?"

"If these guys cannot fight together, how can I fight with either side without turning the other side against me?"

"They surely would not dare face you!"

"Not on their own maybe, but has it not always been the case that the biggest threat to Scotland is not Englishmen, but rather Scotsman who would stab their countrymen in the back for a little favour from London?"

"Aye, but surely there is a big difference between a no mark like Livingston at Lanark and a leader like the Earl of Buchan?"

"Not really, Livingston was sooking in for his own personal advancement. The Comyns and the Bruces are not so much different, only they are playing for much higher stakes. The Scottish Crown."

"So you think that if, say, Bruce fought with you then the Comyns might join Longshanks?"

"It is not a certainty, but it is a possibility. And vice versa, of course. Either side would no doubt be at least tempted to fight against the other with a hope to kill their opponents off and clear their own side's route to the crown. Or they might just undermine our efforts, hoping to achieve the same result without actually declaring for Longshanks. I am relying on the good will and support of all the landowners between the border and the Central Belt to make my plan for Longshanks work. All it takes is for one single Lord to leave supplies for the English and my whole plan could fall down. We need the buggers weakened in every way before we fight to swing the balance in our favour."

"The more you talk the more sure I am that you should not do this on your own. Can't you talk to them, both sides, and make them see sense? Make them see that by everyone pulling together we can win."

"The really sad thing is that you are right, Malc. If all the Scots came together as one and fought as one, nobody could defeat us. I might not know a lot of history, but I do know that the Romans came and we beat them, the Angles and Saxons came and we beat them, the Vikings came and we beat them. We have repulsed all comers until now by fighting together. Now we are in danger of letting the weakest force we have opposed beat us because we are too busy fighting amongst ourselves."

"Do you really think you can win?"

"Of course I do. It won't be easy, but aye, we can do it. We will do it. What's troubling you, big brother?"

"You don't know the history of this period do you?"

"A wee bit, but not really anything about this time, except I seem to have assumed the role of the warrior that I was imitating for my party."

"Well, to be honest, that is what is worrying me. I was intrigued when I heard, so I learned a wee bit about it."

"And?"

"And William Wallace earned credit fighting near Stirling, but he died the following year just outside Edinburgh."

"You think we are history repeating itself?"

"You don't?"

William sat down at the table and thought about it. Meantime Malcolm got them both some more ale.

"Let's assume we are on some kind of merry go round, what would be the purpose of it?"

"I don't know, Wull. Is there a purpose?"

"When I think about it, and I do think about it a lot, one thing seems certain to me. We are not here by accident. We didn't fall through a worm hole or a time warp or anything like that. Something put us here, and if something put us here there must be a reason for it."

"Like what, what possible reason could there be for plucking a couple of nobodies out of the twentieth century and sticking us here? Really, what could be the point?"

"What I think is that we are here to do things differently."

"In what way?"

"For instance, what did you find out about the real William Wallace and Stirling? Was it the same?"

"Right, I see what you are getting at. I don't think it was quite the same. I can't be hundred per cent sure, but I'm pretty sure if it had been such a convincing Scottish win I would remember that."

"Like every Scotsman knows the score from Wembley in 1967, but hardly any other year."

"For me it's the rugby scores, but yes that's what I mean. You remember the wins more clearly."

"So, maybe we have changed history a wee bit. Maybe I won't die at Edinburgh."

"Fuck, I hope not. You have no idea what it is like for me, the guilt I feel."

"The fuck have you got to be guilty about? None of this is down to you."

"Whatever, but here I am about to marry the woman of my dreams, ready to live happily ever after in our own place, safe and sound. Safe because of you. Safe in your place, not ours. Meanwhile you are off putting your life on the line almost every day of your life."

"It's our place, Malcolm. You are my brother, my only family. What is mine is yours. I love the outdoors, always have, but I could never be a farmer. If we are back for a purpose, my purpose is to fight. That is what I was trained for, and it's those skills that are helping me to improve things here. You were ever the reliable big brother. You looked after Dad, kept him from drinking himself to death while I was never there for him. It's the same now, you look after things at home, I go off and kick the bad guy's ass."

"Not forever, Wull. You promised I could go with you and I will go."

William sighed. "I know. But only when you have to. If you have to."

Part VI

Rise and Fall

Chapter 30: April 1298

The Red Comyn

"Excuse me, Sir William, but there is someone here who insists on speaking with you." Alan Boyd appeared flustered and William wondered who could be causing this brave soul such discomfort.

"It is not unusual for people to want to talk to me, Alan. What is wrong with you?"

"It's a Comyn. The Red Comyn."

"As in the John Comyn who earned his release following Dunbar by fighting for Longshanks against the French?"

"The same," replied the young man who brushed Alan aside as he swept into the room. The newcomer was finely dressed, his long strawberry blond hair cascading in waves over his broad shoulders.

Standing to greet his guest, William was pleased to notice the briefest hint of alarm cross the face of the man he now towered over. Not one to normally take pleasure in intimidating people by his physical presence, nevertheless Comyn appeared to have too much self-confidence for any one individual. William was pleased to remove a little of it from him. "To the best of my knowledge, Sir John, you are Longshanks man. What brings you to me? I hope for your sake that you are not relaying messages from the King of England."

Recovering his composure somewhat, Comyn replied "Nobody, not even the King of England, makes a messenger boy out of me."

"Bold words. I believe Longshanks has made messenger of more powerful men than you."

"I dare say, but those men owe their allegiance, and therefore all they have, to Longshanks."

"And you don't?"

"Indeed I don't. I owe all to the King of Scots and no one else."

"Yet you fought for Longshanks against the French, our allies."

"And for that all debt to Edward was repaid. It is usual for valuable men who are captured in a battle to be ransomed. In this case my ransom, like many other of our countrymen, was to fight in Flanders.

I have done so, debt paid. I return to my home a free man, with no obligation to any man save my kin and our King John."

"It pleases me to hear you say so. Tell me, why do you stop to visit me rather than go first to your kin?"

"Scotland is in grave danger. As you are the leader of the nation's army I thought it only right that I warn you and tell you all I know before attending to family matters."

William had no issue with the Comyns as such. Although they were somewhat antagonistic towards him, he realised that this was because his home was in Kyle close to the Carrick lands of their enemy Robert Bruce, who was known to be close with the High Steward. It was no mystery that the Comyns were suspicious of his motives. He hoped in time that he could allay those fears and gain their trust. They were a powerful family and commanded a great many men. Perhaps here was an opportunity to make a move in that direction. He had not heard a lot of the young John Comyn, son and heir of the Lord of Badenoch but, arrogance aside, he liked what he had heard from him so far. "I am grateful to you for your patriotism, please make yourself comfortable. You must be tired and hungry. Alan, arrange food and wine for our guest."

"Of course, Sir William," Alan answered and turned and headed off, leaving the two alone.

"Do you want to wait until you have eaten, Sir John?"

"No, Sir William, I am still anxious to get home. As you know I fought alongside Edward, and I confess that I had no problems with him while in Flanders. For all his faults, he is easy on anyone who does his job well. I did my job well and so I gained his confidence. To be honest, he believes that I will still be fighting for him when he comes north later in the year."

"Hopefully you are not here to tell me that you will do so."

"It would be foolish to do that and still expect to go home to my family, would it not?"

"Collaborators are particularly despised by me, that is well known. Assuming you have heard that then you would be extremely foolish to think you could come to me under such circumstances and be welcomed. So, what do you have to tell me?"

"Because Edward trusts me, I was privy to his plans. You may be aware that plans have been prepared last year in readiness for his return. He intends to move against you a soon as he possibly can."

"He could be here in a few weeks, then?"

"He probably could, but he is not expecting a quick victory; your victory at Stirling has impressed him immensely. Therefore, he is moving his court to York to make it easier to run a long campaign rather than having to go all the way back to London."

"York. That almost certainly means he plans to attack us on the east. Will it take him a long time to move to York?"

"Probably not, but it gives you some breathing space. Most of the other preparations were already well under way."

"It will help me tremendously if I have an idea when he might attack. Do you know if he will ready his forces before or after he moves to York?"

"My understanding is that he will get his court in place first, but has warned his nobles to be ready to go at short notice as soon as he gives the word."

"So, we are in April. It is a long way from London to York; it will probably take him the best part of a month to get everything he needs up to York. That would take us to probably some time in May. Then allow another month for the word to be sent to all parts of his kingdom, and for everyone to muster at York. Probably June. That would then see him cross the border probably in late June or early July at the earliest."

"That sounds about right to me, although I admit I had not worked it out that way."

"It's all about the planning. Longshanks knows that and plans well. Scotland's weak point has always been rushing to react when he puts his plan into action. This time I intend to be fully prepared when he arrives. Ah, here comes your food and wine. We do not have anything fancy, but although plain, the food is nonetheless wholesome."

While they ate the two men continued the discussion. William was keen to learn anything he could to help his own preparations. "You got to watch Longshanks up close. Did you learn anything that could help us?"

Comyn reflected before answering, "It's hard to pinpoint a weakness. He is very thorough, methodical. Like yourself he does not like to leave things to chance. Having said that, he is very good at improvising when things do not go exactly to plan."

"When do they ever?" William queried.

"Indeed. What he does not like is anyone questioning his decisions. He can be become very irritable if someone suggests that there is a better way to do anything that he has personally planned. His temper can be very short."

"Really? That might be very helpful. There is always another way to do things. Often there is a better way to do it. Nobody has all the answers; you should always be ready to listen to advice, even if you do not take it."

There was still a gap in William's plans and he decided it was worthwhile bringing Comyn into his confidence. It was a risk, because he was not completely sure that he would not report back to Longshanks, but he felt that it was a risk worth taking. "Our own plans are fairly well advanced, right up to the battle itself."

"How can they be so?"

"I won't bore you with the details," William replied, but in truth he was hedging his bets. He had already decided not to give anyone else the full plan and only tell the participants on a need to know basis. That Comyn could warn Longshanks was a worry, but then again the list of men he felt he could not trust completely was quite a long one. Comyn only needed to know about the battle itself. "I plan to fight on this side of the Forth. Your lands are to the north, so it is in your family's interest to ensure that the invaders go no further."

"We do have lands in the south-west too," Comyn reminded him.

"Aye, I know, and by the same thought process, if Longshanks is stopped in Lothian he will not progress north nor will he return via the south-west. All those lands will avoid conflict with a Scottish win."

"That is true. Are you confident of victory?"

"I have a good plan, but it is not complete. The battle will be fought and won by the common people, much as they did at Stirling."

"That was indeed a fine victory. Edward flew into a total rage when he heard. Losing to the Scots was bad enough, but when he found out that it was not the massed ranks of the Scottish nobility, it was almost too much for him to bear. It took him almost a whole week to calm down and become rational about it."

"How did he rationalise it?"

"In his overinflated ego he reasoned that the main reason the English lost was because he was not in personal command."

"Was he not interested in our tactics?"

"Of course, but overall he dismissed it as a lack of good leadership, insisted he would not have been caught in such an obvious trap. Also, of course, he notes that Sir Andrew Moray has since died and assumes that most of the credit was his"

"Then we shall have to ensure future traps are less obvious," William said with a smile. It was good news to him that the King of England was underestimating him. Long may that continue.

"You have a trap for him, then?" Comyn asked. All at once William felt that he had already said too much to this man whom he had never met before, and who was about to return home to the part of Scotland where William almost certainly had more enemies than anywhere else. He decided to play his cards even closer to his chest from thereon in.

"It would be foolish to expect to get away with such a move again, and certainly against the wisdom of Longshanks," he replied with a shrug to indicate that he accepted he would be facing a greater challenge next time. Weighing up how much he could safely tell Comyn, he settled on the thing that would be well known anyway. No point hiding it, the Red Comyn would find out anyway as soon as he got home. "We are short on cavalry and archers. Most of my plan is fairly well set, but there is a reluctance among the senior nobles to commit to my plan."

"I will speak to my kin as a matter of urgency, I'm sure we can work something out. I must admit I am surprised that you are struggling for support with the likes of The High Steward, Carrick and Douglas known supporters of yours."

"You have not heard? Douglas was taken prisoner again some time after the fiasco at Irvine and is back in jail at Berwick. Had that not been so I am sure he would be with me. Even so, he would not bring sufficient horse for my needs."

"I am indeed sorry to hear that," Comyn stated. William was sure that he was lying. In the east–west power struggle, Douglas was a loose cannon and it would a relief to Comyn that he would not have to deal with him. "What about the others?"

"I had already decided to fight in the east. The west coast nobles are reluctant to leave their lands unprotected to fight so far from home. More so since they are not as sure as I that Longshanks will come up the east."

"That is understandable, but now that you know that he will definitely strike there, will they change their minds?"

"With respect, Sir John, if I go to them and tell them I have a Comyn's word for it, they will be even less likely to believe it. Should they leave their properties unprotected they will be just as worried about an assault from Comyn lands in the south west as they are about Longshanks."

"That is a reasonable assumption, and probably correct. It is my intention to try to heal this rift between us for the good of the country. Perhaps the best way to start is to show that we in the north-east are prepared to risk all for the whole country. I will do more than promise to ask my kin to assist you, I give you my personal guarantee that we will bring five hundred horse, even if I have to lead them myself. Bowmen you will have to source yourself." With that Comyn stood and offered his hand to William, who could do not less than take it and embrace his new brother in arms.

When Comyn had departed a figure appeared for the shadows where he had been monitoring the conversation. "I don't trust him, William. I don't trust him at all."

"I hear you, Thomas. I would rather not have to depend on him myself, but it may come to that."

"Watch your back, my friend."

"I will. And I will have to rely on you even more. How are you getting on recruiting ships?"

"Very well. We will have at least eight ships on our side, maybe a few more."

"Good. If Comyn does betray us he will almost certainly alert his English friends to our plan to remove all supplies from his probable routes."

"You did not tell him about that."

"No, but he will hear of it; it is no great secret this side of the border."

"What can you do about it?"

"It's what you can do, Thomas. Get as many ships as you can – the

English may well send more ships than we originally anticipated."

"You have more money available to pay them?"

"I promise you as much as you need. Nothing is more important for the entire country than a victory over Longshanks."

"As you wish," Thomas assured him. "I go without delay. Do not fear, I promise you no supplies will reach Scotland."

"That is more than I can hope for, my friend. I only ask for your best efforts. That will be good enough."

Chapter 31: July 1298

Invasion

"My God, Norfolk, it would seem that that mad Scotsman has done more damage to his own country than possibly even we could have achieved. Twenty miles across the border and not as much as a loaf of bread or a jug of milk to be found. Where are all the people? Where are all the animals?"

The Earl of Norfolk had no answers; none of them did. All he could do was express his own concerns. "Will our current supplies last, Sire? Should we perhaps delay and send for more supplies?"

"That would take too long, even if we got them, which I doubt since I am not there to ensure they are sent. While we wait these troops will eat their way through our remaining supplies. No, we must go on. Send word that we need to pick up the pace. Let's find these peasants while we all still have full bellies. I heard a rumour that supplies might be scarce on the route. Although I didn't imagine things could be this bad, I did order extra supplies by ship. We will meet them later."

~~~

A few days later some scouts returned to the Scottish camp. Wallace, informed of their approach, was out to greet them as soon as they arrived. His first concern was for the safety of his own men. "Greetings, Alan. I count seven including you. Everyone is back safely?"

Dismounting next to William and Sir John Graham who had also heard the return, Alan Boyd smiled cheerily. "Aye, Sir William, we are all safe and well. We were able to mix with the invaders without being challenged. They are camped at Temple Liston, a few miles from Edinburgh. Seems that the English king is becoming increasingly frustrated by the failure to locate either us, or sufficient supplies to feed all of his men. Almost to a man the English army seems tired, hungry and irritable. One man I spoke to claimed to be close to the Bishop of Durham and swore that their king is seriously considering retiring home."

"Excellent!" William was grinning as he clapped Alan on the shoulder, and as he turned to the other returning men, thanking each for their efforts. "You have worked hard and must be tired, but if I ask more of you are you able?"

Alan, as always, was first to answer. "Anything, my Lord, what do you need of us?" He turned and started to climb back onto his horse.

"Whoa, steady on. Not right now. Get yourselves food and a bit of rest. Your work is much later. I will send a man to ensure Longshanks knows where we are. Your job is to ensure they get here tomorrow."

~~~

"Sire, the Earl of March asks to see you. He says he has important information about the Scottish army."

Edward's mood improved noticeably. "Ah, it is reassuring to know that not all of our Scottish friends have forsaken us. Bring him in immediately."

The Earl of March was ushered in moments later, his fat face practically bursting with the excitement of being the person who would earn the gratitude of the English King. "My liege, I bring good news of those rascals who have being running from you."

"You know where they are?"

"Indeed I do, Sire."

"Well, out with it then, time is almost as short as my patience. Where are they?"

"Sire, they are camped barely a dozen miles from here on the road to Stirling."

"Are they indeed? It's too late today, but we will leave at first light. By this time tomorrow I will have the head of that common outlaw on a spike outside my tent." Then, as his excitement receded, he added, "You are sure that they will still be there tomorrow? They won't just keep running away when they learn we are coming?"

"No, Sire. I was visited by a friend today who brought word from the Scottish camp. It seems that they have heard that you are low on supplies, the men are in bad shape and fighting amongst themselves and you are about to go home."

"That is not too far from the truth. The only supply ship to dock so far was carrying wine. In retrospect I was foolish to allow the wine to be brought to camp. Drinking wine on empty stomachs on top of all the other frustrations led to fights breaking out in the camp. By far the worst of it, it seems, was a melee involving the Welshmen. I was not overly confident of their commitment, and after being taunted by some of the others they foolishly attacked the Earl of Hereford's men. Over a hundred men dead and we have not yet seen a Scottish soldier! Most of them Welshmen, mind, so it's not too great a loss. At least I won't have to pay them now."

March was keen to keep his lord's spirits up, especially since he had not yet rewarded him for his news. "That is what I heard, and also the Scots. To your advantage I hear that they are celebrating your misfortune. I would venture that when you surprise them tomorrow they will still all be too drunk or hungover to put up any resistance."

"Good news, indeed. Although I normally relish a good fight, I will be glad to put this rebellion down. You will be joining me on the field, Earl?"

Not expecting this request the Earl hurriedly blurted out his excuses. "For the battle, my Liege? Obviously I would love to be beside you, but you had not requested my services. My men are not gathered, let alone prepared."

"I was informed that all of my Scottish nobles had rallied behind this Wallace creature. That is why I did not summon anyone."

"I am always yours, my King. Had I known I would surely have my full contingent at the ready."

"Yet I found no more help or supplies in your lands than anywhere else in this accursed country."

"It is true that this Wallace and his peasants have been scouring the country and removing pretty much everything. I barely have any food left myself, Sire."

"You couldn't try to warn me? You couldn't stand up for yourself, let alone me?"

The Earl of March was almost beginning to regret bringing his news. Rather than the reward he expected for betraying his countrymen, he was on the receiving end of Edward's ire. He could only reply, "I am sorry, Sire, but I do not have enough men to stand against an entire army. As far as I was aware these bandits were everywhere, stopping anyone from going about their legitimate business. I feared that sending a message to you would have meant certain death for my messenger. In any case, there was so much going on I felt sure that you must have been aware of it. It seems to have been no secret;

everyone around here was aware of it."

Longshanks mood was not getting any better, indeed it was steadily getting worse. "Well, I did not know because nobody thought to tell me, you wretched little man. Take yourself out of my sight before I do something we will both regret."

Dejected, the Earl turned and hurried from the tent, proving the time old truth: nobody likes a snake. His pace increased as he realised that Edward was rushing out behind him. Dunbar need not have worried, Edward was not coming after him to punish him, in fact he had almost forgotten he existed by that point. With more important things on his mind he shouted to his generals, "We know where the Scots are! Order all your men to pack everything up. It's a fine enough night, we will all of us sleep under the stars tonight ready to move at first light. Tomorrow we bring the rebels to their knees."

Cheers went up through all of the camp as the news spread. After all of this time chasing an enemy as elusive as food had become, every man relished the thought of a quick victory and hopefully a quick journey home.

Chapter 32: 21 July 1298

The night before

As the short summer night reached its darkest hour another wave of noise spread through the English camp. This time the excitement had turned to dread.

"Wake up, wake up, the Scots have found us before we found them. They attack in the night. Every man wake up and fight for your lives!"

Alan Boyd and his fellow scouts rushed through the English camp, urging everybody awake and into battle readiness. Just outside the camp a couple of dozen Scots clashed metal, banged pots, shouted and hollered in an effort to make themselves sound like a much larger group. The English camp was bedlam. Men were falling over each other, horses were loosed and ran in all and any direction, often sending bodies flying in their wake.

Of the frightened horses, the one who did the most damage was the English King's own mount. In its panic to escape the melee it ran straight over Edward, using his ribs as a springboard and leaving it's rider in agony on the ground.

"What in God's name is going on?" Edward shouted through his pain.

"Sire, I believe the Scots have launched a sneak attack in the night," the Earl of Lincoln responded.

Edward struggled to his feet, holding his side "Where are they, what side are they attacking from?"

"All is confused, I cannot tell. There is uproar in all parts of the camp.

"Well then, it cannot be much of an army if we cannot even see them. Calm the men down; let's get some discipline and learn where to direct our efforts."

Anthony Bek, Bishop of Durham rushed to his king, clearly alarmed, but not at the attack. "Sire, you are injured! What has happened to you?"

Edward brushed him away irritably. "Get off of me, man, my wounds will wait. Let's get this situation under control. Who can tell me what is going on? Does anyone know what is happening?"

Slowly, calm returned to the camp and a realisation that there had been no attack. Not a single person reported any engagement with the enemy. Nobody had been injured, save by accident, nobody had seen a single Scotsman, as far as they could tell.

A few hundred yards away Alan Boyd and his scouts faded into the night and headed back up to their own camp for the night. No sleep for them either that night: there was still much work to do in the morning.

Chapter 33: 22 July 1298

The road to Falkirk

"I am beginning to think that the Earl of Dunbar has indeed switched sides and is helping the Scots lead us astray. We are well on the way to Stirling and still no sign of a Scottish army. If this is just another ploy to lead us away from sustenance I assure you I will personally flay said Earl and hang him out alive for the birds to peck at," Edward moaned to his generals, all of whom were stuck for a response that would not draw more ire from their king. They were saved from having to find something to say by the sudden appearance of a horseman galloping towards them. The rider pulled up just in front of the group.

"Your majesty, my Lords, we have spotted the Scots just off of the road up ahead."

"You are sure it is them?" Edward demanded of the scout. He had endured so many tricks so far in this campaign that he was loath to get over excited about anything. Besides, his broken ribs were agonising.

"Your majesty, a group of Scots, with banners aloft appeared over a hill. It was surely an advance party, so the army cannot be far behind."

"Hmm, Dunbar assured me the Scots were in hiding, trying to avoid a battle. Why would they have an advance party unless they are ready for battle? Perhaps this day will not be as easy as we hoped, gentlemen."

"It may be, Sire, that the Scots, thinking that we were going home, are hoping to pick off any stragglers," the Earl of Hereford ventured.

"Yes, well, that would indeed make sense. It would also fit in with what we know of this Wallace character. He seems to be pretty good at hit and run tactics, catching his targets unawares. Anything to avoid a fair and proper fight."

"Although he did perform well at Stirling—" The Earl of Lincoln was cut off mid-sentence and realised he had spoken unwisely as his king once more flew into a rage.

"He did not perform well. Surrey and Cressingham performed badly.

It is not the same thing. Had I been there all this would have been avoided because I would not have fallen for his blatant traps. Instead I would have crushed them all and Wallace would be as dead as his partner Moray and we would be in full control of the whole of this wretched country again. Just as we were after my last visit here. For the love of God I cannot help but feel aggrieved that every time I earn myself something some incompetent fools manage to lose it again as soon as my back is turned. Make no mistake, I will crush these Scots under my heel and I will not leave until the place is completely defeated. I will not leave a single person alive or running free that is not totally submitted to me."

"Of course, Sire, forgive me. Of course we will right all those mistakes and set this country straight again," Lincoln grovelled.

Edward was in no mood to compromise over anything at that moment in time. Giving Lincoln his death-stare he averred, "I will put things to right. Me, Edward your King and Lord. I will sort out this mess that is not mine. Then I, and I alone, will ensure that it stays sorted."

For a while they rode on, following the scout to where the Scots had been spotted, Edward nursing his broken ribs, the Earls of Norfolk, Hereford, Lincoln and the Bishop of Durham nursing their wounded pride. At length they reached the other scouts at the point where they had spotted the Scots.

"Well, where are they?" Edward demanded.

"Your majesty, they retreated over that hill yonder." One of the scouts pointed to the south-west of their position.

"And you didn't follow them to see where they went?" Edward was almost purple with rage "What are you paid for? You are scouts, why are you not scouting?"

"Your majesty, we remained here so that you would not pass us by. One of the other scouts, Randolph, is indeed trailing them."

"Good, let us make haste then," Edward allowed, his mood still not calmed.

About a mile further on they caught up with Randolph. Unfortunately for them, and indeed for Randolph, he was not telling them anything on account of being dead, his throat slit.

"This is what happens when you don't stick together," Edward stormed, drawing his sword with the intention of taking his frustrations out on the lead scout. But before he could raise his weapon they were interrupted by a shout.

"Over there, over there! The Scots are yonder."

Following the direction being pointed out they did indeed see, some way off still, what looked like the vanguard of the Scottish army. As a smile finally began to brighten Edward's face they saw the Scots turn and retreat, surely in a panic having seen the force that was coming to tame them.

"Steady now, the Scots are clearly nearby but we must ensure that we know what we are facing before we all go rushing over that hill. Bear in mind last year; we do not want to make the same mistakes of falling into a trap. Let the scouts go ahead and check what exactly is over there," Edward cautioned. For all his frustration and anger he had not lost his sense. Despite his comments to the contrary, he was fully aware that he faced an enemy who had earned respect.

Before they crested the hill one of the scouts returned to tell them that there was no army in sight. For a second time they followed the direction that the Scots had gone.

It was the Bishop of Durham that summoned up the courage to caution his king. "Sire, we have been chasing these peasants for quite some time now. Would it not be wise to have a rest and allow the men some sustenance?"

"What would you feed them, Bishop? Grass? Heather? Gorse? You know as well as I do that our supplies are almost out. We continue until we find these creatures. With victory come the spoils, let every man gorge himself *afterwards.*"

Another half hour of marching and the Scots were sighted yet again. Yet another change of course. This time, though, when the scouts reached the hilltop they saw the Scottish army spread out across the valley.

Chapter 34: 22 July 1298
Battle of Falkirk

"Finally, we have something to vent our anger and frustrations on. Doesn't look like much of an army to me, Lincoln. Very few horses, and those all hidden away at the back. What do you think?"

Happy to be addressed in friendly tones at last, the Earl of Lincoln replied, "Indeed not. I see four large groups of infantry with much smaller groups between them. Not even properly lined up. I swear I have never seen such an arrangement."

"It looks to me like the smaller groups may be archers," the Earl of Hereford ventured.

"Not a huge force at all." Lincoln was eager to regain his place at the forefront of the conversation. "Maybe a few hundred in the larger groups, only a few dozen in the smaller groups."

"This is going to be easier than I had hoped. Looks like Moray was indeed the brains behind the tactics at Stirling last year." Edward smiled at his generals. "Let the cavalry take the glory. Release the horses first. As soon as they are clear send the infantry in behind them to clear up. It won't be long before we can let the men eat after all, my dear Bishop." He turned back to Lincoln. "Pick a handful of your best knights and tell them to make sure they get Wallace. I would quite like to speak to him face to face, but if he doesn't survive the battle I will get over it."

"As you wish, Sire. My men are more than up to the task. I will tell them to take him alive." Lincoln was chuffed that he seemed to be the King's favourite at that time. He was brought back down to earth by the reply, though.

"Tell them no such thing. No risks. If he cannot be taken easily they must kill him. Do not underestimate that man; we have all heard of his exploits with that overgrown weapon of his."

~~~

As the English cavalry charged, William smiled and said to Sir John Graham, "They have taken the bait, a full-on assault it is."

Graham was suffering from pre-fight nerves.

"You are sure our defences will hold, Sir William? Sharpened sticks against heavily armoured knights."

William had based his defences on the ancient Greek phalanxes. In his opinion those formations had two weaknesses. Firstly, although the rows of closely packed shields were hard to penetrate, they were vulnerable at the ends. Secondly, on uneven ground it was difficult to keep the tightly packed formation and any gap could be quickly exploited. For those reasons he had decided to have his men stationary and in an elliptical formation that left no gaps, no weak spots. He called his formations shield throngs to emphasise the reliance on the many closely packed shields that gave the group a degree of rigidity.

Not offended by his deputy's doubt, William replied, "We are about to find out. The enemy have already made their first mistake by rushing in without properly surveying the battlefield. I must admit that I am a little surprised by the lack of caution."

"Take credit for that, you have gone to a lot of trouble to unsettle their plans and bring them here tired and hungry. If they make mistakes, that is because you have led them to do so."

"We shall see. They are approaching our first line of defence and still do not slow."

After a downhill charge the ground levelled off and the leading knights came within shouting distance of the Scots. Focussing on the enemy ahead, the riders began to raise their weapons in readiness for the clash just as the first horses stumbled in the camouflaged pits. A war horse at full gallop is not easy to manoeuvre, and while the first knights were thrown off as their mounts stumbled into holes, many of those who were not pierced by the sharp stakes buried in the pits were trampled by the ensuing horses.

At his vantage point high above the field, King Edward cursed as he watched his first wave grind to a halt. He had already lost as many as two hundred knights and his mood did not improve as he realised that those knights who had managed to pick their way between the pits and fallen comrades found themselves unable to advance due to the boggy ground.

"Where are they going now?" Edward asked nobody as the Scottish archers began to unleash their arrows on the enemy now within their range.

"Sire, there appears to be a bog in front of the Scottish lines, our men are forced to go around," Hereford replied.

"I can see that for myself, do you think I am blind or a fool?" Edward raged. "The ground is too soft for the horses, send down the infantry."

On the other side of the valley Sir John Graham smiled at William. "So far so good. Should I send in our horses?"

"Aye, go get them ready. As soon as all the English horses are well clear of the causeway, release them."

Graham rode across to the gap between the third and fourth shield throngs. Judging that the route was clear enough he signalled the people standing there to withdraw into the woods behind them. As the wee folk, the non-combatants, mainly women and children who had been deployed to help disguise William's plan for his cavalry, began to melt away into the woods, Graham turned to urge the Scottish cavalry on.

"Where the fuck are you going?" Graham shouted, shocked to see John Comyn lead his men into the woods with the wee folk. A few of the retreating Scotsmen turned to Graham and shrugged. They took their orders from Comyn only and his order had been to withdraw.

"Comyn, you bastard! Bring your men back here!" Graham demanded, but the horse continued to merge into the wood. John Comyn did not so much as glance back."

"I swear, upon my life, I will kill you, Comyn!" Graham looked across the Scottish lines to where William stood cursing, his shouts lost amongst the noise of the thousands of men between them. Looking back between the shield throngs Graham could see the causeway through the bog that he should have been charging across to attack the advancing English infantry while the English cavalry was still trying to break down the Scottish defences.

At either end of the Scottish lines the shield throngs were holding strong. William watched with pride as his brave men held firm as wave after wave of heavily armoured English knights charged ineffectively against them, only for they or their mount or both to become impaled on the stakes held firm by the defenders. Each time a stake was engaged its holder would release it and fall back to be replaced by another while he picked a new one from the supplies in the middle of the formation. Meantime, the men holding the shields were replaced on the initially few occasions one of them was killed or wounded. William had spent weeks training these men to do just that.

When the English infantry reached the Shield throngs, having been able to cross the bog without sinking as the horseman had done, they were no more able to penetrate these giant prickly hedgehogs than the cavalry were.

High across the valley Edward could see that the battle was not going well. "Bring forward the Welshmen" he ordered.

"But, Sire, they cannot possibly hit the Scots without also wounding our own men," the Bishop of Durham cautioned.

"Those fools continue to throw themselves against seemingly impenetrable objects. They are getting themselves killed anyway. Deploy the archers right now and have them fire as many arrows as they can as quickly as they can. Our men will soon work out that they need to pull back for now."

In truth Edward may have been amenable to a pause while his men were pulled back but his patience was completely worn away after the frustrations of the entire campaign so far, and his ribs were giving him so much pain that he feared he was going to pass out. The last thing he wanted was to have to leave another battle to lesser mortals who then went on to lose. He intended to see this battle through, but he did not want it to last a minute longer than was necessary.

The Welsh archers had more advanced weaponry than their Scottish counterparts, having superior bows and more deadly arrows that they were able to fire more quickly. As they unleashed their arrows at up to fourteen arrows per man per minute, the deadly hail at first reduced the numbers on both sides until the English did indeed realise their only option was to fall back.

As the hail of missiles falling inside the shield throngs began to take a heavy toll on the Scots, William realised that a battle that had started exactly as he had hoped and planned was quickly going wrong. Those defensive formations, so impregnable a few minutes ago, were now being decimated and losing too many men to hold out against another onslaught. While the English leaders were marshalling their infantry for another attack he called to Sir John Graham, "We are lost, order the men to fall back into the wood." He himself rode to the field to save as many men as he could.

William rode across the field, cutting his own path through the English ranks, imploring the men still standing in the shield throngs to retreat. His big heart was breaking for all the dead and dying comrades that he was unable to save. The smooth operation of the shield throngs was mainly due to the management of those few souls in the middle spaces marshalling men and materials and ensuring both resources arrived wherever they were needed. Those men, while protected from the main thrust, had no defence at all against the deadly downpour of Welsh arrows. In the first shield throng, MacDuff, who had cleared the Kingdom of Fife of all Englishmen and collaborators, had fallen, he and his aides resembling more pin cushions than men.

Between the shield throngs lay the corpses of Sir John Stewart of Bonkill, brother of the High Steward and his entire contingent of Scottish archers, felled by the superior weaponry of their Celtic cousins. Those that had survived the hail of arrows were left helplessly exposed when the second cavalry charge came and swept them away like dry grass in a storm.

Fighting a rearguard action, the Scots fled from the superior weaponry of their foes. William paused from urging them back to swing his war hammer, crushing the skull of a black stallion. Watching as it fell, adjusting to follow up against its rider he was distracted by the sight of a familiar face. Just beyond where the knight had fallen lay Walter Hose, the top of his head missing. Loyal Walter had been in the group that had spent the previous night and morning harassing and leading on Edward's army, but had nevertheless insisted on taking charge of the third shield throng.

Wriggling out from under his mount, the fallen knight stabbed at William while he was off guard. Unfortunately for the knight his opponent had been drilled to react on instinct and his hammer fell, as if on its own accord, glancing off of the lunging sword just enough that the thrust missed its target. The hammer continued on its merciless errand to crush the chest of the unlucky Englishman.

Back on the field the remains of the English cavalry chased down the retreating Scots. William, with John Graham and the few remaining Scottish horse rode to intercept them. Standing up in his stirrups, making sure the enemy knew who he was, William drew the English horse away from his men, giving them the breathing space they needed to reach safety. With Graham beside him they hacked their way through the English knights. Although Lincoln's chosen men had not reached the Scottish command on the first charge, all of the remaining knights were aware of the king's order that Wallace must be killed or captured at all cost.

When William could see that most of his men had reached relative safety, he fought his own way back to the treeline. As soon as he reached the trees he threw himself from his horse into the undergrowth, unmindful of the scrapes and scratches he picked up as he crashed to the ground and rolled to safety. As he sprang up ready to rejoin the fight he witnessed the good and faithful Sir John Graham fall from his steed with an axe planted in his back. Another good man gone. Would this calamity never end?

There was no time to dwell on this latest tragedy. William reached for his short sword and turned to face his pursuers. The knight immediately behind had been so intent on watching William that he was swept from his horse by a low hanging branch. Behind him the following knight was dismounted when his horse stumbled over the fallen knight, the horse landing on the fallen man , causing injuries that would lead to his death. Before he could rise the second knight was pinned to the ground by William's sword.

English knights struggled to penetrate the tightly packed wood. Only a few made it any distance in, despite the desire to be the man who brought the head of Wallace to the king. That man would surely be very well rewarded indeed. Those that did discovered a host of traps that had been set to counter such an offensive. More holes had been dug to trip horses. Branches sharpened at the height of a rider, allowing those on foot to pass unharmed. Many men were poised with knives, ready to loose branches which sprung back into surprised riders. Like the previous year at Stirling, the armoured English knights found themselves unable to move easily in a terrain that suited the home team so much better.

Chapter 35: July/August 1298

The victor tries to take the spoils

"It was a great victory, you have righted a wrong today, Sire. The Scots are routed and fled."

Edward, still very much in pain, was in no mood to be soft soaped. "Wallace has escaped and you think that we have had a great victory, Hereford? Until that villain submits to my majesty or is dead, I will not feel that I have earned a victory. How many men did we lose today?"

The Bishop of Durham answered that question. "It is hard to tell for sure but I believe we have over two thousand dead or severely wounded and not expected to live."

"Two thousand. How many dead Scotsmen?"

"We estimate that nearly half of the men on the field this morning are still there now."

"Half? What kind of number is that. How many?"

"Between two and three thousand my Lord."

"Would you say that they had over six thousand facing us Hereford?"

"I do not know the full figure, Sire."

"But you know that they lost *almost* half. I would say that there were no more than a thousand in each of those strange hedgehog formations. Probably no more than a thousand outside of them. That makes five thousand, wouldn't you agree?"

"I cannot argue with his Majesty's maths."

"So we lost over two thousand and they lost over two thousand. A commanding victory indeed. You have the rest of the day to regroup your men and bury the dead. Tomorrow we pursue this Wallace. I do not intend to leave this God forsaken country until I know that he knows I beat him."

~~~

Arriving the next day at Stirling Castle, Edward expected to face some resistance. Instead he found the town all but empty and the castle laid waste. The King was in obvious physical discomfort and

Lincoln sought to limit his distress.

"It is the same as before. Wherever we go these scoundrels have removed all sustenance and comfort. I beseech you, Sire, let us return to York and have your injuries properly attended to."

Once more the King flew into a rage. "York! You would have us retreat without the victory! Never! I came here to put the Scots back in their place and I will not leave until I have finished the job."

Lincoln was admonished, but nevertheless remained concerned for his King's health. Risking further ire, he continued, "Your Majesty is suffering unnecessarily. At least let us find somewhere that you can rest for a few days to recover your strength."

Edward could not accept anything less than total victory, but even he had to admit that his chest needed proper attention.

"Okay, send scouts, find us somewhere to rest for a couple of days. Then we continue. I will not go back to England until we bring this Wallace to heel."

For the next three weeks the King of England sheltered in a nearby convent while his injuries healed.

As soon as he felt well enough Edward led his men into Fife, where he attempted to get some satisfaction by laying waste to most of the kingdom. Excusing his behaviour by accusing MacDuff of treason for evicting the English administrators from Fife and joining with Wallace against him, he wreaked havoc in his wake but left the county without the satisfaction of taking anything of note.

It was the same story wherever he went. Always he learned that Wallace had been there before him and there was nothing and no one of any importance for him to lay his hands on. Edward found himself wondering: did Wallace know where he was going or was the whole country empty?

After a few weeks the English army arrived at Ayr. "I believe this county is the origin of most of our troubles," he told Lincoln on the approach to Ayr Castle. "We will settle in here for a while, locate those that irk us and dispense some English justice. As you know I sent word south; there should be supplies waiting for us at Ayr harbour."

Unhappily for Edward he found no more comfort in Kyle than he had elsewhere in Scotland during this campaign. Like others before it, Ayr Castle had been destroyed, rendering it useless to him. Worse news followed. Waiting for him at the castle were sailors, not soldiers. English sailors.

"What is the meaning of this? Why are you here?"

"Our ship was attacked, your Majesty. The Red Reaver himself. Most of the crew perished and he took the ship. We managed to escape and swim ashore only to find that the Scots were clearing the town."

"Wallace?" Edward guessed. Realising that they did not know of whom he spoke he added, "Really big man, carries a sword as long as a man."

"We saw nobody like that. The man in charge was called Carrick."

Edward was livid. Things kept going from bad to worse. The Earl of Carrick had given his word at Irvine two years earlier and had been quiet since, as far as Edward was aware. At least that gave Edward another focus. If he could not find Wallace, he would take his frustration out on Carrick.

With a face like thunder, Edward barked at his men, "Carrick is just south of here. Let us go vent our anger on the Earl and replenish our supplies from his stocks."

But moving south through Carrick, Edward became even more frustrated. Not only could he still find no sign of the elusive Wallace, but neither was there any sign of the Earl of Carrick in his own lands. Finally, after crossing the border back into his own kingdom, Edward sought shelter in Carlisle Castle. The constable of the castle was Robert Bruce senior, Lord of Annandale, but he only had more bad news for his master.

"I am sorry you Majesty, but the castle stores have been raided while everyone's attention was turned north and there is scarcely a supply in the whole area around us."

"What!" Again his face purpled with rage. Blood pressure through the roof, the English King was wondering when his bad fortune would ever end. "How dare you stand there and tell me a fortress as strong as this has been raided. How could such a thing happen?"

"I am afraid that it was done by stealth, your Majesty. The perpetrator claimed to have been sent by you to replenish your supplies which were running low."

"Who, man, who did this?"

"It was my own son, the Earl of Carrick."

Chapter 36: September 1298

Reflections

The door opened slowly and Malcolm braced himself, dagger in hand, as a dark shape emerged into his home.

"Are you going to stab me, brother? That's a fine welcome home I must say."

Malcolm surprised his brother by exploding in to tears and hurling himself upon him.

"You're alive, Wull, I'm so relieved to see you."

William extricated himself from his brother's bear hug and held him at arm's length. "You're greeting, what's happened? What have I missed? Is Mary okay?"

"We're all fine, ya big daftie. We heard about the battle, but nobody had any news of you. I thought you were dead. History repeating itself."

"What do you mean?"

"Remember that the books I read had you dead by now. You lost the battle, but you are alive. You are still here. The William Wallace of our future history lives on. You can still make a difference."

"Can I? That was my best shot. Months in the planning, and it all went almost perfectly right up to the end. I won't get a second chance at that. The Red Comyn betrayed me and handed Longshanks the victory."

"Aye, I heard about that, there is a lot of anger around here against the Comyns."

"Understandable. I'm fucking raging myself, of course, but it doesn't help."

"Are you saying you don't want to rip Comyn apart?"

"Of course I do. But we can't afford to have Scotsmen fighting amongst themselves. It has got to be united we stand, because divided we will certainly fall. This is not about me and my feelings. No man is bigger than the nation."

"You're not going to make Comyn pay?" Malcolm asked, astonished.

"When I can, but now may not be the time. If I can take Comyn out without starting a civil war I will not hesitate. He's got it coming. But it's not something I can rush into. Make no mistake, Longshanks will be back so we have to be able to resist him." Willian leaned back in his chair and sighed heavily. "For fuck's sake, I thought that this period would be simpler, not bogged down by high politics like the twentieth century. Yet here I am, not able to do the right thing to avoid pissing off people I need on my side."

"Why do you need them? Why not fight on this side of the country? You would be guaranteed the Steward, Carrick and just about every fighting man in the west."

"Would I though? Would Carrick be any more likely to play second fiddle to me than Comyn? You are talking about men who want to be king. Their egos will not allow them to see another man take the glory of defeating Longshanks. Do not for a minute presume that the outcome would have been any different had I fought here in the west. What it does show is that Comyn does not have the balls to be king."

"How?"

"The clever thing for him to have done would have been to follow my plan through. That would have meant that it would have been he who killed, captured or at least put to flight the King of England."

"That makes sense." Malcolm agreed. "So why do you think he didn't?"

"It can only be that he saw me still standing in his way and felt he could not take me out."

"Would you have stood in his way if he had made a bid for the crown?"

"The funny thing is, I don't know if I would have. The man is just back in the country having been captured defending it. If his first action had been to be the man who captured or killed Longshanks, then he would have as good a claim, if not better, than anybody else. If that gave him the consensus then I could have supported him. It's a lot of ifs though."

"You can't support him now though, so will you stand in his way in future?"

"Fucking right I will. There are thousands of Scottish lives on his head. A king should protect his countrymen, not sacrifice them."

"Then you need to carry on, Wull. You're the only one who can do it."

William was somewhat dejected. "How can I ask anyone to follow me now? Who would join me now in any case?"

"Look, Wull, you're on a bit of a downer. That's understandable. But you're still here and life goes on. You said yourself we must be here for a reason. Just because you have not figured out why yet doesn't mean you should stop playing the game."

"The game? Aye, it's a fucking game all right. Whose game? Nobody knows. What are the rules of the game? Nobody knows. What's the object of the game? Nobody knows. What is the fucking point? I sure as fuck don't know. Right now I feel like I don't know anything."

"What you need is time to think. How long is it since you were completely on your own?"

"It's been a while. I've hardly had five minutes since we got here."

"Why don't you take yourself off for a few days. Have a proper think. No point rushing into any decisions if you don't have to. The world will still be here when you get back."

"That's what I'm worried about." William laughed suddenly, then clapped his brother on the shoulder. "As always, you have the right practical advice. I'll do that. See you in a few days."

~~~

Some days later William returned to the farm, rested and clear-headed. "Do you know what I wish I could change about Scotland's future?" he asked his brother.

"Make it a republic?" Malcolm answered him, expecting of course that William was referring to their current situation.

"Bings."

"Bings?"

"Aye, bings. I've had a wander about for a few days trying to clear my head so that I could get a fresh perspective. As I went it really struck me that one of the biggest differences in the landscape, apart from buildings of course, was the lack of bings. I suppose it's a few hundred years until the Industrial Revolution and if I could I would have it that the industrialists found a better way to store their waste. Wee man-made hills are no match for the real thing. Nature knows what she is doing, we should try to interfere less."

"Wow, you really have cleared your head. But you're getting a wee bit ahead of yourself, don't you think? Have you figured out what to do about these times?"

"Aye. Better not waste any more time, there's a lot of work to do. How's my horse doing?"

"Blacky? He's enjoying the peace and quiet, I think. You'll find him out in the back field enj—"

"What is it?" William asked, spinning to face whatever had left his brother slack-jawed, hand automatically on the hilt of his sword.

"Alan Boyd! I thought you were dead." William had believed that both of his old friends had perished in the battle. Seeing Alan alive, and hopefully well, gave him a boost.

"Aye, I'm a ghost come to haunt you. Are you scared?" All three men laughed as they had a group hug.

"But really, Alan, I asked about, nobody saw you. What happened to you?"

"Last thing I remember was some knight swinging a big hammer towards me and then a big flash. I was really lucky, he must not have connected properly. Don't get me wrong, it was sore, still is a bit, but I think what saved me was tiredness."

"Tiredness, are you serious?"

"Aye. Under normal circumstances, even if I had been knocked out, I would have got back up within a few minutes, probably. I think that I had had so little sleep that when I went down my body just switched off. I woke up goodness knows how long afterwards with a woman pulling my arm. The battle was long past and the locals were clearing up a bit, burying the dead. I could have been buried alive."

Fate is fickle, William thought. If there was a plan, it clearly was not only for him. It confirmed his own conclusion that they were all just pawns in some greater being's game. That being the case, there was no point resisting. He would carry on as best he could and if he took the wrong road he felt sure that somebody or something would point him back in the right direction.

Chapter 37: October 1298

A vote of no confidence

"It is quite simple, Sir William. Despite your victory at Stirling, or perhaps because of it, you and your people's army cannot defeat King Edward. Not without the backing of the nobles, and you do not have our confidence," the Earl of Buchan summarised.

"I had the beating of him at Falkirk had not your nephew ran away and left us open to what followed," William insisted, pointing the finger at the Red Comyn. "The blood of two thousand Scotsmen is on his head."

Comyn spat back, "Your recklessness would have had us all killed. It was clear to me, and those around me…"

'Aye, spread the guilt you weasel' William thought.

"… that we would be cut down long before we reached the archers. We were outnumbered by the knights Edward had in reserve. Better equipped and better armoured, we were no match for them in open battle. That is if we even reached them. Those bowmen would probably have cut us down before we came within shouting distance."

"Two years ago I was arguing that we should not be facing greater numbers like that and I was derided because that is how you have always done it. Now, all of a sudden you do not have the stomach for it. You know full well that the plan was that you should have been able to outmanoeuvre the heavy horse and focus on dispersing the bowmen. Those archers were the difference between winning and losing that day."

"According to you, but yours is only one opinion and it is a minority view," John Comyn senior pitched in, leading to a chorus of shouts from all corners as to the rights and wrongs of it.

At length William raised his hands and shouted over the rabble. "Enough. Enough already." By his reckoning his supporters were outnumbered by about three to one. Clearly the Comyn faction had been busy preparing for this. Too late he realised that he had spent too much time wallowing in self-pity when he should have been out and about garnering support. As order retuned, slowly, to the gathering he continued, "We should vote on whether I remain as Guardian and leader of the army."

"No," Buchan insisted "We should vote only on whether you remain Guardian. By the outcome of that vote we can decide how to proceed with everything else."

Knowing that this was a vote he would lose, William decided that discretion was the better part of valour. "My Lords, I have given my best for Scotland. If you believe that I have served her badly, and I can see that most of you do, then the only honourable thing I can do is resign as Guardian. I do not want to force any of you to pick a side in this argument. It is my intention, my wish, to continue the fight and I remain ready to serve the new Guardians, as will all my men, I am sure."

"Resignation accepted," Buchan announced curtly. "Now, since you are no longer a member of the nobility, please leave this gathering."

William was still outside when the meeting ended almost an hour later. William Lamberton, Bishop of St Andrews was the first to go to the ex-Guardian. "We were almost overwhelmed by the pressure from the Comyns and their allies. Clearly they were planning this while we had our minds on other things."

"Aye, I had worked that out myself. Did the rest of the meeting go the same way? Are we now under Comyn control?"

"They pushed hard for it, but they had miscalculated the support for them. The Earl of Lennox was foremost amongst those who spoke up for you, and several of the others were swayed by him."

This was heartening news and William's spirits lifted considerably. "Don't keep me wondering, what was the outcome?"

"There is only one Comyn Guardian, but it is the Red Comyn. His father and uncle insisted on passing the responsibility to the younger generation. In doing so they left themselves open to counter-attack and had to accept the Earl of Carrick."

"That will be a tense arrangement, those men hate each other with a passion."

"Indeed they do. With those two already appointed there was a shortage of volunteers to join them. Nobody wanted to get caught in the middle of that pair."

"So there are only two Guardians until one of them kills the other? After all the complaints about my tenure as sole Guardian, are they really happy to face a situation where a sole Guardian really does want to be king?" William was completely gobsmacked at this news. It was the last thing he had expected, or wanted.

"Well, no." Lamberton answered. "Nobody in the room could accept that, with the possible exception of Bruce and Comyn themselves. Even so, they would probably spend every waking minute looking over their shoulder."

"Certainly, and the temptation to pre-empt the other man's strike would be immense," William agreed, relieved. "So who else is there?"

"By a process of elimination, I think, I was chosen as the third Guardian. I have no doubt that my job is mainly to keep the other two from killing each other. It will be no easy task."

"You sell yourself short, Bishop. I can think of no one more suitable to be a Guardian."

"Not everyone thought so. It was noted that I owe my position to you, but it was also argued that I had your backing despite my ties to the Comyns and Balliols. On balance enough of them were prepared to accept that I was neutral to pass the vote. Or perhaps it was just that I was the only man foolish enough to take the role."

"So, where do I fit in to the new regime?" William wondered, and to himself he further wondered 'Can I fit in? Will I be able to work with the man who betrayed me?' The appointment of the Red Comyn as Guardian was the worst possible outcome for him. A slap in the face to him and a slight to every Scottish life lost at Falkirk.

"There was no agreement. Many argued for you to continue as leader of the army. However, others argued against this. These are powerful men and, quite simply, they do not want to share any of their power with you."

"I see." In a way it was a relief for William. He was sure he could not take orders from Comyn. But what was his purpose now?

"If you want my advice, go back to Kyle. Let time add some perspective to all this. Winter is almost upon us; let us see how things look in the spring."

"You are a good man, Bishop. I cannot argue with you. Good luck to you, I think you will need it."

"Go in peace, William. And do not worry about me, God will take care of me."

William was not so sure about how well God would look after anyone. The Bishop of Glasgow was also a good man, yet he languished in the Tower of London.

Chapter 38: Winter 1298/9

Malcolm was incensed. "How can they possibly do this to you after all that you have given them?"

His brother was more circumspect; the journey home to Ellerslie had given him time to reflect. "It's only politics, Malc, some things never change."

"Fucking politicians are no better now than in the twentieth century! Those bastards owe you more than they can ever repay. It's a fucking disgrace. How can you be so calm about it? What are you going to do?

"There is absolutely no point getting all worked up about something we cannot change. As to what I am going to do, I have plenty of time to think about it, I hope."

"You hope? What do you mean by that?" Malcolm was alarmed. What was his brother not telling him?

"I have to consider that I have enemies that may not be content to let me live quietly here. After all, we found ourselves here after somebody took revenge while I was trying to live peacefully."

"Aye. Then again, maybe that would be for the best." Malcolm raised his hand to shush his brother when he tried to argue. "Maybe our time here is over after all. Maybe we need another event to send us home."

"That is an interesting thought. You know, I have found myself thinking less and less about my former life. I am not entirely sure I would want to go back now. There is a lot to like here. It would be nice to see Dad, though. When I do think about things, it is mostly Dad I think about. Would you really like to go back, though? You are a happily married man, I assume. What about Mary?"

Malcolm had already thought about it, many times. "You know Mary, twentieth-century Mary, was divorced. I had thought about asking her out several times. If we went back, that would be just about the first thing I would do. I am very happily married, we are soulmates, but I think it would be the same if we went back."

"Malc, I'm sorry, I never really thought enough about how you were, are, dealing with all this. Do you really miss it?"

"Aye, Wull, I do. I can see how this life would suit you, but I'm still a twentieth-century boy. I miss my friends, I miss the school, I even miss the kids, I miss the rugby and the telly and the music and, and, … just so many things."

William went over and put an arm around his brother, who was desperately fighting back his tears. "I'm sorry, Malcolm, I can't help thinking you are suffering all of this because of me. I wouldn't blame you at all if you resented it."

Malcolm straightened up, his expression now shocked. "Never think that. I have loved you since the minute you were born. I could never hate you. I would die for you, brother. Whyever we are here, I do not blame you at all. Whatever our purpose, I am behind you all the way."

"Thanks, Malc, I appreciate that. What do you say we step up that training I was always promising you?" William realised that unless by some other miracle they did go back to the future, his reluctance to train his brother to fight properly had now left them both exposed.

Winter came and went. Malcolm learned well and made a fine soldier. His new-found confidence transformed him to the point that William genuinely regretted not training him sooner and wondered if he had made a mistake not taking his brother with him. On a crisp March morning Malcolm had a surprise for his brother.

"You're going to be an uncle," he told William with a huge grin on his face.

William gripped him in a bear hug. "That's brilliant, congratulations. Where's Mary?" Then, worriedly realising he had not seen his sister in law yet added, "Is she okay?"

"She's still in bed, seems to have a wee bit of the morning sickness. I'm sure she'll be fine, she's from good stock."

William was not convinced; he knew how quickly a healthy person could deteriorate without access to modern medicines. Andrew Moray's death still haunted him. "Don't take any chances with her health, you take good care of her."

"Aye, aye, don't panic, Wull. We've already discussed it. Mary says it's common in her family, but we're going to get her sister to move in and help her. If you don't mind of course."

"Okay, good. Of course I don't mind. You do whatever is necessary to look after that wee lassie and the wean."

They were interrupted by a loud knocking at the door. William opened the door cautiously, not knowing who may be calling, or why. All their friends were in the habit of just giving a quick knock and entering.

"Bishop!" William exclaimed. "It is great to see you, come away in."

"Good to see you too, William. I hope you are all well."

"We are all good. Better than good, we are having a baby!" William told him excitedly.

The bishop was a little confused and asked, "You and Malcolm are having a baby? How does that work?"

William laughed heartily. "Sorry, I mean the family is having a baby. Malcolm and Mary are having a baby."

"Congratulations, Malcolm, may God bless you all."

"Thank you, Bishop." Malcolm smiled back. Realising that the visit must be for an important reason, for it was a long, long way to St Andrews, he continued, "You don't mind if I leave you? I need to go and fetch Mary's sister."

"Not at all, Malcolm, don't let me interfere with your arrangements. I just wanted a word with William."

When Malcolm had gone William enquired, "So what brings you all the way across the country? It must be serious."

"Not at all. I have a favour to ask of you."

"A favour? That sounds personal. Not government business, then."

"Well, actually, yes and no. I have been working with our friends overseas for quite some time. It predates my appointment as Guardian, and since I do not want to make it official government business I would like to suggest that you take a break from fighting and try your hand at diplomacy."

"Diplomacy? Do you really see me as a diplomat?"

"I know for a fact that the King of France thinks very highly of you, as do many other European leaders. I have some letters that I was planning to take to Paris myself. I would like you to take them. Have a rest, see how well you are regarded abroad. Help me to get our King released, and see if you can persuade King Philip to give Scotland more than just encouragement."

William had not forgotten how the Red Reaver had reacted at their first meeting. "Do you want me as a messenger boy? Is that what I am reduced to?"

"Not at all, William, not at all. This is not about delivering the message, but about being able to carry the argument forward. Think about it, please, do not be insulted. I assure you that if you will not do this then I will have to go myself as I had planned. There is no one else I would trust to do this. No one."

"If you go yourself then it will have to be government business. You seem reluctant to involve your fellow Guardians in this mission."

"I have been proceeding very carefully with this. Obviously the Earl of Carrick would be very reluctant to see King John return. I am not sure that John Comyn would be any more keen. In fact, I suspect that either one of my fellow Guardians might be tempted to try and scupper my plans. This much you and I agree on, our efforts are not for our own personal advancement, but for whatever is best for the country."

"If I go, do I have your word that my brother and his family will be safe?"

"I am one step ahead of you on that. I dropped in on the Steward before I came here. He is very happy for you to go and gives his assurance that Malcolm will be taken care of."

"In that case, I thank you for the offer, but I would like some time to think it over."

"Of course, of course. I have made arrangements for the first Saturday in April. If I do not hear back positively from you before then I shall go myself."

~~~

Several days later William visited his good friend Thomas.

"What do you think? Are they just trying to get rid of me?" William asked.

"What I think is that God loves me. I can see no other reason why he has sent you to me with this news now," a beaming Thomas answered.

William was dumbfounded. This was not at all the reaction he had expected. In truth, he had come to his friend expecting a bit of sympathy and understanding. "I don't understand, you seem unduly happy about this. Surely it is not because you felt insulted when I asked you to help deliver letters to the merchants last year?"

"No, no, William, you have not heard my news."

"You have news that has a bearing on this?"

"I have been told that my King, Philip, has heard of my exploits against his sworn enemy, Edward, and will grant me a royal pardon. I can go home."

"That is good news, Thomas, I am happy for you. But what has that got to do with me?"

"Well, I am happy, but I am also worried. I have had no direct word from the king himself, and I do still have enemies in France. It will be so much better if we go to Paris together. What an adventure we could have, and if it goes wrong we can fight our way back to Scotland together. For all the fighting we have both done, we have never fought together. Should my enemies find me and I am killed in France fighting side by side with the great Sir William Wallace, I will die an extremely happy man."

"You are crazy, you know that, right? And you want me to go to a foreign country to be killed for a lunatic?"

"Don't worry, my friend, I swear there is no one in the whole of France who could kill you. Probably not in the whole world."

"You are full of shit, Thomas. Nevertheless, it will probably be quiet here for a while until Longshanks figures out his next move. I think I am going to go. Yes, let's do it. France, here we come!"

Part VII

France

Chapter 39: May 1299

The Red Reaver

After a relatively smooth crossing (according to Thomas; William found it extremely uncomfortable) and a bawdy night in Dunkirk, where Thomas had many friends, the pair set off for Paris. As the days passed Thomas became unusually quiet and William thought that it might be the distance from the sea. One cool May evening, as they sat beneath a large oak after eating their evening meal, Thomas finally opened up.

"It is not at all that I long for the sea, for the sea is not in my blood, as many imagine. I am apprehensive because I go to seek forgiveness from my brother whom I love dearly. If the news is false, if he rejects me, it will break my heart. He may as well kill me for I will lose that part of me that will always be France."

"Your brother? It was my understanding that we were going to meet the King. In any case, that is my mission, for I have important missives from the Bishop of St Andrews that I must deliver."

"Yes, we go to see the King, but to me he is much more than a King. Philip was born and brought up at Fontainebleau, not very far away from my home, in Longueville of course. My father was a well-respected man at the court of Philip's father and as children we would play together often. We grew up like brothers and that is the love that I have for him, as my brother. After his older brother Louis died and he became heir we saw each other less and less until I was old enough to go to court. He loved me still and ensured I had a good life in Paris"

William was intrigued by this and wanted to know more. When Thomas got that far-away look in his eyes again and went quiet, he enquired, "So tell me, what happened that the King's best friend, brother even, is now an outlaw?"

Thomas took another long draught of wine, sighed and patted his groin. "This my friend, how much trouble has this caused me, I should cut it off."

"Come on, Thomas, stop teasing and tell me the story, what happened between you and the King? Surely your cock is not what came between you?"

Laughing, Thomas told him, "It is not what you think, there was nothing sexual between me and Philip, or between me and any of Philip's women. There was a very beautiful woman who held me in her spell, but sadly she was promised to another. We could not be together but would meet secretly as often as we could. She loved me even as much as I loved her."

"This girl was married then?" William asked.

"No, not married. Her father, the Count de Angoulême, had promised her to another, though. Such is the way of these things in France, everything is political. Also she had a bad-tempered brother. Now, it seems, the Count is dead and it may be safe for me to return to France."

The Red Reaver told William his story.

~~~

Some years earlier Thomas and Beatrice lay softly in each other's arms after making love, when the door flew open and crashed against the wall.

"Hugh! Leave him alone, he has not wronged me!" the young lady cried, rising naked from the bed and trying to stop her brother slaying her unarmed lover.

Her brother roughly pushed her aside. "You may not feel wronged, but this man has dishonoured the entire family and I must kill him to restore some of our reputation."

By now Thomas had wriggled into his breeches and was ducking and diving in an attempt to avoid the angry young man's weapon. "My lord," he beseeched him, "you will not restore your family's honour by cold-blooded murder. At the very least we should settle this away from here in a civilised manner."

Knowing that Thomas was right, Hugh reluctantly lowered his sword and spat out, "Very well. I will wait for you in the park at noon where we will finish this." He turned and left while he still had the self-control to keep himself from running Thomas through where he stood half dressed.

At noon the two antagonists faced each other and once more Thomas attempted to avoid any bloodshed.

"Sir Hugh, I have wronged your family and you are right to be angry. My only defence is that I have become so enchanted by your beautiful sister that sense and reason can find no room in my head because of my love for her. Please accept my humble apologies and let me be banished from here, never to bring shame to your family ever more. There is no need for anyone to die today."

Hugh had not calmed down in the slightest since the earlier confrontation. In fact he had not calmed down at all since he first heard the news of the secret lovers.

"There is every reason for you to die, you blaggard, and die you shall!" he spat as he drew his sword and lunged at Thomas.

Although caught off guard, Thomas was able to avoid this initial attack and drew his own sword in order to defend himself. After a couple of minutes of defensive swordplay, during which Thomas continued to beg Hugh to desist, his aggressor drew blood when in frustration he swung wildly, catching Thomas on the cheek, leaving the scar which he still bears. The drawing of blood galvanised both men. To Hugh it was a sign that he had the upper hand, but to Thomas it was a sign that he could not play a containing game endlessly. As is ever the case, the best form of defence is attack and Thomas went on the offensive, driving his opponent back until he had him backed up against a wall.

"Once again I beg you, let us solve this without a killing. I do not want to cause your family any more grief. Please drop your sword and I will leave, and you and your family will never see me again."

Thomas made the mistake of withdrawing his sword from the other man's throat as a gesture of goodwill. This gesture was repaid by a knee in the groin and a head butt which left Thomas floored and in considerable pain. Now it was Hugh's turn to be lax when he had the advantage. He stood beside Thomas and took his time gloating, fixing his stare on Thomas, savouring the moment before plunging his sword at the prone man below him. Not a lot of time, only a few seconds, but enough to let Thomas gather his wits, channel his adrenalin and recover enough to be able to roll from the assault and spring up while plunging his own sword upwards. His blade pierced Hugh just below the ribcage and exited through his right shoulder. Even as he impaled this angry young man who had been trying to kill him, a tear slipped from Thomas's eye, as he realised his own happy life had just ended with the same blow that had killed the hapless Hugh.

Beatrice, who had been in tears the whole time, imploring both men to stop, let out a wail of grief and threw herself on her brother.

Raising her head to look at her love, who was babbling his apologies, she found she had no words for him and buried her face back into the bloody corpse of her brother.

~~~

The next day Thomas was brought, in chains, before the King. "Sir Thomas, you are charged with the murder of Sir Hugh de Lusignan, and of bringing his family into disrepute. How do you answer?"

Looking at the Count, who was standing just a few feet from the King, Thomas answered, "I killed him, as you all know. I regret Sir Hugh's death deeply and offer no defence for my actions. I accept your judgement on this, my King."

Philip also regarded the Count as he addressed Thomas for the benefit of all. "Very well, you leave me no alternative. Take the prisoner to the dungeons. He will be hanged as soon as the proper arrangements can be made."

~~~

Thomas was kneeling in his cell praying to his God for forgiveness when the door swung open. He turned to see a hooded figure approach. Realising that his execution was not to be public after all he stood and spread his arms to accept his punishment. No blow came, instead a voice he recognised very well whispered, "Thomas, my old friend, it grieves me that this situation has arisen. The count is a very powerful man and must have satisfaction in this."

"Your Majesty, why are you here?"

"You may still call me Philip for I love you still. Because of the love I have for you I cannot watch you die."

Thomas began to answer, but Philip put his fingers to his lips. "There is very little time, you must be quiet and just listen. You know the way out of here, go quickly. There is a horse ready for you. Make all haste, for when this is discovered in the morning I will have to send soldiers after you. You must not let them catch you because you cannot be allowed to escape a second time. Do you understand?" Thomas nodded his agreement with tears filling his eyes, not for relief at having his life given back to him, but for the love that Philip showed him.

Thomas made good progress all the way to Dunkirk, where he was hoping to catch a ship to anywhere and begin a new life. At the port his hopes were dashed since an English ship was blockading the harbour and no boats were able to leave. Knowing that the King's men were probably not too far behind he decided the only option was to get drunk and enjoy his last few hours as much as he could. He had rediscovered his zest for life while on the run only to find that there was no life for him. Yes, he could keep running, but where could he go? Sooner or later, most likely sooner, he would be caught and would not be able to resist his pursuers; he had already killed too many people. Only one, but one too many. Best to relax and make the best of what time he had left, and where better to enjoy wine, women and song than at a busy port?

While singing and drinking with a ragtag bunch of sailors from various countries, Thomas was trying to decide which young lady would have the pleasure of accompanying him upstairs next. He had already shared his love with two beauties; if he was going he was definitely going with a bang or three. When talk turned to the English ship anchored a few hundred yards offshore Thomas had an inspiration.

"Instead of cowering here allowing those damned Englishmen to dictate what we can and cannot do here, why don't we go out there and sort the bastards out?"

All around the table, indeed as word spread all around the inn, drunken sailors shouted their agreement. After a few minutes of egging each other on, a couple of dozen men found themselves in rowing boats heading out to sea. Despite their best intentions of sneaking up on the target ship, the boats made an incredible racket, shouting and singing, wagering on who would board the English ship first, who would throw the most Englishmen overboard. All the while they continued to imbibe the various bottles of wine and rum they had brought with them.

Probably because the wind and the sea were making almost as much noise as the men in the row-boats, they reached the ship without an alarm being raised. As they raced to climb up to the deck a head appeared over the side looking to see what those strange noises were. Unfortunately for the lackadaisical look-out he popped his head over the side just above the leading climber. Before he could figure out if what he was seeing was real or a drunken illusion, a hand reached up and heaved him overboard. A great cheer went up and all the men climbed with even greater enthusiasm. Once on deck there was no one else to be seen. Complacency had led the crew to drink themselves into a drunken stupor such that even if the noise of the boarding had awoken them, they were in no fit state to fight back.

"What do we do now?" Thomas was asked.

"Me? I don't know. Seemed like a good idea when we were on dry land, but I've never been on a ship before. Where is everybody?"

" I expect they will be below deck sleeping. Otherwise we would be in a fight."

"Can we lock them in? Deal with them in the morning?"

"Aye, aye captain," one of the Dutch sailors replied and hurried off towards the ladders.

"Wait a minute, I am not the captain, I am not even a sailor," Thomas objected.

"Well, you are now. This was your idea, therefore you are in charge. We can't go back now, we are all pirates now, we'll get hanged more than likely."

And so began the outlaw career of the man who would come to be known by all as the Red Reaver.

~~~

"You're kidding," William said.

"Not at all. Every word is true. We could not go back. Well, I could not go back anyway, but once we had taken the ship nobody could go back so we just sailed about and learned how to be pirates. Everyone else was already an accomplished seaman, I just learned as we went."

"What about the original crew, what happened to them?"

"In the morning we found the weapons store and then let the men out. The boats we had come out in were still tied to the side of the ship, so we let them take them and take their chances ashore."

"I suppose since they were blockading the port that they may not have fared too well."

"Probably not, but then we all have to pay for our past misdeeds at some point, do we not?"

"Yes we do, in this life or the next."

"So, now it is your turn, William. There is a great mystery about where you came from. I've told you my story, now you must tell me yours."

"If only I could, Thomas, there is no one on this earth I would rather tell it to." If there was one person that William would have liked to confide in, it was indeed Thomas. However, there was no way that he could make his real story sound like anything other than a fantasy. To tell Thomas ran the risk of him thinking his companion was either a madman or an out and out liar, neither of which would be good for the remainder of their trip. "The truth is that even after all this time I have no recollection of anything since before Malcolm and I were attacked. Sometimes I have crazy dreams that I find hard to understand, but whether that is memories or imagination I cannot tell. Either way there is nothing I can put into words that would make any sense."

"What amazes me is that with the skills you have, and your sheer physical size, no one else remembers anything about you either."

"Maybe they are all dead, Thomas. Like if I told you my secrets I would have to kill you too."

"You are not even funny, William. Let's get some sleep, we should reach Paris tomorrow."

~~~

Sometime during the following afternoon as they approached the French capital and could see the tops of the tallest buildings grow clearer in the distance, they were approached by half a dozen horsemen who blocked the road, forcing them to stop.

"Who are you, where are you going, and what is your business in Paris?" demanded the ringleader, a haughty young man with no neck and a face like a bulldog.

Thomas dismounted and approached William, whispering, "These men mean me harm. I recognise a couple of them, they are connected to the Count de Angoulême. I have never fought on a horse before, I will take my chances on the ground. This is not your fight, you have important business with the King. Do not let this impede you."

"If you think for one second I would leave you to fight alone then I am deeply disappointed that you could have such a low opinion of me. You have risked your life many times over for me and for Scotland. It is nice to have an opportunity to repay some of that." William too dismounted. In truth he was not offended; he knew Thomas was only being polite and fully expected him to back him up. Walking towards the others he held up his letters and told them, "I am Sir William Wallace, formerly Guardian of the Kingdom of Scotland. I come to speak with your King and deliver to him correspondence from the Bishop of St Andrews, Scotland's foremost man of God."

"Then go in peace, Sir William, we will not detain you. Your companion, though, I believe we have business with him."

"Is that so? Then why don't you get down off of your horse and speak to us face to face? This gentleman is my guide. Since this is my first visit to France I need someone to show me the way."

"If that is so, I myself will be happy to escort you after we have dealt with Sir Thomas."

By this time all the riders had dismounted and spread out so that William and Thomas were surrounded.

"Sir Thomas will also be seeking an audience with the King and I am sure he will accept his judgement. I cannot in all conscience look your King in the eye if I stand by and watch you take his law into your hands."

"So be it. We will escort you both to Paris. If you lay down your weapons, I give you my word that neither of you will be harmed."

William held his arms out with his palms upwards "I am unarmed, sir, my sword is on my horse as you can see."

Meantime Thomas was removing the belt holding his scabbard and lowering it to the ground. As his assailant looked away to check that William's sword was indeed fastened to his horse, as it was, Thomas drew his sword from its scabbard and ran through the ringleader. The move was so fast that the others were momentarily stunned, needing just a little bit of time to let their brains catch up with and process what was happening. That little bit of time was all that the two friends needed. Thomas withdrew his bloodied sword and carried out an almost identical manoeuvre on the man to his right. Meanwhile William threw himself into a roll and took the legs from his closest attacker, taking out his sgian dubh as he went. In what was almost the same fluid action he plunged the knife into the falling man's neck, even as he began to twist and launch himself at the next target. As William swung wide to avoid a jab from a short sword he hooked his arm around the fellow's neck and buried his blade up to the hilt in the Frenchman's ribs.

The fight had barely lasted ten seconds and the odds had shortened from six against two to evens so quickly that the remaining two Frenchmen turned tail, threw themselves on their horses and galloped away as fast as they could. Neither Thomas nor William made any attempt to stop them. As they watched the dust settle behind them William looked at his friend and said simply, "Looks like our holiday is over."

Chapter 40: May 1299

Paris

Just after entering the city of Paris, William and Thomas were confronted by a troop of the King's Guards. As they approached William asked his friend, "Do you think these troops are here for us?"

"It seems likely, perhaps we will be arrested for murder. It is probably unwise to try to flee. I suggest we accept whatever they say and leave ourselves at the King's mercy. You will be okay, I think, for me at least it will be an end, one way or the other."

"They have stopped and a single horseman approaches. That must be a good sign, surely?"

Before Thomas could respond the rider reached them and greeted them with, "I am the captain of the King's Guard. His Majesty has heard of your difficulties earlier and has sent us to escort you to the palace. Please follow me." Without waiting for a reply the captain turned and trotted back in the direction he had come from.

"That was a bit non-committal. Are they our friends or not, do you think?" William asked.

"It is not their job to be friendly. Best we just go with them and see how we are received at the palace."

As the two followed behind the captain the other guards fell in behind them. All through the city people flocked to see the mysterious strangers who were being escorted by the King's own men. In general the crowd were friendly, some even waving, cheering and shouting greetings. "I feel like a visiting head of state," William whispered to his friend."

"Well, you are. Just a little delayed." Thomas smiled back at him. "Enjoy the ride and hope that your visit remains friendly."

The royal palace on the Île de la Cité was an imposing conglomeration of buildings that had sprung up over the centuries, some of them fairly recent, with even more under construction. Philip was an ambitious man in all respects. The pair were shown to an impressive apartment and instructed to remain there until sent for. "If we are prisoners, Thomas, I could get used to being an outlaw,"

William joked.

"Believe me, my friend, if we were really prisoners we would not be nearly so comfortable. Although the guards posted outside those doors do concern me slightly."

Many days passed and the only contact with the outside world was when servants brought them food, always accompanied by a pair of guards. Despite repeated attempts the pair were unable to extract any information either from the servants, who said they knew nothing, or the guards, who refused to say anything at all. However, that aside they were not ill-treated. The apartment was sumptuous and the food and drink were excellent. Finally, almost two weeks after they had arrived, the doors opened and this time an elaborately dressed gentlemen instruct them, "Please follow me, gentlemen. His Majesty will see you now."

They were led though many halls and corridors, all bristling with finely dressed people, most of whom greeted them cordially as they passed. Many of them spoke to them both by name, leading William to venture, "It would seem we are welcome here. I wonder why we have been held for so long?"

Thomas made no reply, merely shrugging his shoulders. At length their guide, who had not introduced himself nor answered any of their questions as to what was occurring, stopped before a pair of large, ornately carved doors and rapped sharply with his cane. The doors swung open to reveal a large, high-ceilinged, ornately decorated hall. Philip was seated on a raised platform at the far end and beckoned for them to approach.

"Welcome, my dear friends," Philip said as he rose to greet them. "It is a pleasure to at last meet the renowned Sir William Wallace, our good friend from the Kingdom of Scotland." He kissed William on both cheeks. Then he turned to Thomas. "My very dear old friend. We have heard many tales of your heroics in protecting our ships from the English. Welcome home, Thomas." He embraced his boyhood friend warmly and sincerely.

William was on a diplomatic mission, but it was new to him and he had questions he wanted answered. "It is a pleasure to meet you, your Majesty, but I was wondering why we have been held here so long?"

Philip laughed and announced to the room, "Sir William is a great warrior, and they say no one understands war better. It would seem that his role as an international diplomat does not come so easily to him." To William he said, in lower tones, "Forgive me, Sir William, but your arrival put me in a delicate position. Since you have been straight with me, I will be straight with you. We have recently negotiated a truce with King Edward of England. As part of that agreement there will be a wedding between my daughter, the beautiful Princess Isabella, and the English Prince Edward. There is a lot at stake, so I could not be seen to be sheltering two of my new friend Edward's enemies."

"So why did you take us in?" William wanted to know.

"I could hardly turn you away, where would you have gone? What would you have done? As I said, I will be honest with you. While you were under my safety I wrote to Edward telling him you were here."

"You would have turned us over to King Edward?" William asked, slightly aghast. This was a possibility he had not considered. Sure enough, this diplomacy game was a tough one. He would need to up his game.

"It does not matter, my friend. We all do what we need to do to protect our countries, do we not? In any case, as you can surmise, Edward has lost all interest in both of you. As long as you remain in France, you are no concern of his."

"It is not my intention to remain in France, your Majesty."

"Perhaps not, but we both know that you are more welcome here in France than you will be by the men who replaced you as leader in Scotland. They feel you are as much a threat to their ambitions as Edward is."

"You are remarkably well informed."

"I too am good at my job, Sir William. Also, one of the letters you brought from the Bishop of St Andrews addressed your situation. The good Bishop is a friend of yours, of course, and informs me of the current situation in Scotland and asks me to look after you. He fears for your safety should you return."

This was a blow to William, and once again something he had not really foreseen. That Comyn would wish him dead was no surprise, but was Bruce also his enemy? Sadly he could see that it could be the case. Although the Earl of Carrick had been prominent in the defensive strategy before, during and after the Battle of Falkirk, he had nevertheless always stopped short of directly supporting William. Either man would probably feel that William stood in the way of their ambitions to wear the crown.

Philip interrupted his thoughts. "I see that my news has unsettled you, Sir William. Nevertheless, be sure that I am your friend and have much to offer you. We will speak more later. For now, please let yourself enjoy our beautiful city and country." He turned to Thomas. "And from my dear, dear old friend, I ask your forgiveness. We have treated you harshly and are glad that you have returned home to us."

"What has changed, your Majesty? The last time we spoke you banished me from the kingdom."

"I was wrong. It seems that the young lady was as much to blame as you, if not even more so."

"How so?"

"Even after she married she continued to enjoy the company of other young men," Philip told him with a shrug.

"The family do not hold the same view as you do; they tried to kill me."

"We know all about that. We have spoken to the new Count and cautioned him. We have his word upon his honour that you will not be harmed. This issue is at an end. Sir Thomas, I have sent word to your family, you should go see them soon. Take Sir William. I will send for you when I have news."

Chapter 41: July 1299

John Balliol

William enjoyed his time at Longueville almost as much as Thomas, and he felt welcome there in a way that he no longer did in Scotland. It was the first real holiday he had had in years, centuries even. For the most part the weather held good and the friends spent most days hunting, fishing and swimming. Evenings were spent meeting friends old and new in different parts of the surrounding countryside. Thomas had not lost either his appetite for, or charm with, the fairer sex. Although not himself much of charmer in those situations, William nevertheless found that he was almost as popular with the girls as Thomas.

All too soon they received a summons to return to Paris. Welcoming them back, Philip got straight down to business after the initial pleasantries.

"You will be pleased to learn, Sir William, that we have secured the release of your King John."

"Amazed would be a better word. Has he returned to Scotland? Was he welcomed back?"

"No, Edward would not allow that. He is here in France, and has asked to meet you."

"In France? Why does he not go home?"

"Well, he is home. He has lands in France, including at Troyes where he is now. Some of my men will escort you there tomorrow. He is expecting you."

"Is this part of your agreement with King Edward?"

"Not at all. This is what your Bishop of St Andrews has been working on. It says much for his discretion that even someone such as you was not aware of it."

"I am learning new things all the time. It seems there is a surprise round every corner lately."

"Do not worry, my friend, you are amongst the first to know. I do not think that even your Scottish nobles know of this yet."

"Thank you, your Majesty, for informing me. I will of course travel to see him tomorrow. Many good men have died in his name. We shall see what they died for."

~~~

The following day when William arrived at Troyes, he was surprised to learn that the Bishop of St Andrews, William Lamberton, was already there. John Balliol came to greet him, with the bishop by his side.

"Welcome to my home, Sir William. It is indeed a pleasure to meet you, the man who has become a legend in our own lifetimes."

"The pleasure is all mine, your Majesty, "William replied with a bow. Then turning to address the cleric he continued, "Congratulations to you, Bishop, it is always a pleasure to see such a good friend. How are things back in Scotland?"

"There are rumblings from south of the border. King Edward may be planning a campaign, but he is meeting some resistance from his barons. I argued for your return, but the other Guardians seem to think that you would be a distraction."

As they went inside William was reflective. Perhaps if the Guardians did not want him back, his best bet would be to return with the King.

Once seated, William showed his lack of diplomatic skills by getting straight to the point. "If we are here to discuss putting you back on your Scottish throne, your Majesty, shouldn't we have the other Guardians present?"

"I am afraid that is out of the question. In order to be released here I had to swear an oath that I would never rise up against King Edward," Balliol said matter-of-factly, as if it was a matter of no consequence.

"Are you going to abide by that?" William asked, exasperated, knowing the answer; it was written all over Balliol's pudgy face. "Surely you agree that an oath taken under duress, as yours was, cannot be held to be legally enforceable."

Balliol simply shrugged.

This was the man he had fought for. This was the man thousands had sacrificed their lives for. His heart wept for all the good men who had died for this apology for a king who was sitting in front of him meekly accepting whatever the King of England dictated to him. So many good men! Fathers, sons, brothers, husbands. It was taking all of William's self-control to stop himself taking Balliol by the shoulders and giving him a good shake.

The Bishop stood up and put his hand on William's shoulder. "I can see that you are upset, William, and understandably so. However, things are not as straightforward as they may at first seem. There are many parts to this deal. Firstly, with King John being in France he comes under pressure from King Philip who has agreed to do what he can to ensure King John does not return to Scotland. Secondly, the church has played a major part in this deal, as you are well aware, so that our King has also had to give his word to the Pope. You cannot expect him to break that oath. Thirdly, and perhaps most significantly, Edward Balliol remains in England under the care of his maternal grandfather, the Earl of Surrey."

"So, your son is held hostage and you cannot return for fear that he will be killed, is that it?" William asked. It was at least a reason, not a good one, but something.

"Not that. I do not fear that. Edward is in no danger. I am sure that Surrey loves the boy and would not allow him to come to any harm. In any case, King Edward will want to keep him safe and ensure that the heir to the Scottish crown is completely under his control. That is why he wants us both alive for now."

"For now, yes, but should anything happen to you, Longshanks can march into Scotland claiming to fight with and for the legitimate King of Scots. All of this puts you in grave danger I would say."

Now William was even more conflicted. He felt nothing but contempt for the man sitting opposite him, but nevertheless his continued existence seemed to be the best prospect Scotland had of resisting Longshanks.

"That is a worry for us all," the Bishop agreed. "The prospect of a new King moves ever further away. Should the King die or relinquish his crown there would almost certainly be war between the Comyn and Bruce factions, which Edward would no doubt sit back and enjoy. Before the dust could settle the two Edwards would move in and vanquish whoever remained, which might not be a lot."

"So, tell me, your Majesty, why not just abdicate publicly in favour of your son? Surely that at least keeps the power in your family for your descendants."

"My father-in-law has been turning my son against me so that he now despises me. I could not bear to give him the throne, son or not. In any case, he would be the willing puppet that King Edward desires. He tried to make one of me, and God forgive me, I took too long to stand up to him properly. I fear that my son would be a willing servant and I cannot allow that. At times I wish that I had not been given the crown, that Bruce had been awarded it to suffer the humiliations that I have had to endure. I would rather die than see King Edward gain even a morsel of advantage, but I will live as long as I possibly can for the same end."

William doubted that anyone would have so easily acquiesced to Longshanks' demands, although he was aware that the Earl of Carrick's father was unstintingly loyal to the King of England. How his own father, the original competitor, would have fared he could not guess. Perhaps no better than Balliol. Lamberton was right about one thing, it was not simple.

"Then why I am here? What is it that you expect of me? I have been fighting and leading men to their deaths for you. Do you want more blood?"

"No, I do not want any more blood, and believe me I regret every dropped spilled as much as you do."

"I sincerely doubt that. How many tears have you shed for any of them?"

"Sir William, do not speak to your King that way. Be respectful," the Bishop chided him.

"Then he should not demean the sacrifice all those Scotsmen have made for him," William growled back.

"He is right, Bishop, I am undeserving. To tell you the truth, seeing you now, knowing you have the passion to complement your fighting abilities I have changed my mind. No longer do I wish that Bruce had been crowned instead of me. I wish that you were King before any of us."

"That could never be. If he has not done so already the Bishop should tell you of the esteem the Scottish nobles hold me in. Even if that were not so, I would never be King. Not ever, and especially not now. Perhaps it would be best if there were no Kings."

Balliol allowed himself a small laugh. "How would that work, if everyone was fighting all the time over every last thing because there was no one to keep them in line? That could never work."

Chapter 42: August 1299

Changed loyalties

William returned to Paris disillusioned. He had intended to return to Scotland and find a way to continue the struggle. It was always going to be a difficult return with the Red Comyn holding so much power, but he had hoped to carve out a place with the Steward. Now, though, it was hard to imagine asking anyone to risk their life for John Balliol.

King Philip was sympathetic. "So you are disappointed in your King John. I should perhaps have warned you, but I thought it best you find out for yourself."

"That is as it must be. I can only judge on what I myself can see. It is usually a mistake to rely on the opinions and judgements of others."

The two of them were walking in the Palace gardens. William had developed a liking for Philip, and the respect was mutual. Although what came next was still unexpected. Philip stopped and turned towards William, his expression serious. "It seems to me that you are not able to go back to Scotland and fight for your King. That is a great pity, a man like you should always have a cause to fight for."

"I don't know that a man needs to fight, but you are right that I do not have anyone to fight for back home. I do have a brother, though, and land. Perhaps I should just settle down."

Philip laughed. "And be a farmer? You are not a farmer. You need action, intrigue, a cause."

"Do you say so?"

"I know so, and so do you. Let your brother have the farm. You can go visit him, or better still, let him come to France and farm here."

"You have lost me completely, your Majesty. What are you trying to say to me?"

"I have work for you. You and your friend, our friend, Thomas. Your brother too if it pleases you."

"My brother is not a soldier."

"I am not offering him a war. Happily, right at this moment I do not have a war, although that may change at any time. What I do have though are two worries that I could use a man of your capabilities to

help me with. One of them is your old friend, King Edward."
William's eyebrows raised involuntarily at the mere mention of
Longshanks. "The other is the Knights Templar; you know of
them?"

"I have heard of them, but do not know a lot about them." William
answered. That was only partially true. His interest in the history of
warfare had covered much of that organisation, but at the same time
he did not know of anything specific to that period in France.

"Both of these forces would like to rule in France. For that reason I
need to keep an eye on them and their movements. Unfortunately I
fear I may be called away to Flanders again; the truce there is very
fragile. I would like you and Thomas to go to La Rochelle where the
Templars have a strong presence and keep an eye on them for me."

"And Edward?"

"There are always wars and rumours of wars. Although we are
officially at peace, it seems that Edward may be plotting to take
some parts of France that he considers to be his by right."

"How so?"

Philip allowed himself a little chuckle. "Ancestors of Edward held
lands in France, in Gascony, Normandy, Anjou, Maine, and Poitou.
He feels that all of these lands should be his, in particular Gascony."

"So La Rochelle is kind of in the middle of the disputed lands, is it
not?"

Still smiling smugly, Philip said, "Yes, it is, shall we say,
strategically situated. Edward held most of these territories,
particularly in and around Gascony until recently. As part of an
earlier agreement he gave up those lands. Although there was a
possibility that those lands may have been returned to him, he did
not fulfil the requirements for this. I had no choice therefore but to
rule that he should forfeit them completely. I suspect that is at least
part of the reason why he is so keen to get hold of it, its wine and the
income from it. He is a little upset at having to pay for wine that he
considers his own."

"I can see that he would be a bit put out by that. Presumably he does
not agree with your judgement or the reasons for it?"

"Edward is an extremely arrogant and presumptuous man," Philip
stated with no hint of irony. Pot and kettle sprung immediately to
William's mind, but he said nothing. Philip continued, "Since the

area has been under the control of English overlords for so long, many of the residents are more inclined to give fealty to Edward than to me. That is something that will change in due course, but it will take much time. There have been some skirmishes back and forth over a few years now. Some towns have changed hands several times. For now they are all under my control and I would really like to keep it that way "

"Why me? Don't you have your own people in that area?"

"I have heard many tales of your adventures. What impressed me most was the way that you were able to gather information and plan your movements around that. There are a great many of your countrymen in Paris; take some time to meet them. Choose the best of them. I will pay for as many men as you need, within reason."

"If I am agreeable, what about Thomas? What is his role in this?"

"Thomas has already agreed. I spoke to him while you were in Troyes. You will run a vineyard and he will take care of the ships exporting wine from your place and others. Between you both I hope to learn about all comings and goings in that region by land and sea."

"Run a vineyard? You just said, truthfully, that I am not a farmer, yet you offer me a vineyard."

"It will be your base. The vineyard will run with or without you. If you go you will live there and keep the profits. If you do not go, I will keep the income. Neither of us are farmers."

"You seem to have it all worked out," William said with an air of acceptance.

Philip smiled. "You will do it?"

William had nothing else to do, but was reluctant to commit. "Let me think it over. I will speak to Thomas and let you know."

"As you wish. Meantime I will arrange somewhere for you to meet your new recruits."

"You do not like to take no for an answer, do you?"

"I don't expect to have to. This will be good for you. The climate is much better for you in the South of France than back in Scotland."

"The rain is warmer, no doubt," William joked.

~~~

A few days later William and Thomas were interviewing exiled Scots for their new venture, having agreed with King Philip that the crown would underwrite the cost of a dozen good men to be used as information gatherers and up to two hundred soldiers to be trained for lightning attacks as and when required. It occurred to William that Philip might just be wanting all of the Scots out of Paris.

The last of those interviewed was Sir William de Vieuxpont, a veteran of Philip's campaigns in Flanders.

"Thank you, Sir William, you are just the type of man we are going to need right away. I will come and find you in a few days. Be ready to travel when I do."

"Of course, my Lord. May I just say what a pleasure it is to be working with you. Although I have been away from Scotland, news of you has reached us here nevertheless."

"I thank you again. I hope that I live up to your expectations."

"I am sure you will. There was talk of a retainer?" Vieuxpont asked hopefully.

Thomas answered this query. "That is correct. You and the others we choose will be paid in advance, when we travel."

"Not now? Are we not to be trusted with the King's gold?"

"If it were up to me, yes, you would be paid now in order to help prepare for this mission. However, the King is reluctant to put temptation in anyone's way. He worries that there may be a temptation to spend the money right away on wine, women and song as it were. We will not have the time to go looking for missing men and dragging them out of inns or brothels. Nothing personal, just a precaution."

Vieuxpont was obviously disappointed, but saw no gain in labouring the point. "That is a pity, but I do understand. See you both soon."

Turning to Thomas as Vieuxpont left, William said, "We now have the numbers. Are you sure you want to do this?"

"My friend, I am almost in heaven. Here I am back in France, with my best friend and about to get a new ship paid for by my King. What more could a man ask for, I ask you?"

"Well, he could ask for a cause he believed in, a good reason for asking men to risk their lives."

"Living is a risk in itself. We are offering these men, most of whom have no motivation and no direction in their lives, an opportunity to do something worthwhile. Why do you worry about that?"

"About two thousand men died at Falkirk fighting for a just cause. There is not a night that it does not haunt my dreams. I worry about asking men to die for a cause that I do not even believe in myself. Personally, I do not care whether Aquitaine or any other place belongs to Edward or Philip or the Pope. Honestly, it just feels wrong to ask Scotsmen to die in a foreign land."

"Perhaps you should let them decide where they want to die and what they would die for. You are not forcing anyone to do anything. All of these men have a choice. As do you."

"You are right, of course. It is just that I fear my choice is to go to La Rochelle and risk the lives of a few volunteers, or return to Scotland where I may be responsible for the deaths of many more. I wish there was another way."

What William really wished for, but could not explain to his friend, was to be back in the twentieth century with his father and brother. Now not only did he not know how his father was, but also he had heard nothing of Malcolm since he left Scotland. For all he knew his brother was dead, and if so how could he not hold himself responsible for that? Malcolm had wanted to fight and William had overruled him. He should have kept him close and maybe he would be with him now. Or maybe he would be dead. Was that the key? They had been sent back in time together, but William had made every effort to keep Malcolm safe, as he saw it. What if he was wrong? What if Malcolm had a bigger part to play and William had thwarted those plans? Could that be why they both now appeared to be in limbo, with no sense of purpose?

Chapter 43: Autumn 1299

La Rochelle

La Rochelle was a beautiful town overlooking the Bay of Biscay. The dock area was dominated by the Château Vauclair, a four-towered castle of white sandstone built by Henry II, the great-grandfather of Edward I, in his capacity as Duke of Aquitaine. William's vineyard was just outside the town and from there he despatched his spies to tour the countryside and towns garnering any information that could prove useful. Thomas spent the first part of his time refitting his ship as a ruse for getting to know everyone connected to the port and watching all the comings and goings.

"That man there, the tall one in the middle with the slight limp, that is Guillaume de Liège, the commander of the Knights Templar here. If you want to get close to anyone, he is your man," Thomas told William as they stood opposite the Templars' headquarters watching the comings and goings.

"You have seen nothing suspicious in or around the port?" William asked him.

"Nothing at all. Plenty of activity and the Templars seem to have a hand in most of it, but nothing suspicious at all. If you ask me, it is not a religious order at all, but just a cover for an international trading business. They own most of the mills in the area and pay no taxes. It is hard to compete. He is coming over."

"Good afternoon." The Templar Commander, approached, smiling amiably. "It is good to catch the two of you together. Let us talk."

"It is indeed an honour to be recognised by a busy man like you," Thomas replied. "What interest can we possibly hold for you?"

"Come now, let's not pretend. I know that you have been sent here by King Philip to keep an eye on us. The King is insecure and sees everyone as a threat. He will see you as a threat eventually; be careful."

William immediately took a liking to the straight-talking Templar. "You are well informed, sir. You may be pleased to know that our report to the King will be favourable to you. We will be happy, on our part, to share information with you and your men. You may also be aware that our purpose here is also to keep an eye on events in the surrounding areas, in particular any news connected to the King of England."

"Yes, I know you have a history with King Edward. Seems strange to continue your quarrel with him so far from home." When William did not respond, Guillaume continued, "I thank you for your offer, but we Templars rely on no one for our protection, or for information. Nor do we fear anyone, be he knight or be he King, for we have the Lord God on our side."

"Of course. Thomas and I meant no disrespect. However, we would appreciate it if you would let us know if you hear anything that may be of interest to us."

Guillaume appeared to think about it for a few moments then answered, "Since we are going to be living in close proximity to each other we may as well be civil. You will be aware, Sir William, that we have a small presence on Scotland." William nodded an acknowledgement. "Your Bishop of St Andrews is an admirable man and it seems he has a great fondness for you, and by extension also for you, Sir Thomas. I can tell you that things are relatively quiet in Scotland and the bishop has asked us to tell you that he will keep you informed of developments."

"That is a comfort to me. He made no mention of my brother?"

"He made no mention of anyone. You should be reassured by that. Had there been anything of interest you can be sure he would have told you."

"Thank you, Sir Guillaume, I cannot tell you how relieved I am after speaking to you today. I am deeply in your debt."

"In my opinion you are serving the wrong master. Be sure that King Philip will use you for his own ends and cast you off when he no longer needs you."

Thomas was moved to defend his old friend. "With respect, Lord Commander, I have known the King since childhood. He has ever been kind to me."

"Kind? Do you really think so? Tell me then, as one of his oldest and dearest friends, what titles has he bestowed on you? What great lands are at your command? He has it in his power to reward you well for your loyalty, after all have you not been fighting his wars with England for years?"

Thomas was visibly troubled by this but said nothing. But in his head a seed had been planted.

Guillaume continued, "Yes, you know I speak true. And you, Sir William, what has he given you? A vineyard! One vineyard. If he really wanted you to stay in France and fight for him would he not have made you a Count at least? With a snap of his fingers he could have married you off to a rich widow and made a true nobleman of you."

"Maybe the King knows me better than you do, Sir Guillaume. I am not a man to be bought and sold."

"And yet here you are, bought for some grapes."

"That is not how I see it." William was considering that he may have misjudged the Commander. Was he trying to insult them and provoke a fight? Did he see them as a threat? Did he really have something to hide?

"Forgive me, gentlemen. I am a plain-speaking man and sometimes I unintentionally upset people unnecessarily. All I meant to say was that I believe that I know the King better than either of you. Judging you both to be honourable men, I simply wish to advise you to be careful in your dealings with your master. He is a coldly calculating animal with the survival instincts of a snake."

William was willing to give the Templar the benefit of the doubt. "Am I to assume that you and the King are not close friends then?" he joked.

The commander smiled himself. "How insightful you are. I can see that you are in no need of my warnings. Good day, gentlemen."

William looked at Thomas and with eyebrows raised asked, "What was that about really?"

Thomas shrugged and replied, "I am not entirely sure. Although I have the feeling that he was sizing us up and has decided we are no threat to him."

"That is probably true. He has a great many well-armed and well-trained men at his disposal. Let's hope we do not end up on the wrong side of him."

Chapter 44: Winter 1301/2
Battle for La Rochelle

"They have taken Sir William de Vieuxpont!" William told his assembled scouts. Almost three years after he had arrived in France this was the first sign of anything untoward. Of all of his scouts, Vieuxpont had been the most consistent, never once being late with his report. William had given it a week and then gone himself to investigate. "It seems that the men who took him were working for the English crown. He was ambushed just outside Blaye and it seems he was taken via Bordeaux to London. We must assume that Longshanks has set his eyes back on France while Philip is away in Flanders. From now on I want you all to work in pairs at all times and be even more vigilant. I will send word to Paris for reinforcements."

"It will take time for a force to get here from Paris. Are we not vulnerable meantime?" one of the men wanted to know.

"By the same token, it will take time for any invasion force to come from England."

"If they are not already on the way," another scout ventured.

"You are right, of course. Good to see you are all still thinking. As far as we know nothing is underway. Sir Thomas?"

"I have many friends at sea and get information all the time. At best I have a good idea of all ship movements near enough to be of concern. At worst though, any ship heading straight for us could arrive before we have enough time to prepare," Thomas answered.

"That is why we must be vigilant at all times. Of course the biggest danger still comes from those loyal to the Duke of Aquitaine. That is why it is essential that we increase our watchfulness while being even more discreet. We need to be aware of any build-up of arms, or any talk of such, as soon as possible. All our lives may depend on that information."

When the others had gone Thomas asked, "Should we inform the Templars?"

"Yes, I plan to do that next. They will not give us any assistance, that has been made quite plain, but it is only polite to warn them.

After all, as religious men they will probably be busy with burials in the aftermath."

So it transpired when William took the news to the Lord Commander. "Thank you for informing us, but this is a wordly matter. The affairs of the Kings of France and England do not concern us. We fight for the King of Kings and only he. However, we will pray for your safety."

~~~

When the attack came it was not overland from the south, but by sea. Five ships laden with troops and horses had set out from the south coast of England and were within sight of La Rochelle before William and his men knew anything about it. Had they been able to land right away they would have gained a huge advantage. Fortunately for the defenders the assailants arrived at low tide and could not access the harbour.

"Where shall we deploy our men, Thomas? Where will they land, do you think?"

Thomas pointed. "If they know the layout of the town, and we must assume that they do, then of course that will be the best place for them to have room to unload. It is too late now for me to get my ship out and take the fight to them. I will stay here and fight beside you."

As the foreign vessels eased into port the two friends held their men back, to some dissent. "Surely we should be right down there to cut them down as they disembark? Is it not foolish to allow them the time to get into formation?" asked Iain McDougal from the Western Isles.

"We do not yet know what we face. Only fools rush in."

"Nonsense, you have lost your touch. This easy living has made you go soft." McDougal, over six feet tall himself with a face lost amongst wild orange hair and beard that looked like neither had ever been trimmed, was a formidable fighter with a fear of nothing and no one.

William, well aware of his critic's reputation, refrained from a debate but instead told him, "I am glad you are so keen to die, I need a volunteer to lead the charge, on my command – on my command, mark you – and you are he. Pick a dozen men, but wait for my order to attack."

"Is that wise?" Thomas whispered.

Keeping his own voice low William answered, "If I was commanding this mission I would have archers ready to provide cover for my men as they got off. If they do it is unwise to go to early. If they do not it is unwise to go too late. Our loudmouth friend will find out which it is."

"If there are no archers he will claim the glory."

"If there are he may die."

"You will let him?"

William did not answer directly, but turned to McDougal and his men. "Now is the time, but I warn you that there may be archers. Keep your shields raised above your head until you're two paces away. Do not lower them too early."

As the men, shouting their battle cries, ran at the knights climbing down from the first ship those Englishmen already on dry land lined up ready but did not advance.

"I was right." William raised his hands and shouted after the running Scotsmen, "Get those shields up!" He did not bother to order them back, knowing that they would not come. Their blood was well and truly up, that death or glory mindset that William despised for the number of Scots that had died unnecessarily. Even as he roared, the first volley of arrows flew up from the ship, luckily not hitting anyone. However, the archers now adjusted their range and fired again, this time to better effect. Two Scots fell, one dead with an arrow in his throat, another stopped by an arrow in his thigh. Despite his warnings, William could not see a single shield above chest height. The archers stopped when the defenders were about thirty yards from the ship. Less than half of them reached the assembled knights and there was the sound of metal upon metal, roars of aggression and yells of pain as the few threw themselves against the now thirty or so knights ranged against them.

Within five minutes all twelve of the first wave of Scots lay dead or dying for the loss of only four Englishmen. The remainder of the Scots were venting their frustration at being held back, but William commanded them: "Hold still until they charge. Any man who goes before that will be cut down as surely as those poor souls. As it is, we are going to be heavily outnumbered. We may all die here today. Let us die well, and let us take as many of our enemy as we can with us."

When the invading force were fully assembled they numbered almost a thousand men, facing less than two hundred. Happy that the odds were heavily in their favour the charge was called and they advanced at pace up the docks. William stood in front of his men with his arm raised until the insurgents were about a hundred yards from him. With a mighty yell he lowered his hand but did not move. It took those at the front of the charge a few moments to realise why the Scots had not moved to meet them. As the rumblings got louder they turned to see five hundred barrels of wine rolling towards them. All the arrows in the world would not have slowed the progress of William's first trap. Knights were bowled over like skittles as the wine ended up in the harbour, accompanied by almost a hundred and seventy battered and broken knights.

Slowly the Englishmen regrouped, still the Scots held their ground. Still William stood five paces in front of the lines of Scotsmen. Having learned nothing from the first setback the invaders once more surged forward. This time William waited until they were less than twenty yards from him before moving swiftly to his right. As he did so the line behind him parted to reveal two stacks of timber. Realising too late what was happening the onrushing knights clashed with those behind as they tried to avoid William's second line of defence. When the Scots had cleared the front of the wood piles a man holding a heavy hammer stepped forward and knocked out the pegs that were holding the foremost logs in place. Slowly the whole of both piles started to move and then gather pace, bouncing forward into the oncoming army. By the time the dust had cleared William's small force were facing shorter odds of around three to one.

"Okay, men, now it is your time for glory. Cut them down before they can regroup." Rushing forward, swinging his long sword double-handed he hacked at his enemy before anyone could get close enough to him to do him harm. Just behind and to his left Thomas was singing as he fought and all around swords clashed or struck shields or took life and limb.

The Scots were still heavily outnumbered and in the main were no match for their well-disciplined opponents. The number of defenders dwindled at a faster rate than the attackers, and William and Thomas found themselves back to back, fighting for their lives. While regretting that he was going to die so far from home and, it now seemed, almost pointlessly, he heard battle cries, not from his enemy but from the direction of the town. Within seconds some of those facing him began to turn away and engage others and a few minutes later the remaining English were running for their ships, pursued by the familiar red-on-white emblems of the Knights Templars.

Lacking the energy to join the chase they watched the English retreat. A voice they recognised spoke from behind William and Thomas. "You fight very well. It seemed such a pity to let you die."

"Lord commander, we are truly grateful for your unexpected intervention. We owe you our lives."

"You are most welcome. As far as I can tell, I have lost no men today, God has looked after us."

"That is indeed a blessing, though we have lost many. Can I ask you, why did you come? You made it very clear that it was not your fight."

"That is correct, but many men believe that we Templars hoard great treasures. We were not aiding you, simply ensuring that no trouble came to our chapel." The Lord Commander paused for a moment. "In any case, Sir William, while praying for you and your men I believe that God spoke to me, instructing me not to let you die. It would seem he has a purpose for you. You and Sir Thomas fight very well, why don't you take the oath and join us? If God has a purpose for you, I am certain that it is not to aid the King of France. Join us and help us liberate the Holy Lands."

"I am flattered, of course, Sir Guillaume. Let me ask my God for guidance. If he instructs me I will join you gladly."

"And you, Sir Thomas?"

"Lord Commander, you obviously have not heard of my reputation. Holy vows would be unbearable for a man of my disposition."

The Lord Commander laughed and clapped Thomas on the shoulder before turning to his own men and taking control of the clearing up operation. The surviving Englishmen were allowed to leave on a single ship and the Templar fleet had now been expanded with the capture of the remaining English ships. Another gift from God.

Thomas was curious. "Would you really go with them on a Crusade?"

William had the tiniest hint of a smile on his face as he answered, "My God will indeed guide me, Thomas. But my God is Scottish."

Part VIII

End of an Era

Chapter 45: January 1303

Au revoir to France

William returned from his meeting with the Lord Commander in a seething rage. Thomas was taken aback; he had never seen his friend this agitated, even at times of the most extreme pressure. Not even after the betrayal at Falkirk. Thomas himself had a cool head under pressure and did not let the big man's mood panic him.

"That must have been quite a chat. What has disturbed you so? What is on your mind my friend?"

"Regicide!"

"That is a bit strong. And dangerous, even for you. Philip has caused this mood?"

"Four years we have given him and how does he repay us? Betrayal, that's how! The Lord Commander has confirmed that Philip is about to sign a treaty with the King of England that will hand vast areas of France back to him. Including this part. He is about to make us subject to Longshanks and he has not even had the common decency to mention it to us."

"I can see why you are angry, it puts you in a very bad position. But you must calm down, my friend. If any man could get to Philip and kill him it is you, but it will not help. Come, let us drink some wine and consider our options." Thomas went off to fetch a carafe of the vineyard's finest.

When Thomas returned with the wine William had himself more under control. "I'm sorry, old friend. It's not even Philip, I am scunnered with myself. Four years spent protecting France when I should have been back in Scotland."

"Scotland would have been difficult for you under Carrick and Comyn. Now that Comyn is himself Lord of Badenoch and effectively sole Guardian what role can you play? Perhaps we should go to Flanders in exchange for land there. What do you think?"

"Fuck the land, any land. My father would be ashamed of me if he could see me here, lord of the manor. Comyn or not, I must return to Scotland and fight to free the land, not just from England, but from the entire system of overlordship. Men should not own other men.

Common people, the majority of the people, should not owe themselves to others just because those others stole their land. They can only claim it, and keep it, with the acquiescence of the masses. Is it time that someone stood up and said 'No more!' Let the people fight for themselves, for each other, not for some arrogant 'aristocrat' who claims to have been born better. We all come into the world the same way. We all bring nothing with us and take nothing when we go. From this day forward I fight for no King; rather I fight for no kings."

Chapter 46: February 1303

Home

"A hundred thousand welcomes to Scotland's prodigal son," the Bishop of St Andrews said as he embraced William. "We must kill the fatted calf today."

"Good idea, we are starving, are we not, Thomas?"

"Indeed we are. We brought you some wine."

"Thank you, where is it?"

"It's on the way from the docks. We didn't wait for it to be unloaded; it will be here shortly."

"How much wine did you bring me?"

"Fifty barrels."

"Fifty barrels? That is a bit excessive, don't you think."

"It is also with the compliments of Sir Guillaume. I didn't know you two knew each other."

"Well, you know, we both get around, we have bumped into each other once or twice. Nice man, as you will know. But why so much wine?"

"When we heard of Philip's arrangement with Longshanks we realised it was time to come home. The Lord Commander offered us passage in a Templar ship. There was some spare capacity so Thomas and I loaded some wine we had produced that was sitting at the docks."

"William, you should know that I cannot accept stolen goods," the bishop laughed.

"Not stolen at all, Bishop. Call it severance pay. Would you rather we had left it for Longshanks? We loaded what we could and destroyed anything we had to leave behind."

"Okay, in that case I accept, thank you both."

~~~

Later, after the beef, the conversation turned more serious. "What will you do now? Things have changed while you have been away."

"As they must. My next stop must be to my brother. Do you have news of him?"

"Malcolm is doing quite well. He seems to have come out of his shell a bit."

"In what way."

"He seems more, shall we say, assertive."

"That sounds good. I think. In what way?"

"He was summoned to a parliament held in Peebles. Sir David Graham had requested the Guardians award him the land at Ellerslie. He had some dubious claim on it, but to me it seemed like a bit of a set-up to strip you of your property. Everyone expected Malcolm to meekly accept what was being proposed but he defended you brilliantly. His arguments were so good that Graham attacked him only to find that your brother is no pushover. I must say he produced some very unusual moves, a lot of jumping about with arms and legs flailing. Graham literally did not know what hit him."

"Malcolm gave him a kicking, did he?" William laughed out loud, sorry that he had missed that. It seemed that his brother had indeed been practising his Bruce Lee moves, and put them to good use.

"He certainly got the better of him, although I confess I did not see it all. Graham was backed by the Comyns. I believe it was their idea. The Earl of Carrick and I argued for you and Malcolm. When the fighting started I witnessed the Lord of Badenoch grab Bruce by the throat before I was floored by a punch from the Earl of Buchan."

"That is outrageous!" William was incensed at the physical attack on the young Bishop. Although many bishops were also warriors, for example the Bishop of Glasgow and even the Pope, William Lamberton was always focussed on diplomacy and solving things through dialogue.

"Most of those gathered agreed and the violence actually served to swing the sympathies of the parliament against Graham and the Comyns. When the dust had settled, not only had the land been confirmed as yours, but it was agreed that should anything befall you the land would go to Malcolm."

"Well done, Malcolm, I must congratulate him. What is the general situation in Scotland? I hear that the Lord of Badenoch is in the ascendency?"

"Yes, although officially the single Guardian is Sir John de Soulis."

"I hear he is King John's man."

"Indeed. After the King was released from Papal custody he moved to his ancestral lands in Picardy, as you no doubt are aware. From there he seemed to be trying to arrange his return. He sent letters confirming de Soulis as his proxy."

"How did the others take that?"

"Not well, as you can imagine. Carrick could see that his days were numbered and joined his father in giving allegiance to Longshanks."

"That is disappointing," William stated flatly. In his mind, though, it was a good thing. If he was going to see his country move forward without a King it would be easier to remove Bruce while he was aligned to England.

"With Carrick out of the way, so to speak, Badenoch became encouraged. He effectively took control and undermined de Soulis at every opportunity. Fearing for his life, de Soulis fled and is with Balliol in Picardy."

"Then Comyn is effectively in charge?"

"He is very headstrong, as you well know, and there is no one strong enough to stand up to him. Carrick could have kept him in check. But by declaring for Edward he has effectively ruled himself out of the race."

"My single biggest regret is not killing Comyn after the betrayal at Falkirk. I was trying to avoid the kind of situation we are in anyway. That was a mistake; I should have taken him out."

"He expected that. You would have had a very difficult task getting to him on his own."

"Oh, if I had wanted to reach him, nothing and nobody would have stopped me." It occurred to William that if he had gone wrong in what he truly believed was his mission to correct history, then it was either when he trusted Comyn before Falkirk or failing to take him out afterwards. Still, there was nothing he could do about that right now. He had to focus on what he could do.

"What of my men? Do any of them still resist, or have they chosen another side?"

"Many of them fight on from Ettrick. Sir John Graham leads them now. I am sure they will be heartened by your return. Will you return to them?"

"If they will have me back, I have plans for them. I intend to settle things once and for all."

Chapter 47: February 1303

Uncle Billy

"Come and meet baby Alan. I swear he has Dad's eyes and smile," Malcolm urged his brother after the initial bear hugs had subsided.

"Baby Alan? Really? Congratulations both of you. I could not be more pleased. All that time I spent worrying about you and you were doing great without me to hold you back." William was genuinely pleased and untypically his eyes brimmed with tears of joy for his brother and sister-in-law.

"Here he is," Mary said as she handed the tiny bundle over to meet his uncle.

William took him gingerly, genuinely afraid to hurt the wee soul. "He is beautiful. He does have Dad's eyes, but these tiny wee ears are so like Mum's."

"Do you think so?" Malcolm asked as he bent to take a closer look at his son. "Oh aye, so they are. He's got that same wee folded in bit at the top, how did I not see that?"

"Probably because you are too busy staring dreamily into his eyes to see anything else. Like when he needs changed," Mary laughed.

"You won't mind sharing space with this wee whirlwind will you? He is not usually this quiet."

"I wouldn't, of course not. But I won't be staying."

"William, you have done your bit. Let the others take the strain. At least stay a while, get to know the wee fellow," Mary implored.

Malcolm added, "Mary's right. Scotland has changed while you were away. Comyn is the main man now and because of that Bruce has aligned with England. It seems that there is no way back for John Balliol. You don't have a side in this fight."

"I am on Scotland's side and I must continue the fight for a free country. Not just free of English interference, but free of tyranny in any shape or form. I will fight with, and for, the people of Scotland to earn their right to choose a government that works for them. Not only for the privileged few."

Malcolm knew what his brother meant. He was talking about democracy, but he could not discuss it in front of his wife who would not, could not understand. The real problem was that apart from the brothers, no one would understand the concept. Now really was not the time.

Later, when the brothers were alone, Malcolm picked up the earlier conversation. "You are way out of time to introduce something as radical as government for the people by the people. Absolutely nobody will understand the concept. Even if any did, how could it possibly be implemented? There is no infrastructure, no way to nominate and elect representatives. There are not even any trade guilds, let alone political parties."

William sighed. "I know. I will not live to see such a country, but I feel that I must try to at least do the groundwork. Maybe this is why we are here. You can join me, you were always much more active politically than me."

"I would help if I could, but where do you start? There literally isn't anything to work with."

"That is where you are wrong. The people of Scotland defeated an English army at Stirling, and could have, should have, done it again at Falkirk. Those men believed in themselves. Themselves, Malc, not a King or an Earl or a Lord. They fought and won without the ruling class; we need to build on that and expand it. That is where we start. Ettrick Forest will be the foundation for a Scottish revolution."

"Still, they were following you. You gave them belief, yes, but that belief is more in you than in themselves. I don't think for a minute that many, if any, of them think they could do anything remotely like that without you. Do you see what I mean?"

"Aye, I do. And you are right. It's the timing again, it's too soon, as you said. What should I do, then? I can't do nothing, I can't stand by and not fight. But I can't fight for John Balliol, and I sure as fuck will not fight for John Comyn."

"You need to think about how to get where you want to go rather than focussing on the destination. If a fully democratic country is your goal then you know where you want to be and you know where you are, you just need to work out the route from A to B. Think of it as a battle. Just like Stirling or Falkirk. What steps do you need to take to achieve your ultimate goal?"

"Thanks, Malc. On the plus side, this gives me an excuse to stay here for a while. Time to think, time to plan, time to be an uncle."

Chapter 48: March 1303

Ettrick Forest

"You really need to be more careful, Sir Simon," a voice whispered in his ear while a big hand clamped over his mouth stopping him from making a sound. The gentle pressure of a sharp blade against his throat meant he was unable to struggle.

All at once he was released and spun to face his assailant. He feared the worst.

"William! When did you get back?" he roared as he stepped forward and embraced his old comrade in arms.

"A few days ago, I am surprised you have not heard."

"We do not have as large a network as there used to be. Most of our information comes from going out and seeking. Very few venture as far into the forest as this."

"That is no reason to be lax with look-outs. You could be dead and no one would know. How many men could I kill quietly before anyone noticed?"

"Oh oh! He's back. Better get our act together, boys!" Alan Boyd shouted for all to hear, and soon bodies were jostling with each other, all eager to welcome their former leader back. Alan, as always, was at the front of the queue.

Later, after the camp security had been overhauled and each man reminded of his duties and obligations, William, Thomas, Simon and Alan had time to catch up properly. Thomas was a fine storyteller but while he was regaling them with heavily embellished tales of their time in France, William could see that the others were impatient to tell their own tale.

"Thomas, you are taking up all of the time, save some tales for later. Alan, you look as if you are itching to tell something, what is it?"

"The tale is not mine to tell, Sir Simon has just led a hugely successful mission which will thrill you."

Simon was indeed eager to tell and immediately boasted, "You are not the only one capable of catching folks unawares. Several days ago our scouts came back with news that an English army headed by Sir John Segrave was rampaging east of here and seemingly heading for Edinburgh. We set out almost immediately to intercept them. When we reached Biggar we met up with a force led by your old friend the Lord of Badenoch."

"With friends like that, who needs enemies?" Thomas interrupted.

"He is not my favourite person either, I admit, but nevertheless he and his men have probably done more than even we have this last year or so."

"What a pity he wasn't as keen for a fight at Falkirk!" Thomas interjected and then spat on the fire.

William observed, "The difference is that he is fighting for himself now, not John Balliol, and certainly not me."

"There is bad blood between you; perhaps I should not recount this tale," Simon said with a sigh. Alan too looked crestfallen.

"Do not make allowances for Comyn, Thomas and I are eager to hear of your adventures. If you cross paths with Comyn is does not detract from you at all."

"Thank you, William. Anyway, by the time we met up we were getting reports of the English setting up camp near Roslin. It was late afternoon and like us, Comyn had been travelling all day already. That notwithstanding, it was decided that we should march overnight and take them by surprise."

"That was a brave decision, it must be almost twenty-five miles. Was it yours?"

"To be honest, I am not entirely sure who mentioned it first. We all just understood that it was the only thing to do. Within the hour we were under way, about eight thousand in total, probably about as many of Comyn's men as ours, although most of the horses were theirs. We marched in two-hour bursts then rested and many men swapped horses so that no one was more tired than they needed to be. It was dusk when we found them, but most of them were already up and about. We had the advantage that although they had more horses, almost none of them were in action. The fight was ferocious so I cannot tell much more than my own involvement. I'm sure Alan will have a different perspective. If we were outnumbered it was not by much, probably no more than ten thousand against us. For my part I slew four or five, including Sir Ralph Manton. We lost a few ourselves, of course, but we got by far the better of them. I would estimate that we lost about a thousand, the English probably lost over half and the rest fled."

"That is indeed a tremendous victory. A few of those and the balance will swing greatly in our favour." William spoke with a great deal of excitement.

"You have not even hard the best part."

"There is more?"

"Oh aye, there's more. Not all the English survivors got away. We took several prisoners, including Sir John Segrave, who had been wounded."

"That is a good catch. Where is he now? You have no prisoners here. Does Comyn have him?"

"Unfortunately not. It had seemed that we had faced too small an army and we soon found out why. Not long after we set off after the battle, we were assailed by another group of about the same size. Had they arrived earlier we may have had an even more serious problem. As it was we were of course tired by the overnight march and having fought a battle already. To our advantage, we had swapped our horses for English ones and had more of us on horseback than before and had also picked the best of the weapons available and stored the rest. Plus of course we had the thrill and momentum of having won a great victory. Unfortunately, during the clash our prisoners, including Segrave, slipped away."

"Two battles in one day is exceptional in itself. Two battles after an overnight march is almost unbelievable." Both William and Thomas were already deeply regretting not having come back to Scotland sooner. To have missed that day on the twenty-fourth of February would always be a disappointment for them.

"Not to give too much away, you should let me finish. The best is yet to come. Not only did we take on and defeat a second troop of about ten thousand men, but not too long after that second great fight we defeated a third troop."

"Oh, come on now, you are pulling my leg, surely! I cannot believe that such a feat is humanly possible." William was searching the faces of Simon and Alan, expecting to see a smirk, but there was none. Many other men had gathered round and were themselves getting pretty worked up, replaying amongst themselves the most memorable parts of that incredible night and day so that eventually William turned back to Simon and could only say, somewhat in awe,

"It is true, you did that, you actually fought three battles after a twenty-odd-mile march and won all three! They will surely sings songs about that day until the end of time."

"And deservedly so," Thomas added walking around, congratulating all the men, hugging and kissing them all with tears in his eyes. William joined him and the mood in the camp went up another notch as men who had fought with the man they almost worshipped revelled in the admiration he proclaimed for them."

A shout went up: "Who is like us?"

"Damned few!" came the reply, or words to that effect.

"They are ready to take over the world," Thomas observed with a grin.

"Just Scotland will do for me," William replied solemnly, and to Simon asked, "How many of your men survived all that fighting?"

The question brought Simon back down to earth. With a sigh he answered, "We left here with almost five thousand men. There are barely two thousand now."

"Scotland will have to do, that is far too few for the whole world. I hope that we have enough men left to hold on to what we've got. I hate to pour cold water on such a momentous achievement, but just like after Stirling, Longshanks will be back. Only this time we do not have the numbers to take him on in a set piece battle. Let us hope we do have the numbers to undermine any gains he makes"

~~~

As William had feared, the Scottish euphoria did not last long. Longshanks came north and swept almost all before him. He consolidated his gains by strengthening strongholds and building new ones. Few castles or towns remained under Scottish control. As winter closed in the resistance fighters huddled in their camp deep in the forest and reflected on a mixed year.

"Our victory at Roslin seems like a dream now," Simon said with a sigh. "All of that hope of an end to the wars with England drifted away like the smoke from that fire."

"Longshanks' ambitions are only limited by the quality of the men serving him," William observed. "It seems now he has realised that if he wants a job done well he has to do it himself. This is why I returned. His peace with France allows him to focus his efforts solely on Scotland. I fear that he will not leave this time until he is completely sure of total victory."

"I suppose the best part of John Comyn claiming all the credit for the win at Roslin is that Longshanks has focussed his efforts on the Comyn lands in the north-east and the south-west. Perhaps the fact that he is not hounding us shows that we are not doing enough."

"We can never do enough, as long as a single foreign administration holds sway in a single Scottish town. Do not fool yourself that Longshanks has forgotten about us. Unless Comyn can pull out another great victory, this time against Longshanks himself, he will eventually yield. It is just a matter of time."

"That would be a great pity."

"Unfortunately it is inevitable. When it does happen Longshanks will turn his full focus to whatever resistance remains. That will probably only be us."

"Let him come here, we still have lessons to teach him," Alan Boyd said defiantly.

"Aye, if we could lure him into the forest we would have a great advantage. He is no fool, though, and he knows that as well as we do. That is why he will not come," William told them.

"But if he really wants us he will need to come and find us surely?" Simon asked.

"Longshanks makes his own rules to suit himself. In my opinion, he will be happy enough to see us penned in here not doing any damage. Only if we venture out can we inflict any harm on his administration. He knows that and will wait. Do not be surprised if he goes after the things we love to lure us out. I intend to bring my brother and his family here for safety. The rest of you should consider doing the same."

Chapter 49: February 1304

First betrayal

On a cold but clear February day William and Simon led a force of some forty men on a raid on Peebles. Before they could reach the town they were intercepted by a larger force of about a hundred heavily armed men.

"That does not look like the normal guard on its rounds," Simon remarked. "I can see Robert de Clifford and William de Latimer to the fore."

"Let us spread out and try to stretch their lines so that we can pick them off singly. We are too heavily outnumbered for a head-on clash," William suggested.

Simon replied, "We won three in a row about this time last year. We can defeat this lot."

"With respect, look at the banners. This looks like an elite force; there are probably no weak spots in that formation if we allow them to hold it." William veered off to the right and shouted to his men. "Try to draw them off! Take them one at a time."

Simon Fraser continued straight and most of the men followed him. A few, Alan Boyd chief amongst them, strung out on either side riding as if to swing around behind the charging Englishmen. As William neared the now-stretched English line he stood up in his stirrups and raised his big axe in his left hand. By manoeuvring nimbly, he managed to avoid the assaults of the first three assailants. The first he struck with a perfectly timed backswing that found the space between the man's armour and his helmet, almost severing his head from his body. A second knight, as he swung his own axe overhead leaving himself exposed, fell as a fierce swing forward direct into his abdomen pierced his armour and tore through internal organs. Realising he was not getting that weapon back William released it before the falling enemy could drag him off balance and reached for his hammer. The third knight avoided William's blow just as easily as William avoided his, but was slower to recover as both men pulled their mounts round and fell from his horse as William's hammer tore flesh and smashed bone in his thigh. He died some hours of intense agony later.

William was having a good battle, but a quick glance towards the thick of the action showed that his compatriots were faring about as badly as he had feared. Turning to head for the thick of it he was faced by a familiar figure who easily dodged the swing of his hammer but did not attempt his own assault. "William, it is me, Robert, Carrick. You are outnumbered and will lose today. Segrave has hand-picked his best men to get you and Simon."

"If you are the best of England, Carrick, then I have nothing to fear for it is you, not I, who is fighting his last battle."

But Bruce continued to turn and evade William's blows. "Do this not for yourself, but for all of your men. You have been betrayed. One of your men waits for us on the edge of the forest. All of your men are to be put to the sword. There are thousands of foot soldiers behind us; it will be a massacre."

It made sense to William. To face such a force as they were facing could not just be bad luck. Not sure how to judge Bruce, he pulled off and rode towards the main fight, urging his men as best he could. "Retreat! Save the camp, we are betrayed and trapped."

Only eight of the original group reached the relative safety of the forest, where they were able to use their intimate knowledge of the terrain to shake their pursuers. William was heartened to see that Simon and Alan were among the survivors.

"Leave the forest!" William yelled when he arrived back at camp. "We have been betrayed! Thousands of soldiers advance on us even as we speak. This is not the time to make a stand. Save yourselves."

As the men began to clear out, Malcolm asked his brother, "Are we not going? Do we make a stand here?"

"No, Malc, it is not your time to die. Go home, if it is safe to do so. If not go to the Steward, or the monastery. Keep yourself safe."

"I will not leave you alone here."

"Your first duty is to your wife and children. Ensure their safety. If you must die, die for them, not for me." Malcolm still hesitated but William pushed him and insisted, "Go now, save your family."

~~~

It took the invaders another two hours to reach the camp, which they found totally deserted. From his concealment William watched and listened as de Clifford grabbed a man by the scruff and shouted angrily in his face. "Where are they? You promised me the rebels but they are not here. You had better not be leading us on a chase or I promise you that you will suffer for it."

"No, my Lord, I would not. I assure you that they were here this morning. As soon as the raiding party rode out I left for our rendezvous. There were still hundreds of people here then."

"Then where are they now?" Clifford roared.

"I would venture that your informer found a conscience and warned off his companions. After all, he probably thought that you would be happy with the ringleaders." William was not surprised to hear the voice of Robert Bruce. What was he up to?

"We may as well get out of here while the light is still strong enough to see by."

While Clifford led his troops back the way that they had come, William eased himself out of his hiding place and started to follow them, intending to pick off the stragglers. Before he could reach the last man he disappeared from sight. William carefully moved to where he had been to find the grinning figure of Alan Boyd leaning over the bleeding body of the soldier. William mouthed, 'What are you doing?' to him and got the whispered reply, "What you taught me. Come on, they are getting away."

The pair chipped away at the rear of the army until finally they got their hands on the man they really wanted to speak to.

Between them, William at the head with a hand over the prisoners mouth, they carried the man away until they judged they were far enough to risk a shout from their captive.

"Well then, John, what do you have to say for yourself in your defence?" William asked curtly.

The portly prisoner, eyes almost popping out of his head, his entire body quivering with fear, spluttered a few garbled unintelligible words. Alan slapped him hard, leaving a clear red handprint on his face. "If you want to live to see another day you better start trying to explain yourself."

John's mind grasped at the merest hint that he might survive this. "They took my family, my wife and children, and said that if I did not help them capture you I would never see them again."

"Who took them?"

"I don't know, some English soldiers."

"They did not tell you who they were?"

"No, I swear. When we went to bring our families as you suggested, Sir William, they were waiting for me."

William was suspicious "Waiting for you? Waiting where?"

"They were in my house."

"Why, man, why did they target you? How did they even know where to look for you? How did they know about you, of all the hundreds of men that were here?"

John's mouth was working but no sound was coming out. Alan slapped him again, drawing blood from his lip. "We can't hear you, how did they know?"

The traitor sat on the ground blubbering like a baby.

Now sobbing so loudly that his words were disjointed he replied, "It's my wife, my lord. She made me do it."

"Your wife? What are you talking about? What kind of a man blames his wife for his failings?"

"When I got home the soldiers were in my house. My wife had gone to them and asked for safe passage back to England."

"Back to England?"

"My wife is English. From Leicester. She wants us to go there."

"And just like that you gave away the lives of your comrades. Hundreds might have died here and you would have gone to England a happy man."

"Please just kill me, please."

"I am not going to kill you," William said and turned away.

John was momentarily relieved, hardly daring to hope that he might be spared. He turned to Alan, his hopes crashing as he realised Sir William had only said that he would not kill him. Alan returned his stare, his face contorted with disgust and then said, "I am not going to kill you either."

In total disbelief John turned back to see that Willian had not left, but returned with his war hammer. "You didn't really think that you were going to walk away from this, did you?" He swung his hammer in an arc over his head and pulverised John's right foot and ankle. The traitor looked down, still in shock and the pain not yet registering, to see that his leg ended in a jellied mess. Blood and bone were splattered over all three of them.

As he finally started to scream Alan told him, "I hope that you are still alive when the animals start to eat you."

Chapter 50: Spring 1304

Outlaw

"We are officially outlaws, William," Simon announced on his return to camp.

"Officially? Have we not always been outlaws to Longshanks?" William asked.

"Aye, but now it seems we are outlaws in our own country. I have just seen the Earl of Lennox. Peace has been declared. All the nobles who had not already done so have submitted to Longshanks. Apparently the Lord of Badenoch, assuming the role of Guardian, has negotiated a good deal for most of Scotland."

"And what exactly is a good deal for most of Scotland?"

"There are to be no reprisals or disinheritance and Scottish law is to be upheld. It seems that Longshanks tires of trying to bend Scotland to his will and accepts that unless he leaves the country to its own devices and accepts pledges of overlordship the country will rise up against him as soon as he goes home."

"I would have hoped that it would rise up anyway, Simon."

"Perhaps, perhaps not. The Red Comyn, as sole Guardian, sees himself as King in all but name. I suspect that he intends to consolidate that position with Longshanks at his back as long as the King of England lives."

"And when the old bastard dies?"

"The expectation is that Comyn will make a bid for the crown and few will oppose him."

"I will oppose him," William stated unnecessarily

"As will I, which is why you and I are specifically excluded from the treaty that they have signed."

"How are we excluded?"

"Longshanks reserves the right to annul the treaty unless we two are handed over to him."

"They all agreed to this?"

"All of them. They all signed."

"What a difference a year makes. The end of winter and the start of spring always seems to usher in a big change. Two years ago I returned to find that you and Comyn had had a huge success and Scotland seemed to be in the ascendency."

"Although I do remember that you warned me of reprisals."

"Sadly we were not up to resisting this round of invasion and a year ago we were being hunted in our own den. Now this."

"You could go back to France, I suppose."

"That was a mistake last time and it would be worse this time. I will continue to fight to remove any English administration wherever I find it until such time Scotland is completely free of English interference." Addressing his old friend he asked, "What about you, Thomas? This may be an appropriate time for you to return home."

"I am hurt that you even suggest such a thing. I will be by your side till the end," Thomas pledged.

"As will I, until death," Simon affirmed and the three men embraced.

Chapter 51: Summer/Autumn 1304

Dwindling resistance

"Sir William, I have served you unquestioningly and love you like a brother," Alan Boyd said seriously. "But I am afraid I am ordered by the Steward to return to Kyle. He claims the war is over."

"William embraced Alan. "I have had no better nor more faithful follower than you. I also love you like a brother and wish you only well. Our lives as outlaws are not for those who have a choice. Go in peace."

When Alan had left, Simon mused, "Once you commanded tens of thousands of men, now we are down to single figures. Are you sure you want to continue?"

"Absolutely! We will do what we can. Take from the occupiers what we can and what we do not need we will give to the poorest. We will keep the flame alive, and when the time comes, as it must, people will know where to come. Who knows what next year will bring?"

"I'll drink to that!" Thomas exclaimed, raising his goblet, and the others joined him.

~~~

After a spring and summer of wandering, the last of the resistance fighters happened upon a small group of English soldiers on the banks of the River Earn. It was during a prolonged spell of dry, hot weather, and the men were relaxing, some lying on the river bank, others swimming and splashing where the river widened into a pool. William, riding in front, held up a hand to stop the group, then dismounted and signalled them all to keep quiet.

"Looks like about a couple of dozen soldiers enjoying a day out," he told his men. William was annoyed that an invading force could be so casual, eating and drinking and having fun as if they did not have a care in the world. As he stood and watched them for a few moment his anger grew, not at the Englishmen, but at all his fellow Scots who had allowed this situation to develop. How any Scotsman with a shred of pride could allow the country to come to such a state that invaders could relax and play carefree like children, baffled him.

After a few minutes, during which time not a single Englishman had even noticed the armed group less than a hundred yards from them, William snapped. The others were waiting for a signal, expecting a plan of action. This time there were no whispered orders, no thought of how best to take advantage of the situation. Withdrawing his two handed sword from the sheath on his back, William let out an animal roar and set off towards the frolicking soldiers at a run. At first the soldiers did not react. It had been so long since there had been any trouble on any of their patrols, or since they had even heard talk of any trouble, that at first they just could not comprehend what was happening. When William had approached to within a few yards of the nearest soldier a panicked voice from the water screamed out:

"Fuck! It's William fucking Wallace."

Realisation that this was an actual attack came too late for the poor soldiers. Before that first cry was completed it was being drowned out by shouts and screams as Wallace swung his big sword down in an arc and cleaved in two a man still rising to his feet. The Scots rampaged past the internal organs spread on the grass, slashing and stabbing while their opponents scrambled to retrieve weapons carelessly cast aside an hour earlier. A single Englishman, butt naked, climbed the far bank and chanced to look back to see the river run red, carrying corpses and body parts towards its meeting with the Tay.

Chapter 52: August 1305

Second Betrayal

When the end came it was, predictably, a betrayal by fellow Scots. After the incident at the River Earn the group had mostly gone their separate ways. It was an unspoken realisation amongst them that they were pissing in the wind. William was awakened early from his slumber by an incessant knocking on the door.

"Sir William, Sir William!" rasped an urgent voice trying to find the balance between a shout and a whisper. "You have to hurry, the English are coming. Sir William, please hurry. Can you hear me, Sir William?"

William removed the crates blocking the door and opened it to a late summer morning. As he squinted against the rising sun and stooped to come out through the small door he asked, "Where are they? How many?" Realising that there were too many blurred figures facing him he reached for his sword as two men holding a large sack jumped from the roof behind him and enveloped him. Even as he struggled to free himself he could feel himself being bound tightly as men circled him, winding rope all around the length of his body. By the time he hit the ground he resembled a giant maggot writhing and struggling to be free of its cocoon.

"There is no point struggling, Sir William. Even if you could get free you are too heavily outnumbered, even for you. Best you come quietly with some dignity."

Recognising the voice William spat out, "And what would you know about dignity, John de Menteith? Are you not selling yours for English gold?"

"You do not understand; the war is over, we lost. You are not taken by the English. You are apprehended on the instructions of the Guardian as a disturber of the peace."

"If John Comyn wants me, why does he not come for me himself? Untie me and I will do you no harm. Take me to Comyn and let him face me man to man. Let God decide which of us is the most deserving in combat."

"I am afraid that will not be possible. I have my instructions and those are to hand you over to Sir John Segrave in fulfilment of the treaty signed between our two countries. You are a barrier to peace, William. If you continue to attack and kill Edward's soldiers he will be forced to retaliate. You will be responsible for the deaths of many of your countrymen. And for what? It seems that it is only your pride, your pig-headedness that makes you continue a war that is long past."

Much as William hated to admit it, and he would not do so out loud, not here and now at any rate, Menteith was right. However many Englishmen he killed there would always be others to take their place, and if they could not stop him they would resort to other ways to bring him to heel. "So it ends," he said wearily "If I am an outlaw in Scotland, take me to Comyn. Let me be judged in Scotland and hanged in Scotland. I would much rather die in Scotland than as public entertainment in London."

Alas, this last wish was in vain. William remained bound for seventeen days as he was jogged and jostled in the back of a cart with stops only to change guards and horses.

Chapter 53: August 1305

A bed for the night

When the sack was finally removed from his head, William looked around and saw with some amazement that he appeared to be in a house. Surely the Tower of London did not have such fine floors and panelling. "Where am I?" was the obvious question, but if he expected an answer he was disappointed.

The door slammed behind him and he heard the sound of bolts sliding home and a key turning in the lock. No point trying the door; there was bound to be a small army of heavily armed men on the other side even if it would open. Looking around more carefully, William could see traces of where pieces of furniture had been hurriedly removed, so that all that was left was a bed and a table with two chairs. How strange! A bed, a real bed. It had been so long since William had lain in such comfort that he really could not remember how long it actually was. The table and chairs was an even greater puzzle. He was undoubtedly a prisoner – his hands were still bound – but what prisoner has such comforts? Some years earlier he had wondered where he was only to realise the real question was not where but when. Now it seemed the real question was not where but why?

William sat down on the bed. It did not have the same level of comfort as a twentieth-century mattress, but it was a fair step up from what he had become accustomed to. 'Oh well, may as well make the best of a bad situation,' he said to himself as he lay back on the bed and adjusted his shackles as best he could. Within a minute he was sound asleep.

Some hours later William was awakened by the sound of metal on metal as the bolts on the room door were drawn back. When the key had turned noisily in the lock the door flew open and several burly guards with weapons at the ready rushed into the room. Unlike any other time in recent years the disturbance did not cause William to spring into action. He remained in repose as he watched the guards form two files either side of the door. For a few minutes nobody moved and nobody made a sound. 'This just gets curiouser and curiouser,' William thought. 'Have I taken another leap into the unexpected? Whatever will happen next?'

The guards sprang stiffly to attention as the sound of heavy footstep got louder and louder until a familiar figure entered the room. "It's okay, you can all leave. There will be no trouble here, will there, Sir William?"

'I must be dreaming!' William thought as he rose from the bed to stand facing his visitor, almost close enough to touch. Just about close enough to grab him by the throat and squeeze the life out of him. His visitor was not a stupid nor a careless man. He had assumed, correctly, that William would be too intrigued to discover why he was there, at least initially, to do any harm.

Still waiting for confirmation from the prisoner that there would be no trouble, the guards jumped when King Edward shouted at them. "I said get out! Now! Go!"

Edward walked over to the small table and sat on a chair. "Will you join me, Sir William? I believe we have much to discuss."

William took hold of the other chair, resisted the brief temptation to lift it and bring it down on the head of his nemesis, and sat down.

"I would have you know that I consider you to be a noble and worthy adversary, one of the finest I have ever faced. The present situation is not how I would have liked things to end between us. However, you must be aware that you have almost as many enemies in Scotland as you do in England, in fact probably more."

"Had I had more friends in Scotland it is more likely that I would have been watching your demise many years ago than being at your mercy as I am now" William replied. It was true and there was a tiny flicker across Edward's face that showed that he knew it to be true.

"Nevertheless, here we are. You were expected at the Tower some hours ago, and I hear that there are already rumours of your daring escape doing the rounds. We can make those rumours true, you and I. It is not too late. I am a generous and forgiving liege and am perfectly willing to come to an arrangement with you even at this late hour."

"And why would you be at all interested in doing a deal with me? Surely you know that I have nothing to bargain with?"

"You sell yourself short, Sir William. You have something that no other has, your integrity. People respect and trust you, even most of your enemies accept that you are a man of outstanding moral fibre.

A man like you would be a huge asset to me. I require nothing more than your acceptance of me as your king. Become my man and I will give you more than you ever dreamed of. The Earl of Carrick and the Lord of Badenoch both harbour hopes of becoming King of Scotland when my time is up. Neither of them deserve it and you can help me make sure neither of them achieve it. I am offering you the opportunity to become my warden for Scotland. You will have the power to govern Scotland as you wish, within some small constraints that I give you. I will make sure that everyone who currently pays homage to me, and that is pretty much everyone, knows and accepts that you are to be my agent in Scotland and that your word is my word."

William was not often lost for words, but for a few seconds he could only gawp, open mouthed. The offer had caught him completely off guard and he had no idea how to answer.

Edward misread the hesitation. "I can see that you are interested," he said and a big shit-eating grin spread across his hateful face, making him seem, William thought, almost human.

William was not at all interested. Bemused, yes. Confused, yes. Cynical, yes. But not interested. His mind was working overtime. Although Longshanks appeared to be in complete control in Scotland, he was obviously not completely sure that he was. Did he know something that William did not? Almost certainly, but what could there be that made that much difference? He was old, of course, and probably did not have too long left before having to give an account of himself to a higher authority. William concluded that probably what was worrying Edward was losing all of his gains as he got older and less able to control things, or just knowing that his son would not be able to hold on to Scotland when he succeeded him as King of England.

"You don't have much faith in Bruce or Comyn then, or your own son for that matter, and you want me to secure your legacy for you?"

Edward's countenance changed dramatically and no matter how hard he might try to deny it, William knew he had hit a nerve. Edward knew that Bruce and Comyn were both waiting in the wings for him to die to make a claim for the Scottish crown. Neither were likely to be reliable allies for his son since both were aware of his shortcomings, as was everyone both sides of the border. Both were likely at best to use him to further their own cause and then renege on any promises made when they were king.

"If you think that some of my countrymen are preparing to displace your family, why on earth would you have any hope of me helping you? More than any man I have ever known I would wish you dead."

"Of course you would. That's one of the things I like about you. You're consistent, and because you are consistent I know that if we have an agreement here tonight you will honour it and I will have no more worries over my Scottish lands because of it. Much as I admire you, your time is well past and we both know as it stands you have no influence any more."

"You speak true, I have just said the same myself."

"For that reason I would not have gone to the trouble and expense of arranging for you to be brought here. It just is not necessary. Of course we have gone to the trouble of whipping up the crowds and making tomorrow a bit of an event, but as I said it is not really my idea.

"Last year when I negotiated the peace with your countrymen the chief among them, as you know, was the Lord of Badenoch. The Lord of Badenoch was very willing to come to mutually beneficial arrangements that would guarantee the peace. It all went quite well, I think, but I could tell that he was planning ahead because of two items he was keen to address.

"The first was that he wanted to make me aware of plans the Earl of Carrick had to make a bid for the throne after my demise. He gave me quite a lot of detail and has led to the aforementioned Earl being closely watched at this point.

"The second thing he was keen on was getting rid of you and your acquaintance Sir Simon Fraser. Although I issued warrants for your capture in my name, you should know that it was at his bidding. Of course he was at pains to assure me that you two are very dangerous and implied that with you both on the loose any peace would be fragile at best. He was quite convincing. Afterwards, though, when I gave it more thought, it became clear to me that some of the schemes he had attributed to Carrick were actually his own. His father was one of the original competitors and with Balliol out of the way his main competition is Carrick and I could see that he was planning to get rid of him, or at least marginalise him enough that he did not get in his way. Once he was king he could more easily deal with him.

"You are a different kind of problem, though. You were consistently loyal to king John despite his shortcomings and it is known that despite that you have a very good relationship with the Earl of Carrick. That is why Badenoch is so keen to be rid of you. Of all people you, Sir William Wallace, are the most likely to get in his way. Having seen first-hand how well you fared against even me, the greatest warrior in all Christendom, he is extremely aware that a civil war in Scotland against you, with or without Carrick, was one he could not be sure to win. Your ability to mobilise the common folk and persuade them to die for you is astonishing. You have no idea how much it costs me to go to war; I wish I had your talents in that area, I really do. Anyway, as I understand it Comyn fears you because you have the ability to make Scotland as ungovernable for him as you did for me at one time.

"So there you have it. Scotland is mine, there is nothing you can do about that. You have given it your best efforts but you have failed. It should concern us both what happens to Scotland in the future. When I first got involved following the tragic accident to my dear friend Alexander, it was because your countrymen feared for the results of a civil war between the Bruces and the Comyns and Balliols. They were right to be worried, and they are right to be even more worried now. A war between these two powerful factions is likely to be long and bloody, and everyone in Scotland will suffer much in the process. What is left at the end of that, assuming that there is eventually a clear-cut winner, will probably not be much worth having. You suspect that I am worried about losing Scotland, but the truth is that I, or my successor, will be able to sit back and watch your former comrades in arms tear each other apart and simply walk in and pick up the pieces afterwards. No, my worry is that the pieces that are left will not be worth picking up; they will be too broken to mend for any useful purpose. You have a chance now to put your country on a sound footing. Fair government in your way with appropriate deference and taxes to me, and everyone gains. Except Carrick and Badenoch, that is, but maybe they will not lose as much as they would fighting each other, so that would effectively make them winners also. As I said, many lives depend on what is decided here tonight."

William could see that his captor had a point. He had not had a chance to put any of his thinking into practice since his return from France. Could this be the opportunity he needed? As de facto head of state, could he reform the system enough that there would be no need for anyone to follow him? He briefly imagined a Scotland where the parliament was extended to include not just the nobles, but representatives from all towns, perhaps even democratically elected officials. It could work but there were major problems.

Firstly, he would need to forcibly remove anyone with a reasonable claim on the crown so that there would be no challenge either now or in the future. That was politics though and not war, and was therefore murder plain and simple. He could kill, had killed more men than he could easily count, in war. To execute rivals in such a manner would only make him like a whole host of undesirables over the centuries, none of whose regimes had lasted.

Secondly, even if he could remove all rivals and implement a new regime, how would it work in practice? With no proper communications it could not be run centrally, but for the same reasons giving too much power locally would only lead to a plethora of mini tyrants up and down the country. It would be next to impossible to stop that happening, and the only way to solve it would be similar to point one. Big tyrant kills little tyrant. It would be rule by fear.

Thirdly, and most importantly, it was likely that Longshanks was planning to use William's capitulation to end any resistance to him in Scotland; whether that was as severe as William's option one or not was a moot point. Long term he was not going to leave Scotland alone whoever was in charge. Taxes and demands for military services overseas would likely be unbearable.

Worst of all was one single fact. If he accepted this offer he was accepting Longshanks as de facto ruler of Scotland. Every day that he was in charge, regardless of how he ruled, was one day nearer his beloved country becoming simply Scotlandshire. One simple yes was all it would take to undermine all of the sacrifices made by thousands of honourable Scotsmen over all those years.

"You make a very generous offer," William replied, "but even if I accepted that you had the authority to make such an offer, which I most definitely do not, I am not of noble blood and have no right to govern Scotland."

"But you were sole Guardian of Scotland for a time, is that not as good as being King? Your word was law."

"You misunderstand the position of Guardian. Although I had some degree of control over what happened to the army, all other decision were taken for the benefit of the country in consultation with the leading barons and prelates. I am afraid you have no right to offer such a position and I have no right to accept such an offer. The people of Scotland are sovereign and only they can decide who rules them."

"Nonsense!" Edward cut in, a bit less amiable now, getting short on patience. "The people of Scotland are not sovereign. They have no say on who they owe their allegiance and pay taxes to, they do as they are told, as does everyone else all over the world. I picked the last King of Scotland and I intend to pick the next one, or rather the next man who will govern for me."

"But things have changed in Scotland," William told him, "and they will never be the same. You cannot see it, and most others cannot either, but history will show that it is so. I have shown them what can be done by ordinary people. The army that came close to defeating you at Falkirk was not led by nobles with knights and men-at-arms making up most of the numbers. It was led by me, a commoner and with few exceptions the whole army was the same. Just ordinary Scotsmen who know how to make a difference. You are right that Comyn should be afraid of an army with me at the head, not because of me, but because that army would only be fighting for what was best for Scotland and no one pursuing their own agenda would be able to stand against it. I led the people, but it was still the people, the common folk of Scotland that made the difference and now that they know they can make that difference they will never be the same again."

Edward shook his head.

"You seem to have lost touch with reality, William. Without a leader the people are nothing. They are already back where they were before you misled them and soon you will only be a distant memory, and not a good one for most of those who have suffered because of you. I have offered you a chance to make amends to them, to help them to a better way of life in my peace, but you throw it back in my face with mad ramblings. It's a pity, a great pity. You could have been somebody that history would remember with fondness. Now you will just die as an outlaw and a traitor and soon you will be forgotten.

"I bid you adieu, Sir William. May God forgive you for your folly"

Chapter 54: August 23rd 1305

Execution

When they came for William the following morning he was well rested and ready to face the day, Despite the circumstances,and he was determined to go out with as much dignity as he could muster. Part of him was looking forward to the release. Since his return to Scotland so much had been disappointing. It seemed to him that all of his earlier efforts had been in vain. All those good men dead for nothing. He had only delayed the inevitable. The only comforts had been the brief times snatched with Malcolm and the children. He had a boy and a girl now. William wondered how they were, whether they might grow up safer without him.

Before he could become too maudlin the door flew open and a troop of guards rushed in, weapons at the ready. He briefly considered putting up a fight. Would any of his captors overreact even though he was shackled hand and foot? Probably not. No point going out to face his public battered and bruised. Better to have both eyes open and be able to look his detractors in the eye. With a bit of luck the end would be swift, although he doubted it. 'Hell hath no fury like a lunatic scorned,' he thought.

William was taken through the streets of London to Westminster Hall, at that time a large space with two rows of huge pillars, making it almost seem like it was three separate halls. The journey was not at all pleasant; he was chained in the back of a small cart and the streets were lined by angry citizens who shouted, screamed and threw all sort of crap at him, literally. He stood as straight as he could in the circumstances and attempted to keep his composure, looking back at the crowd and letting them see that he was not intimidated by them or anyone. For the journey in to Westminster his escort made an attempt to keep the crowds at bay and nobody came close enough to do any damage, so that he arrived relatively unscathed.

William was led through a door at the back of the hall so that he had to walk between everyone assembled for the event. It seemed that everyone who was anyone was there and he recognised quite a few faces. Keeping his composure he smiled and greeted those people he recognised, but none of them responded with other than the same kind of verbal abuse that the crowd outside had given him. At least nobody in there was throwing actual shit. At the far end of the room sat a row of men whom William assumed to be the judge and jury. No sign of their King, though; could it be that he was creating an alibi for the previous night by claiming to be out of town? John Segrave was the only one on the bench that William recognised; it had been he who had been in overall charge of William's journey south. Their paths had seemed to cross very frequently in those last few months. William nodded politely to Segrave who nodded back, the only act of courtesy he received from anyone that day.

As William was brought to a halt a few feet in front of the bench someone stood up and, after urging the gathered dignitaries to be quiet, read out the charges.

"William Wallace, you are charged with treason, murder, rape, theft, sacrilege and any number of other offences that would take too long to read out. Treason in that you have defied the will of our anointed King Edward, resisted and removed and even killed his appointed officials, including the Sheriff of Lanark. Further that you have led and encouraged armies to raid into England, killing everyone you came across, including women and children, and laying waste to buildings. That you killed priests and defiled churches. That you allowed and encouraged those in your charge to engage in the foulest of behaviour towards innocent subjects of King Edward. That you conspired with a foreigner power to overthrow our King, namely the King of France."

It was quite a long list and included many things that William had done, but also a great many that he had not. To William it seemed a bit like hearing someone read a sensationalised account from a modern tabloid newspaper: you knew that there was some truth in there somewhere but you were not quite sure what the real truth was. Although in this case William did know what the real truth was. He knew because he was there, to paraphrase one of his favourite Welshmen. When the charges were complete he responded to them.

"My lords, ladies and gentlemen," William mocked, turning full circle and bowing to the audience. "That is quite an impressive list and probably just too much for one man to have achieved in such a short space of time. However, I am flattered that you consider me capable of all of this. Of the great atrocities you accuse me of, crimes against civilians, women, children and clergy I deny completely. I do note, however, that I see gathered here many men who have committed the 'crimes' I am accused of in the name of their King, who is also guilty of those crimes." At this point howls of derision arose and from the bulk of the hall so that he could barely be heard. He continued, speaking directly to the bench in front of him. "Of the other crimes you accuse me off, the ones that I actually did do, I confess to acting as best I could to protect my country from a foreign invasion and as such have committed no crime. As to your main charge of treason against the King of England, your king himself is aware that at no time have I, either in person, in words or acts or by proxy through any other individual neither accepted nor recognised your King Edward as my monarch nor as having any authority whatsoever in Scotland. I am a Scotsman, I was born a Scotsman and will die here today a Scotsman and have at no time gone against the interests of the true King of Scots whom I recognise to be John Balliol."

When the cacophony had died down to a reasonable level the dignitary with the scroll continued. "William Wallace, you are found guilty of all of the crimes alleged against you and are sentenced to be taken from here to the Tower of London where you will be readied and taken to your place of execution. There you will be hung by the neck until you are almost dead, then taken down and emasculated and eviscerated before being beheaded. When you are dead your head will be put on public display as a warning to all other traitors and your body parts sent to all corners of the kingdom to serve as the same warning in those parts."

The ride back to the Tower of London was pretty much the same as the ride in to Westminster. Big crowds lined the streets, hurling abuse, stones, rotten fruit, even excrement. This time, though, there was no attempt by his entourage to stop anyone from climbing onto the cart and assaulting William. All of that specialist training, counter terrorism, interrogation techniques came into play as William retreated into the safe places in his mind and tried to separate himself from the pain, which he knew was soon going to get exponentially worse.

William was temporarily drawn back to reality when a face he knew like his own appeared in front of him. "Forgive me, my friend, I was not there in your time of need. I followed as soon as I heard, but I was unable to catch up with you." Thomas's face showed intense anguish and William raised his chained hands towards him. Thomas took William's hands and kissed them, tears falling from his eyes.

"You should not have come, Thomas. They will kill you also."

"I had to try. You would have done the same for me." William could not argue for it was true.

"Please do not stay and risk capture. Go to Carrick. Warn him that Badenoch has betrayed us. He is trying to use Longshanks to get rid of his enemies. Robert is not safe. Simon is not safe. You are not safe. Please go. Look after my family for me."

"I promise." Thomas said as he dropped down from the cart and melted into the crowd.

~~~

When they reached the tower William was thrown roughly into a small empty cell. There was no offer of food, no last meal, not even a drink of water. The only comfort was a visit from a priest to hear his confession and to administer the last rites. The very nervous priest could at first barely speak when he entered; he was obviously aware of the grisly stories about William, especially the ones about torturing and killing holy men.

"You have nothing to fear from me, Father. Disregard all you have heard about me, for I have never done other than defend the church and those who serve her."

Soon after the priest left William was on the move again. It occurred to him that there could have been no other reason to take him via the Tower than to increase the public spectacle and allow more people to see the monster before it was put down.

At Smithfield the crowd cheered with delight as the huge, naked figure of William Wallace was hoisted up by the noose around his neck. For William this was the easy part. Although not at all pleasant he was in his safe room in his mind, focussed on his breathing as he had been trained to do centuries away. Only he was aware that this was not the first time he had been choked part way to death, and most of the other times had been by his own comrades.

After a few minutes, and before he was in serious danger of dying, the rope was cut and he crashed the few feet into the boards of the platform which had been erected specifically for this event. Ropes were tied around his wrists and ankles and he was stretched out between two posts.

"Hanging is much too good for this devil!" the executioner yelled to the crowd, who responded with cheers. "Much too quick, we all want to enjoy this death don't we?" This raised even more whoops and cheers and whistles from those assembled.

When the executioner brandished a gleaming dagger the crowd became even more excited. "Skin him alive", "Cut his heart out" "Cut off his tongue and his ears, gouge out his eyes" were among the requests. The executioner walked over beside his victim, who was somewhat ironically stretched out almost to the shape of a saltire, and teased the crowd. Placing his knife at various places on William's body he asked, "Here?" next to his eye, and again at his throat, his heart and on down until the point of his blade drew blood from Williams groin. "Yes, here I think!" he shouted as he took his prisoners genitals in his hand and sliced them completely off. William had known what was coming and had tried to steel himself. There is only so much any man can bear though and as the pain tore through his brain and the blood began to spurt from the gaping hole between his legs William opened his mouth and yelped in pain. The executioner held the bleeding cock and balls up and then turned and to the crowds delight rammed them into William's mouth.

It was only a matter of time now before William either bled out or choked, his throat already badly damaged from the hanging. Being experienced in these things the executioner did not want lose his man before he had finished so without too much showboating he took his dagger and with a flourish plunged it into William's side and drew it across his abdomen, allowing intestines and other organs to fall out as he cut. Before his pounding heart failed William had the sensation of floating and tried to look up to where he felt rather than saw a brilliant white light.

The executioner saw William raise his head slightly and then it dropped almost to his chest. The crowd saw it too and many expressed disappointment that the show was over. For those that remained watching the reward was to see William's corpse cut down and beheaded. Perhaps they were just making sure. After that an oversized axe was brought into play to hack the body roughly in to four pieces for distribution throughout the country while the head was placed on a spike for display at the Tower.

Part IX

21st Century

Chapter 55: August 2005

Twenty-first century boy

"Get the doctor, quickly, he is convulsing!" the ward sister shouted to the young nurse.

Five minutes later the doctor ambled in, chiding the nursing staff as he came. "You know there is a DNR on this man. I..." Words failed him as he looked at William sitting up in bed, sipping a glass of water that a nurse was holding to his lips. William, a haunted expression on his face, looked at the doctor, whose mouth was opening and closing soundlessly while his eyes attempted to bulge clean out of their sockets. Two men questioning their sanity, unsure of reality.

After a few moments Doctor Abernethy regained his composure enough to instruct a nurse, "Better call Alan," before crossing to the bedside to carry out an examination.

~~~

"Billy! I knew you would come back, I always knew it," Alan said through tears as he rushed to embrace his son, still propped up but unmoving. "How are you? Are you sore? Can you move?" and to the nurse, when he realised he was not getting any answers, "Is he aware? Can he hear me? Does he recognise me? Is his brain okay?"

"We don't know yet," Abernethy replied from behind him, having followed Alan in. "His vitals are within the normal range, if a little weak. I've got more tests lined up for him, but I must caution you that he will probably never be his old self again. This might be as good as it gets."

Alan turned briefly from gazing at his wee boy's face to tell the doctor, "I told you he would be back. He'll come all the way back." He turned back to his son in time to see his mouth attempt to work, but no sound came out. Helping his son lift his head forward, Alan held the water to his lips and William this time was able to drink properly on his own. Once more he tried to speak and this time a rasp came out, the sound of sandpaper on cork.

"Take your time, Billy, you've got all the time in the world. Have some more water." Once more Alan held the glass up while William drank.

"Malc." This first word brought an old hurt back for Alan. He looked at the doctor with his eyebrows raised in a question.

"Best just to tell him, he will need to know sometime."

"Billy, I'm sorry," Alan told his son, tears welling once more in his eyes "Your brother is dead. Killed in that tragic accident that put you here."

"No. Malc is fine. You are a grandad." The voice was getting stronger and there was no mistaking what he had said. Once more Alan looked to the doctor for a lead. The doctor just shrugged and shook his head.

"William, I am Doctor Abernethy. You have been asleep for quite a long time. Do you know why you are here? Do you remember the accident?"

"No accident. They tried to kill me."

Abernethy spoke to Alan again. "Don't let yourself get too upset by anything he says. We won't know for a while just how well he has recovered, and we may never know what has happened to his mind. Just enjoy having him back at all."

"I'm hungry." This declaration broke the spell and the room, which had been filling up as news of the miracle spread, erupted in laughter and excited chatter. Two nurses raced off to see what they could fetch.

"Bring some soup," the doctor called after them.

William was now smiling, his thin face lighting up. "Dad, you're looking great!"

"Never better, son, never better." In fact where such a tragedy could have turned a man to drink, Alan had gone in the opposite direction. A functioning alcoholic since his wife had died, he had given up the drink after the accident and bought himself a car to avoid the three bus journeys. It was the first he had owned in years. He could not have done it for himself, but it was easy to do for his son when he needed him.

"Your dad has been here every day for over nine years talking to you, reading to you and even giving you physio. If you find you can move at all, that is probably down to your father"

William lifted a bony hand to his father's face, smiled a big cheesy grin and said, "Thanks, Dad, you're the man."

The nurse returned with a bowl of soup and grudgingly let Alan take it from her to feed his son himself. "Careful!" she cautioned him. "It might be too warm."

Alan blew on the spoonful of soup and held it to William's lips. William sipped gently, decided it was okay and leaned forward to take the whole spoonful. "Lentil, my favourite."

The room broke into spontaneous applause. He winked at the nurse who had brought the soup as he swallowed another mouthful. "If you think that was good, wait until they bring me a pie." He grinned.

"Okay, give the man room to eat," Doctor Abernethy ordered, shooing the gawping onlookers out of the cramped room. Turning to the ward staff he added, "Make sure there are no unauthorised visitors, this is not a circus show. From now on nobody comes in here without my say-so." There had to be a book in this, no point giving unrestricted access to anyone else, particularly the press.

William had finished his soup and seemed energised. He lifted his hands and examined his bony fingers and skinny arms. Lifting the blanket to see his emaciated body and legs he quipped, "Looks like most of me has already left."

"Don't worry, young man, you have been asleep a long time and your body has atrophied. However, you seem to be in remarkably good shape mentally. Give it a few weeks. We will feed you up, plenty of physio, we'll get you back up and running, all being well."

'The sooner the better,' William thought. He was reminded of a Steven Segal film he had seen before his adventure. In the movie *Hard To Kill* the Segal character had woken up from a coma and almost immediately had been able to fight off assassins sent to finish him off. Life was not imitating art here. If anyone came for him now he was dead, pure and simple. The big questions that took the edge of his joyous return were: Who had tried to kill him? Did they still want him dead?

Chapter 56: July 2006

Fun in the sun

Kenny jumped, spilling his glass of San Miguel, when a big hand clasped his shoulder and a deep voice boomed, "Tig. You're het!"

Turning round slowly, he squinted against the midday sun as he looked up at the big fella who had disturbed his peace as he relaxed at The Caribe bar near his home in Montemar Costa. "Fuck me! Wee Wullie Wallace! You're not dead!"

William spread his arms, looked himself up and down, and replied, "Alive and kicking, old pal. How's it going?"

"Apart from the sudden heart attack, pretty good. You look a hell of a lot better than the last time I saw you. They said you wouldn't make it."

"They lied." William laughed. "You should keep in touch with folks more, I've been back for months now."

"I've burned too many bridges, Wull. I cannot go back."

"Pish talk. Alan and Walter asked me to give you their best. They would love to see you. In fact, they said they want to come visit you, but don't know where you live. Costa del Sol they said, but he's moved since he went there."

"Really? I do miss the boys. Sorry about Malcolm, by the way. Your big brother was the best of a good bunch."

"Aye, thanks. Actually the reason I tracked you down is because I need to talk to somebody about it all, and you are the only person I know that might hear me out."

"Very mysterious. Better get some beers in then, this sounds intriguing."

"Thanks, I'll have whatever you're drinking, but can we talk later, somewhere private?"

"Of course, come back to my place, I'll make you some dinner."

"You can cook?"

"Oh aye, needs must and all that."

~~~

Later, after they had eaten a passable chilli con carne that Kenny had cooked from scratch, William became serious and said to his host, "Listen, Kenny, you were always the guy that could think outside the box, properly open-minded, so to speak."

"That's only because the other guys were a bit narrow-minded. Not their faults, it's how they were brought up."

"You were brought up much the same as the rest of us."

"No really. My dad was a bit of a nutter. Brilliant with some things, completely off the wall with others. He once insisted he was the centre of the universe?"

"Wow! Really?"

"No shit. For such a clever man he had some weird and wonderful ideas."

"Talking about weird and wonderful, I need to tell you about my last ten years."

"You have been in a coma, what's to tell?"

"Last year was not the first time that I woke up. Right after the crash I woke up in the thirteenth century."

"Fuck off! That is not possible. You must have been dreaming," Kenny insisted dismissively.

"Come on, Kenny, hear me out. You are supposed to be open-minded, are you not?"

"There is a limit, Wull."

"Do you think so? Let me ask you something, what do you know about William Wallace, the Braveheart guy?"

"I remember seeing the film and believing it at first. I also remember wondering why I had never heard of the guy before. In fact, it got me interested in Scottish history, it's a fucking disgrace what we were not told at school."

"Agreed, but hear this. I never saw Braveheart when it first came out, because it did not exist then."

"What? You've lost me, how could it come out if it did not exist?"

"You remember that Malcolm and some other teachers threw a birthday party for me before the 'accident'?"

"Aye, and I'm still pissed off that I wasn't invited."

"Not my fault. It was supposed to be a surprise and it was a school thing. Anyway, the point is that they did a mediaeval thing and I was supposed to be a minor Scottish historical figure with the same name, William Wallace."

"Hold on, William Wallace is no minor figure, a lot of people would say that he is the greatest Scot ever."

"Correct. Now, that is. At the time of the party he was little known, I assure you."

"Wait, wait, wait! You said yourself that Braveheart was already out. You are contradicting yourself."

"No, forget what you think you know and listen to me. Please listen, you are the only person I can talk to about this, apart from a shrink I suppose, who would not believe me. I am telling you that I went back in time, Malcolm as well, and became the Braveheart guy. The movie had not been made at the time I went back, and after I returned I saw it in the hospital. I could hardly believe it, and people were laughing and joking because of the name, little realising that I knew the truth behind the rubbish they were watching."

"Are you trying to tell me that you changed history?"

"Aye, that is exactly what I am saying. Time is not linear, I think that it is somehow concurrent, if you see what I mean."

"Concurrent? You mean everything is happening at the same time?"

"Kind of. Wait a minute." William got up and went to the kitchen, returning with a basin of water. Sitting it down between them he continued, "Imagine that this is kind of life, the universe and everything."

"Hmm." Kenny was far from convinced.

"Just try to imagine it. This is everything in time, it is all connected and if everything goes according to plan it is all nice and peaceful just like the water there."

"Okay, that is what I like, a peaceful life."

"Now, imagine something happens to disturb the status quo." William dipped a finger into the water. "You see what happens?"

"Ripples. You disturb the peace and you get ripples."

"Exactly. Now imagine that as time and space. Something disturbs the natural order of things and it affects everything around it. Different events have different effects, so that you can get tiny wee ripples that hardly affect anything right up to tidal waves that have huge effects for a long time."

"But the ripples go in all directions, even backwards."

"They do. Now this model is only for demonstration purposes, so that in the actual universe the ripples go in all direction, like an explosion, forwards backwards, up, down, sideways, any and all directions. There are probably all sorts of forces at play that affect how far and how strongly things are affected so that the ripples are not consistent. Anyway, here is what I think happened with me and Malcolm." William put a match in the water and waited for the water to calm again. Then he picked the match up and dropped it back at the other side of the bowl.

"Do you see how there are ripples where I picked up the match and where I dropped it?"

"I do."

"Depending on how big an event it is the ripples are stronger or weaker. Where I picked up the ripples are quite gentle and do not travel very far. Where I dropped the match they are stronger and reach further."

"You don't think that the two events would be equal?"

"Probably not, from my own experience. The effect on the modern world was not too great on a global scale. There would be a lot of short-term fallout that would settle down as people adjusted and even forgot. Back in the past the effect was much greater and affected events not just locally, but nationally and even internationally."

"So what about the backward ripples?"

"Well, I cannot say for the mediaeval part, but in the modern world Braveheart kind of proves my point."

"Braveheart? How?"

"Had Braveheart been about when the event occurred I would have known. Malcolm would have known. George Clark, the history teacher, would certainly have known. It did not exist. When I came back not only did it exist, but it had been made and released before the event that picked Malcolm and I up from 1996 and dropped us in 1296."

Kenny thought for a while. William, appreciating that there was a lot to think about – he had had almost ten years to figure this out – left him to his thoughts. Eventually Kenny restarted the conversation.

"Okay, so I think I can see what you are getting at. I think I am going to call your event a time tsunami."

"Time tsunami, I like that." William smiled, happy that Kenny was taking it seriously.

"Assuming that you are correct and that everything is connected in time and space, how did you get from one time to another? Are you suggesting that the crash somehow propelled you through some kind of wormhole or something?"

"That is a good question. The honest answer is, I just don't know. I do have a theory, though."

"Only a theory? You seem so sure about the rest of it," Kenny joked.

"Don't be facetious, it doesn't suit you. I am more confident about what you call the tsunami because I have lived it. I have seen first-hand the changes that were made."

"Wait, you mentioned Braveheart, but how do you know there were changes in the past?"

"Braveheart is still the answer. The historical Wallace went from a minor figure to a national leader and achieved legendary status."

"I see, so there are changes that you are sure about, but there is no evidence for anyone else."

"That is the nature of the beast."

"Let's have your theory, then."

"It is only a theory, of course, but it has caused me to become more religious since it first occurred to me."

"You think God did this to you?"

"Maybe, maybe not. But I do think that a higher power is at work. I remember you used to like computer games, and I see you still do." William pointed out the covers sitting on one of the shelves. "So you will know that in some of these games it is possible to work through a game, even right to the end in some cases, and not be able to complete a game or a level because you have missed some important piece of information or artefact."

"Aye, that can be bloody annoying."

"Well, imagine for a minute that life on earth is a game, or an interconnected series of games. Imagine that whoever is running or playing the game gets so far and finds they cannot progress because something is missing. What do they do?"

"Restore from a saved version or restart the game."

"Of course. In one of our man-made games, yes. Now imagine a game, or games, so sophisticated that they run continuously, concurrently and contiguously."

"Everything at the same time?"

"That's right. So that not only can a character move items about in the game, the controller can move characters about. Not just in their own time and space, but from one time and space to another."

"So you think that you are an important character in this game of life. So important that you are moved about to save the game when and where needed. Is that what you are saying? Lara Croft is really a guy!"

"Yes and no. I think that there is a reason why both Malc and I were sent back."

"Malky, aye, I had nearly forgotten about him. What is his part in all of this?"

"DNA. All the time we were back I had a compulsion to protect him. Something was making me keep him out of harm's way. He was eager to fight and felt really bad about being excluded, but I just kept coming up with reasons for him not to participate. Malc was the main reason I tried to keep all the action away from Ayrshire. So my theory is that certain traits and even memories, actual knowledge are passed down through DNA to unconsciously influence the twentieth-century me."

"If that is the case, then why from Malcolm? Why not from you?"

"I've considered that too, and while I cannot rule out having left offspring, I don't think so. When we first arrived back it was like a rerun of the old gang. Malc and me, Alan and Walter."

"And me?"

"No, you were missing, it was not a complete copy. Some people were there, others not. You remember Mary Barbour?"

"Mary from the dairy? Was she there."

"Not only there, Malc married her. She is one of my ancestors. Anyway, getting back to the thread, Alan and Walter recognised us as two brothers they used to know that had gone away. I think that originally, say version 1 of the game of whatever, one of the brothers died and the other went on to become my nth times great grandfather. Restoring the game allowed Malcolm to reprise the ancestor role while I was needed for knowledge gained hundreds of years later."

"But you said when you went back that you were aware of a historical you."

"Yes, but who knows how many iterations there have been? I was not the first, but probably not even the second or third."

"I think I may be getting it. Do you think that the original Wallace was supposed to do great things but managed to get himself killed too young?"

"I suppose that is what I am saying, aye. This is why I knew you were the right man to talk to about this. What else do you get."

"Well, if you are right about the DNA thing, and I am not sure at all about inherited memories, then maybe it needed the right input. Not just the paternal y-DNA, but the right maternal line to allow the right mix of genes," Kenny suggested.

"Aye, we're both struggling a bit with the technical aspects, but I think your idea is good. As far as the unknown aspects are concerned, after all this time scientists don't know what most of the human brain is for. Same with DNA, only a small percentage has been identified. It has to be possible that more things than just eye and hair colour are passed on."

"I can't deny that. I will certainly take more of an interest in such things from now on."

Chapter 57: August 2006

Revenge is sweet

"You killed my brother. A nicer man you could not meet. Never hurt a soul his entire life, and you killed him. I need to know who gave the order."

"I swear to you, it wasn't me!" Gerry Clark pleaded as the incoming tide reached the spot where he was buried, vertically, in the sand with only his neck and head protruding.

William was hunkered down in front of him, the warm Mediterranean water already seeping into his boots. "We have already been over this. You have always been a cunt that nobody liked. Always too eager to please the man. It was not hard to get old comrades to talk because none of them were ever your friend. It says a lot about a man that he can live so long and not have a single real friend."

"They are all lying. It wasn't me. You said yourself nobody liked me. They are covering for each other and making me the scapegoat."

"I accept that is possible, and I wouldn't blame them if they did. Nevertheless, I have looked into their eyes and I do believe them. You, on the other hand, ran as soon as you saw me. That can only be a guilty conscience. Why else would you run?"

Water was now reaching almost to Gerry's mouth; time was short. "Okay, okay, I did it. But I was only following orders. I'm sorry about your brother, I really am, but he was collateral damage. Shit happens. We have all been there. You have been there. We are all the same, brothers."

"No, Gerry, we are not all the same. The rest of us took care to minimise collateral damage. We all tried to avoid hurting anyone that was not a direct target. You, though, you always enjoyed killing for the sake of it. The more the merrier. In Northern Ireland when the rest of us were taking out individuals with knives and sniper rifles, you were planting bombs and shit. Didn't even get your target most of the time."

"Ah, but I always got my man in the end. The brass didn't mind a few extra Micks getting offed in the process. It was easy for them to blame my bombings on the Irish themselves."

"It will soon be too late for you. You must realise by now that I really am not digging you out of there unless you tell me who gave the order."

"Oh, for fucks sake! You know who gave the order. Now get me out of here."

That was all the confirmation William needed. It was more than he had expected. He stood up, picked up the spade and threw it on the beach.

"Where are you doing? Wallace! You promised that if I talked you would let me go."

William sat down in the surf and bent so that his nose was almost touching Clark "I lied," he said simply as the first wave of salty water reached nose level. The condemned man, eyes bulging, dared not even scream as he held on to life, praying that his last gasp of air would last long enough for the tide to turn.

~~~

When the tide had gone out William recovered his spade and dug down to the drowned man's shoulders. Taking his dagger he removed the head and scraped the sand back over the stump. Placing the head in a bag already partially filled with rocks he waded out until he was waist deep and then threw the bag as far out as he could. He had been careful to choose a secluded beach as far as possible from any kind of traffic. Even so, he knew that the murder would be discovered eventually. No matter, he would finish his mission tonight. Beyond that he had no plans.

~~~

"I need your help, Kenny." William had changed and driven the couple of hours back to Torremolinos.

"Sure, anything. What do you need?"

"I won't lie to you, this is dangerous. If I could do it any other way I would."

"Dangerous, how dangerous?"

"I think you will be okay, I just need you to drive me somewhere and then leave."

"That is dangerous how?"

"I know who killed Malcolm. I am going to even the score."

"Shit, Wull, why don't you just go to the police?"

"I can't. There are some things I haven't told you. You remember I was in the army?"

"Aye, that was years ago. Before you were a teacher."

"Right. Well, I wasn't just army, I was Special Forces."

"You mean like James Bond or something?"

"Not quite, but I was doing black ops, government work."

"What has that got to do with Malcolm? It was an accident, wasn't it?"

"It was supposed to be an assassination. Malcolm was collateral damage."

"Some baddy that you sorted out looking for revenge?"

"Actually, and this is the problem, it was the British government."

"No way! Why?"

"It's a long story. All being well I will fill you in later. Right now there isn't time. The actual assassin is dead. Now I need to get to the man who gave the order before he realises."

"Wullie, you are scaring me. I can't go about shooting people. For fuck's sake, I can't even fight."

"You don't need to get involved. You really do just need to drive me and drop me off."

"That's all? Where is the danger?"

"Just make sure no one gets a good look at you and you should be okay. You will be long gone before anyone has reason to notice you."

"Should be okay?" Kenny was already feeling nauseous and the colour had drained completely from his face. He was so pale he looked as if he had never left Ayrshire.

"Here, take this." William offered his friend a pill.

"What is it?"

"More Dutch courage than a litre of Johnnie Walkers."

Kenny made no move to take the pill. Tears were beginning to spill from his eyes.

"This is for Malcolm, trust me." William urged him.

~~~

In the early hours of the next morning an elderly gentleman escorted a scantily clad young person from the Bunny Lane drag club in Arroyo De La Miel. He opened the back door of the waiting taxi for his date then slid in after. He spoke to the driver in fluent Spanish: "Have you taken me home before?"

"No, sir."

"Okay, head out towards Coin, I will tell you when to turn off."

The driver put the taxi in gear and set off. In the back seat the couple were getting to know each other."

~~~

Extracting himself from the passionate embrace of his hired friend the elderly gentleman instructed, "See the big iron gates just up there on the right? Turn in and wait for the gates to open. When they do, follow the drive past the villa to the smaller outbuilding. We will get out there."

"As you wish, sir," the driver replied and turned as directed towards the huge metal gates. As the taxi slowed to a stop a smaller gate at the right opened and a burly man holding a machine gun walked towards the vehicle. Before he reached it the back window slid down and a voice from the back said crisply, "It's okay, Michael, it's only me."

"Good evening, sir," came the clipped reply and the guard turned and retraced his steps. Moments later the gates swung slowly and silently inwards. When they were wide enough the taxi advanced carefully up the drive to the pool house and stopped.

"No need to get out. Take this, thank you," the passenger said as he generously tossed a one hundred euro note into the driver's lap."

When the pair had gone into the pool house the taxi turned and drove back towards the gate, stopping as soon as the building disappeared from the rear view mirror, and before coming into sight of the main house. Pressing the button on the key fob, the driver released the boot catch and William Wallace climbed out of the car.

He leaned towards the partially open driver's window and whispered, "Thanks, Kenny, you did great. Did anyone get a good look at you?"

"No, nobody bothered with me."

"Good. The gate should have stayed open for you. Just drive

casually straight out. Try not to stop, but don't rush and draw attention to yourself. Leave the car where we picked it up. It'll be fine."

And with that William faded into the bushes and was gone.

~~~

William waited close to the pool house while his target satisfied his carnal urges. Having come this far he was confident that he would not be stopped before he could complete his task. All being well he would only need to kill one person. If things went wrong and he had to kill more, so be it. As Gerry had said, collateral damage happened.

When he first tracked Sir Peter down it was at the very club he had been to that night. After some discreet enquiries he had established that he was a regular who came in every Thursday and always left with a date. Thursday was amateur night, a kind of open mike night where wannabe performers could strut their stuff and hope to secure employment either at Bunny's or at one of the many other smaller clubs who would check in there from time to time on a Thursday. Sir Peter would hire whichever one of the performers ticked enough boxes that night for a private show. The boys were there to make money, and although what Sir Peter required was not standard entertainment, he did pay well over the going rate.

Finally, hours later, it was starting to get light, another taxi arrived to take the guest home. William waited, pistol at the ready in case there was any change in routine and he had to strike early. That would be messy, but as long as Sir Peter died he would leave all other lives in God's hands – including his own.

About five minutes after the taxi had left, Sir Peter emerged naked and walked to the pool. William was surprised to see that the old man had been taking care of himself. Although he must have been roughly the same age as William's father, his body looked like that of a much younger man. Sir Peter slipped into the water, perhaps to clean away his sins, William thought, and breast-stroked to the far end. William emerged from the shadows and slipped inside the building. Sir Peter was on his fourth length when he noticed a figure standing at the edge of the pool. He began to tread water as he took in the interloper and peed a little when he recognised him. William noticed the stain in the water and laughed despite himself.

"I see you are pleased to see me, Sir Peter."

"William, you took me by surprise, that is all. I am indeed pleased to see you. You should have phoned ahead, though. Made an appointment."

"Yes, you would have liked that, wouldn't you? I'm sure there would have been a very nice reception committee waiting for me. No, let's not waste time beating about the bush. You know why I am here and it is not to compliment you on your fitness, although I admit I am impressed. You've done pretty good for a desk jockey."

"William, don't be like that. I know we have had our differences, but that was a long time ago. The world has moved on. You should move on too."

"My brother has not moved anywhere except to the cemetery. Do not approach the edge, I do not want to shoot you," William warned as he raised his pistol.

Sir Peter noticed the silencer. Once more treading water he asked, "What is to stop me shouting for help?"

"You know better than I that no one is close enough to hear you; that is why you do your business here and not at the house. You think you are being discreet. But go ahead, shout for all you are worth. You may be lucky and someone will come, but then I will have to shoot you."

"You always were thorough, William, very meticulous. It is good to see that you have not lost your touch. I can still use a good man like you. Privately, you understand, not government work. The pay is much better, as are the perks."

"Do you really think that you can buy me?"

"Why not? Every man has his price, after all. Look, I really am terribly sorry about your brother. I assure you that he was not supposed to get hurt. He was collateral, field agent's decision. Totally out of my hands."

That may well have been true, but it cut no ice with William. "Field agent? Who was it? Give me a name and I might spare you."

"Come on, William, you know I can't tell you that. Not even with a gun pointed at my head."

"I know, I just wondered how much you wanted to save your own skin. Don't expect Gerry to come to your rescue, though. He lost his head somewhat in all his excitement at seeing me again."

"Ah! I should have known. So what do you want with me then? You have your revenge."

"Gerry was only following orders. Your orders. I want to know why. I was out, a school teacher, no threat to anyone. Why did you order me taken out?"

"You don't know? Really? I thought you had all the answers." Sir Peter chuckled despite the situation.

"Are you going to tell me or do I just shoot you?"

"If I tell you, you will shoot me anyway. Maybe I want to die knowing that you are unfulfilled."

"I give you my word, I will not shoot you if you tell me what I want to know."

"I'm not sure that I believe you, but what the hell, it is worth a gamble." Sir Peter was trying to work out what he could get away with. Even looking down a gun barrel, he could not shake his lifelong dedication to the system. "Donald didn't tell you?"

"How is Donald involved in all of this?"

"Was, William, was. Your old friend had an unfortunate climbing accident just after your unfortunate experience. Our information was that Donald had confided in you about the assassination of Willie MacRae when he got hold of a copy of the McCrone report. We thought you were about to share that with the activist at your school."

"My school was involved?" William was clearly surprised, shocked even.

"You really didn't know, old boy? Well, that is a pity. All of this could have been avoided. Pretty pointless all round, as it turns out."

"What do you mean by that?"

"The McCrone report that we had been trying so hard to suppress since the mid-seventies is now available on the internet. Anyone can read it. Hasn't made a blind bit of difference. The majority of Scots still believe the old too wee, too poor, too stupid line we have been feeding them since forever. At least it proves the too stupid part. But in the nineties things looked different. We had to play it safe."

"Donald told me about McRae and McCrone. Events ten and twenty years before my botched assassination. Why are you ignoring the obvious motive for getting rid of us?"

"I don't understand, old boy." Sir Peter was bluffing: William could tell that he had been counting on Donald not having told him after all.

"Supplying kids to perverts from children's homes. Here you are living it up in Spain, where the age of consent is still only thirteen, and only raised to that in 1999. You with your penchant for young boys."

"Ah! Wasn't sure if you were interested in that."

"Seriously? You don't think that anyone and everyone would be interested in that degeneracy?"

"Look, William, I know what was in those papers. Don't get me wrong, I despise it as much as you do."

"You cannot be serious!"

"I am serious. I like young men, yes. But young men are not still boys. I do not dabble with really young boys, not at all. It goes on, and I regret it. I really do."

"You expect me to believe that? What about the people that do? You know who they are yet you allow them to continue. You condone it."

"No, not at all. In the real world things like that happen and powerful men are involved. You cannot stop them. I cannot stop them. More powerful men than I have been terminated for just asking questions."

"If you want to live, the price is evidence. You give it to me and I'll take my chances over releasing it."

"Now you really are being naïve. You know this goes right to the top. This is not about individuals, it is about the entire system."

"That's what I thought." William sighed as he unscrewed the silencer from his revolver and stuck it in his pocket before holstering the gun. He never thought for a minute that he would get anything from Sir Peter, but he had to try.

More shocked than relieved Sir Peter said, "You were not lying. You really are not going to shoot me." He had reached the shallow end of the pool.

"That was never my intention," William told him as he moved his left foot to the object that had just become visible to Sir Peter.

"What is that?" and then, as realisation struck him, "Oh fuck!"

William kicked the coil of electrical cable into the water. Sir Peter thrashed about like an epileptic dolphin before the replacement circuit breaker eventually tripped, a little too late for Sir Peter.

Printed in Great Britain
by Amazon

54935259R00159